Loving LIEUTENANT LANCASTER

OTHER BOOKS AND AUDIOBOOKS

BY SARAH M. EDEN

THE LANCASTER FAMILY

Seeking Persephone

Courting Miss Lancaster

Romancing Daphne

Loving Lieutenant Lancaster

Christmas at Falstone Castle*
in *All Hearts Come Home for Christmas* anthology

Charming Artemis (Oct. 2021)

STAND-ALONES

Glimmer of Hope

An Unlikely Match

For Elise

The Best-Laid Plans*

THE JONQUIL FAMILY

The Kiss of a Stranger

Friends and Foes

Drops of Gold

As You Are

A Fine Gentleman

For Love or Honor

The Heart of a Vicar

Charming Artemis (Oct. 2021)

THE GENTS

Forget Me Not

*Novella

CHRONOLOGICAL ORDER OF ALL RELATED

SARAH M. EDEN REGENCY-ERA BOOKS

Seeking Persephone
Courting Miss Lancaster
Glimmer of Hope
Romancing Daphne
The Kiss of a Stranger
Friends & Foes
Drops of Gold
For Elise

As You Are
A Fine Gentleman
For Love or Honor
Loving Lieutenant Lancaster
"Christmas at Falstone Castle"
The Heart of a Vicar
"The Best-Laid Plans"
Charming Artemis (Oct. 2021)

Loving LIEUTENANT LANCASTER

A Lancaster Family Romance

FROM *USA TODAY* BEST-SELLING AUTHOR

SARAH M. EDEN

Covenant Communications, Inc.

Published by Covenant Communications, Inc.
American Fork, Utah

Printed in the United States of America
First Printing: June 2018; Second Edition: April 2021

30 29 28 27 26 25 24 23 22 21   10 9 8 7 6 5 4 3 2 1

ISBN: 978-1-52440-525-0

To Nadeoui and Doug
for raising a wonderful son, for welcoming me into your lives
and family, for loving me like one of your own

Acknowledgments

WITH GRATITUDE TO . . .

- Annette Lyon and Luisa Perkins, for making Tuesdays my favorite writing day of the week

- Karen Adair keeping me on task, celebrating even miniscule word counts, cheering me on, and getting me in trouble at writing conferences

- Katherine Eden, for brainstorming this story with me and helping me address all the missing and broken bits of it. You are the best!

- Ginny Miller, for willing and eager proofreading, and for always finding errors I've missed

- Dr. Michael Darley, for helping me keep this body moving, functioning, and thriving, and for giving me hope for the future

- Pam Victorio and Bob Diforio, for endless and unwavering support

- Sam Millburn, for, as always, taking my words and making them better, stronger, and clearer

- My family, for helping out when the nights are long and the editing deadlines tight, for reminding me to take care of myself, and for being amazing

Chapter One

London, August 1816

ONLY A FOOL WOULD IGNORE an edict from the Duke of Kielder, and though Linus Lancaster was many things, he was not a fool.

Thus, as directed in a tersely worded note delivered to his rented London rooms, Linus reported to a very specific location in their club at the appointed hour, prepared to do whatever his universally feared brother-in-law required of him. He was not afraid of the duke—indeed, he liked him quite a lot—but the tone of the summons portended ill, and Linus braced himself for the worst.

He arrived at the club with a moment or two to spare. Nothing at all had changed in the month since he had last dropped in. Adam, the infamous duke himself, had sponsored him for membership shortly after he'd ended his time in the Royal Navy. The club had offered some diversions in those early days of adjustment, but having lived more than half his life at sea, Linus struggled to summon enthusiasm for hours of card games or pointless wagers. While he enjoyed a game of billiards now and then and found some enjoyment in quiet reading, day after day of nothing but idle pursuits had quickly grown tedious. He was, in a word, bored, a state of being he had nearly forgotten existed.

Adam was in the predetermined meeting spot: a somewhat secluded corner of the dark-paneled reading room. The web of scars marring his face pulled in sharp, disapproving angles. The Dangerous Duke, it appeared, was in a foul mood.

Seated beside him was another of Linus's brothers-in-law, Harry Windover, who was as personable as Adam was prickly. Linus took the empty chair near them. He exchanged an abbreviated, silent nod with Adam, then shot a confused look at Harry. "Do we know why we've been summoned?" he asked.

"Adam has chosen to be mysterious," Harry said. "My theory is he wants us to play a guessing game. I'll begin." He narrowed his eyes and stroked his chin. "I've hit upon it. His Grace has grown so inordinately fond of the both of us that he wishes to form our own private club. He will be providing us with matching hatbands and—"

"Shut up, Harry." Adam said that often. Remarkably often, in fact. Anyone listening in for the first time would think Adam disliked his brother-in-law, though that was not at all the case.

"Your turn to guess," Harry said, turning to Linus.

"I've fought more than enough battles in my life; I'll not invite another." Adam nodded. "Wise."

"I will, however, admit myself intrigued by your summons," Linus said. "If you're of a mind to elaborate, I won't object."

Adam's expression hardened. "Your sister has accepted an invitation to a house party."

"Which sister?" Linus had four, after all.

Harry chuckled. "Would we be having this conversation if it were any of them other than his wife?"

Only Persephone's acceptance of an invitation required Adam to do the same. There were few things Adam disliked as much as parties—they being filled with people, whom he did not care for; socializing, which he loathed even more; and the requirement that he be away from home, something he allowed only under extreme duress.

"I still don't understand why Persephone's plans have necessitated this meeting," Linus said.

"Perhaps he means for us to kidnap him so he'll not have to participate in the party," Harry suggested, always one for lightening the mood no matter the necessity.

"You couldn't manage a kidnapping even with your abductee's full cooperation," Adam said.

Harry poked his thumb in Linus's direction. "I'd have the lieutenant, here, to help. He's likely a dab hand at subterfuge and scheming. We'd find ourselves quite in demand amongst gentlemen wishing to escape Society. We could advertise our services, have a few adventures."

"I could use a few adventures," Linus admitted. "Anything to escape the monotony of this life of leisure."

Harry lowered his voice and donned an overblown look of warning. "Do not tell Adam you are bored; he will find something incredibly miserable with which to fill your time."

As much as Linus welcomed both the company and banter, especially since Harry was an expert at the very entertaining ruffling of Adam's feathers, he suspected the duke was not patient enough for the undertaking just then.

"You have been known to skip invitations Persephone has accepted," Linus said, returning to the topic at hand. "Why is this one different?"

"For one," he said, "the party is more than two weeks long. I'll not send her off to Nottinghamshire for a fortnight and not follow her there." Adam, despite his very real preference for solitude, never could bear to be apart from his wife for long. "For another, she made absolutely certain I could not refuse."

Harry's grin grew. "How did she manage that?"

"She threatened to suggest the party be moved to Falstone Castle." Adam's expression grew blacker, something that struck fear into the eyes of everyone else in the room.

"Either you go to the party, or the party comes to you." Linus couldn't help but be impressed with his sister's strategy. "You couldn't refuse after that."

Harry sighed. "Ah, I love the Lancaster women."

The Lancaster *women*. How often Linus had to remind himself that his sisters were grown, even the youngest, who had that year undertaken her second London Season. In his mind's eye, they were still as they'd been when he'd left home so many years earlier: little, struggling, and still quite attached to him.

"I know you too well to think you invited us here simply to bemoan your social obligations," Harry said.

"If I have to go to this party, so do you two." Adam glared at them both, lids lowered enough to render his gaze particularly sinister.

"I have not received an invitation to a house party," Linus told him. "A life in the navy did not leave me so inexperienced with Society as to not know that I cannot simply arrive at a party unwanted."

"You were included in the invitation that arrived at our home. It seems our hostess did not realize you have inflicted your sister with a months' long bout of stubbornness by refusing to live at Falstone House whilst in London."

It had been a point of difficulty between Linus and Persephone, but he'd refused to yield. In his sister's home, he too often felt like a child still.

More than that, he was unnecessary. He had no desire to spend every waking hour constantly bombarded with his own pointlessness.

"I am beginning to suspect I know what house party you are referring to," Harry said. "Athena and I were invited as well."

"Persephone has declared that this will be 'quite the social event.'" Adam's nostrils flared, and a breath growled from him as he quoted obviously verbatim his wife's evaluation.

Another of Harry's laughs began on a snort.

Linus couldn't hold back his amusement any longer. "Our Persephone is quite brave to insist you attend in the same breath she explains why you will be miserable."

"It is not her ready acceptance on my behalf that concerns me most," Adam said. "She has warned me that if I maim or torture anyone in attendance, or otherwise cause any degree of unpleasantness, she will kill me."

Harry's eyes danced with merriment. "You're a little afraid of her, aren't you?"

Adam ignored the question.

"Do you suspect maiming and torture will be particularly difficult for you to avoid?" Linus asked.

"Knowing where the party is being held," Harry said, "the answer to your question is an emphatic yes."

Linus's interest was even more piqued. He looked from one brother-in-law to the other. "Who is hosting the party?"

Adam's mouth turned down in a severe frown.

Once again, Harry answered the question Adam refused to acknowledge. "The Dowager Countess of Lampton."

"Adam intends to maim and torture a dowager?" Linus didn't believe it for a moment.

"Do not be ridiculous," Adam shot back.

"It is her son, the earl, who is in greatest danger, I would wager," Harry said.

Lord Lampton. Linus cast his mind back. He had spent very little time amongst Society, so people did not pop into his thoughts easily. "He is the one who dresses in bright colors, I seem to remember."

"I have never known anyone who preens and prances and generally annoys to the degree he does," Adam said. "He takes delight in being ridiculous. I am required to summon every bit of self-control I possess to simply not run him through every time we meet in Lords."

"I personally think marriage has mellowed the dandified earl," Harry said. "He will always be something of a madcap, but he's not nearly as flamboyant as he once was."

"He wore lime-green pantaloons to Lords not a fortnight ago," Adam said. "And I am absolutely certain he watched me, in particular, for my reaction. I don't know if he was attempting to impress or annoy me."

Linus inserted himself into the discussion once more. "Do you truly think this ludicrous lord will render you murderous?"

"Lampton is practically begging to be strangled," Adam said.

"And you would be more than happy to oblige," Harry added.

Adam nodded slowly and with emphasis. Linus wasn't truly worried. While Adam wasn't overly fond of people and had a tendency to be very forceful when he was put out with someone, he generally knew how to behave, and despite his insistence that Persephone's threats were the reason for his willingness to be civil, he had actually improved considerably over the years.

Harry whistled low. "Adam in the same house as Lord Lampton for a fortnight? We'll never be victorious in this battle, Linus. There will be death and suffering, likely our own."

"Then it is a very good thing for the both of you that you will have a military man on your side." Linus was actually a little excited. Preventing Adam from ruining Persephone's stay in Nottinghamshire and keeping the dandified Lord Lampton from annoying Adam into truly unfriendly behavior would be a tremendous challenge. He needed a challenge.

"You believe we will succeed?" Harry still looked amused despite his obvious doubts.

"Or die trying."

"Do not fret," Adam said, rising from his chair, "if you fail, *you* will not be the one who dies."

"Are you thinking of yourself now?" Harry asked. "Or Lampton?"

"Both," Adam said. "Both."

Chapter Two

Hampton House, Nottinghamshire

ARABELLA HAMPTON'S HEART SANK AS she watched her aunt paw through her meager assortment of dresses, tossing most of them aside. "You will have no need of so many bright colors. A lady's companion is meant to be quietly helpful, not the center of attention."

None of the dresses would truly be considered attention-grabbing, but Arabella had to admit that the robin-egg-blue dress her aunt discarded did not match the image one usually conjured when thinking of a lady's companion—somber, serene, sedate. Browns and grays and dark colors were likely best.

"Surely this green is subdued enough." She held up a wool day dress. It would be warm when winter arrived, and the cut was flattering, a vain argument, perhaps, but a strong one. She felt so very unsure of herself in this new position and needed every bit of buoying she could muster.

Her aunt eyed the dress. "The neckline is a touch low." She tossed the dress on the pile with the others that would not be making the journey with Arabella.

The bodice was so high not even her clavicle showed when she wore it. Perhaps it was more daring than a companion was permitted. She had not lived a life of luxury, being naught but a poor relation in her uncle's house from the time she was seven years old, but being companion to a dowager countess was something different entirely.

Was it wrong of her to hope she would be permitted to wear a cheerful color now and then?

"Lady Lampton has given you an opportunity, Arabella. She could have chosen an experienced companion, one not in need of training or instruction.

And though your youth will prove helpful in fetching things, I can only imagine she would have preferred the companionship of someone nearer her in age and, heavens, somewhere near her in birth. But she chose you, and you would do well to focus all your energy on making certain she does not regret that."

Arabella was not unaware of her good fortune. Truth be told, she was baffled by it. The position had been offered to her only a few days earlier, without preamble, without forewarning. Lady Lampton had simply come and made the offer in a tone of unflinching authority. Arabella's aunt and uncle had managed little beyond an overawed, halting agreement. Arabella had begun packing that very night.

Here was an unforeseen way out of the misery that had been life in her uncle's home. His first wife had passed away many years earlier, bringing a bit of peace to Arabella's life; however, the second Mrs. Hampton was very much like the first one had been.

Better even than escaping, Arabella would be living at Lampton Park, the nearest thing to heaven one could find on earth. She would spend her days amongst the Jonquil family, just as she used to imagine when she was a little girl.

The late earl had been the kindest man in all the world. He had never failed to greet her with the same deference he offered the daughters of the fine local families, though she could claim no real significance, an unwanted and neglected orphan in the care of an aunt and uncle who resented her.

Her earliest memory of the earl was clear, despite the passage of so many years. Her parents had died not long before that day. She had come to the churchyard to place a handful of wildflowers at their graveside but, not knowing how to read, could not find them. Her grief had spilled over as the realization of how very lost they were to her became too much for her tiny heart to bear. He had found her, had taken her in his strong and gentle arms, and had carried her to the place where her mother and father lay, holding her as she cried.

She had sought him out again and again after that, not realizing in her innocence how very presumptuous it was for her to monopolize the time and attention of an earl. At times, she had simply sat beside him and cried; other times, she had told him of her day, of something interesting that had entered her thoughts. He listened no matter the topic. He had held her, laughed with her, reassured her.

He had cared about her when no one else had, and she loved him for it.

"Are you paying any attention?" her aunt demanded, pulling her back to the present.

"I am sorry."

With a *tsk* and a shake of her head, her aunt launched into a scold. "You are meant to be a help to the dowager. If you spend all your time woolgathering, she will quickly grow frustrated with you. You will find yourself without a position. Should that happen, do not think to return here."

Arabella nodded. She would not prove a disappointment for all the world. "I do wish to do a good job, but I am not entirely certain how."

"You do as you are told," was the first instruction. "Do not make trouble. Do not draw attention to yourself nor forget that you are but the smallest step above a servant."

Arabella nodded. That was not so very different from her place in this house, a role she had learned well over the past sixteen years.

"And do not give them reason to be ashamed of you," her aunt added. "The Lampton title is old and respected, no matter that the current holder is a little odd. They are as far above you as the sky itself."

Arabella nodded. How well she knew that truth. She had once asked the earl if she could live with him and be part of his family. Though he had not been unkind in his response, he had told her she could not. "Family stays with family," he had said gently. He had not needed to elaborate. She was not his family. She belonged where she was, and dreams of something better were just that . . . dreams.

"Good." Her aunt pursed her thin lips. "We had best go through your adornments next."

Arabella took out her small shell-covered box, a discarded container she had found behind Sarvol House when she'd gone scavenging at eight years old and in which she kept her few baubles. As quickly and subtly as she could, she pulled from it a slender chain, on which hung a single glass bead. She clutched it in her fist, hidden from view, and handed the box to her aunt. Any of the rest of its contents could be denied her without causing pain, but that chain and bead meant the world to her.

Philip Jonquil, the oldest of the earl's sons, had brought her the simple bit of jewelry shortly after his father's death, having found it among his father's things with a note indicating it was meant for her. She had been but eleven years old. Her dear earl had not forgotten her, even in death. She'd accepted the offering and wept, her heart breaking. Philip, far too young to be bearing such a burden, had, like his father before him, put an arm around her and offered her his strength, comforting her in her grief even as he'd battled his own.

If only she had been permitted to be a part of that family. Among them, she would never have been lonely or broken or forgotten. But eleven years had passed, eleven years without *her* Lord Lampton, eleven years of loneliness and struggle. She was now more than twice the age she had been when she'd received the necklace, the earl's final act of kindness toward her, yet she felt the loss almost as acutely as she had then.

Her aunt dropped the shell box onto Arabella's bed. "All of this will have to remain behind."

Arabella clutched her treasure ever tighter, making absolutely certain it was entirely hidden.

"You will have four dresses and two gowns suitable for dinners or entertainments," her aunt said. "No one will expect you to have jewels or fine hair combs."

Leaving behind what few adornments she had and resigning herself to her most dowdy gowns was a small price to pay. She would be away from her aunt and uncle and the misery they inflicted. Better still, she would be among the Jonquil family, walking the corridors where her dear Lord Lampton had spent his days. Being there, even as a companion rather than an honorary daughter as she'd once dreamed of being, would help fill the void she'd felt all her life.

In Lampton Park, she might at last find home.

Arabella's heart sped as the carriage traveled the manicured drive to the front portico of the Lampton Park manor house. The regal prospect, park land stretching out in all directions, the imposing façade of the grand home, and the stately trees placed at deliberate intervals all declared to new arrivals that this was the seat of an important family. Only a very naive, very lonely little girl would ever believe such a place could be her home simply by asking for it to be.

But it will be now. In a sense. She would be living there, and that would be enough.

Arabella, along with her uncle and aunt, was ushered inside directly to a sitting room where the dowager countess, the late earl's widow, clad, as always, in unrelieved black, received them. Bows and curtsies were exchanged.

"What a pleasure—" Aunt Hampton began.

"I will not keep you," the dowager said. "Your niece and I are perfectly capable of sorting everything on our own."

Aunt and Uncle Hampton could do nothing but accept their dismissal. To argue would be to imply that the dowager was not, in fact, capable of seeing to the business at hand.

Quick as that, Arabella was free of the two people who had controlled every aspect of her life for years. She stood a moment in shock. No matter that she was a grown woman; she'd never been granted any true freedom. She hardly knew what to think.

"I am so pleased you are here." The dowager took her hands and squeezed her fingers.

"You are?"

The dowager's smile grew. "Oh, dear. I can see your aunt and uncle have dampened your enthusiasm." She slipped her arm through Arabella's and guided her from the room and toward the grand staircase. "If I told you we are soon to have a house party, would that lift your spirits?"

Arabella nodded. House parties required a great deal of work. She would have plenty to do, which would help secure her welcome here.

"Wonderful," the dowager said. "For now, though, let us focus on getting you settled."

Arabella ran her hand along the banister as they climbed the stairs. The earl must have often done the same. He had been at home here, happy and content. She could so easily picture him in this place, greeting guests in the entry hall, standing at the top of the stairs. Were he here just now, he would smile at his wife in that way he always had, with love so palpable no one seeing his expression could ever have doubted the depth of his feelings.

He had loved his wife with an open affection few gentlemen allowed. And Arabella knew with absolute certainty that he would have welcomed her here as well, hugging her as he had so often done. Of course, she was much older now, but she wanted to believe that he would not have stopped comforting her with those paternal embraces she had depended upon so much.

"Your room is just down here." The dowager's voice broke the spell of Arabella's reminiscences. "I should warn you, we will be removing to the dower house when the party ends, so you will need to pack again. Let that guide you as you decide which items to pull out and which to keep tucked away until we are settled for good."

The dower house. It made sense. Philip was married, making his wife the true mistress of the Park. That the dowager had remained in residence at the manor house as long as she had was, in all actuality, unusual. Yet Arabella felt more than a twinge of disappointment. The dower house was not the place she had dreamed of all these years. It had not been *his* home.

Still, she would be nearby, which was a comfort, and she would be in a position to help and to be companion to the dowager, which would have pleased the earl. There was great reassurance and a sense of purpose in that.

Philip, the current Lord Lampton, stepped from a room only two doors farther down the corridor than they presently were. He wore a jacket of bright green, not an unusual choice for the flamboyant young earl, though his waistcoat was a subdued grey, the influence of his wife, no doubt.

He grinned when he spotted her. "Arabella." They had known each other all her life, which didn't truly make their use of Christian names entirely proper, but it didn't make it utterly absurd either. "I see Mater was able to steal you away after all. She was very determined to manage the thing."

All the Jonquil brothers had been rather impish growing up. The entire neighborhood had stood in mingled amusement and wariness, wondering what mischief they would get into next. None of the brothers had been as endlessly entertaining as Philip. Arabella had sometimes tiptoed down to the banks of the Trent to watch the brothers enact one of their paper-boat battles or chase each other around the trees and brush. More than once, Philip's antics had set her laughing loudly enough to give away her hiding spot. None of them had chastised her. She had even been invited to join in.

The brothers had all grown more solemn after their father's death. Philip's transformation had been more heartbreaking, owing to the weight he'd then carried and the drastic change it was from his carefree personality. Over time, he had shed that soberness in favor of an almost ridiculous degree of dandification. No one could be entirely certain why. Arabella could not remove from her mind the memory of him, nineteen years old, only days after burying his father, sitting on the low wall of the Hampton House back garden, his arm around her as she'd cried. That was the Philip she remembered and the one she more and more often saw peeking through his mask of frivolity.

"Good afternoon, Lord Lampton." She curtsied, as was proper.

He laughed, the sound so familiar to anyone who had been a child in the neighborhood while he was growing up. "I don't imagine I will ever grow fully accustomed to being called that by someone who knew me when I was a ragamuffin young pup."

"You are a number of years older than I," she said. "That does help a little."

The famous Jonquil smile lit his face. "I'm not quite in my dotage yet."

"Thank the heavens for that," the dowager said. "If you were anywhere near your dotage, that would put me in the realm of an ancient relic."

"Hardly." Philip kissed his mother's cheek. "I haven't forgotten about our planning appointment. I will meet you in the sitting room in a quarter hour, fully prepared to commit myself to all manner of inconvenient and miserable things in the name of your house party."

The dowager nudged him teasingly. "You love those 'inconvenient and miserable things.' Do not attempt to convince me otherwise."

Philip tugged foppishly at his waistcoat. "I do enjoy a gathering."

"What you enjoy is an audience."

He laughed once more, then disappeared down the corridor. The dowager led Arabella to a room at the far end.

"This room was Stanley's," she said. "I am afraid it is not very feminine, but it does afford a nice view of the east garden. When we relocate to the dower house, you can choose from three different bedchambers."

"Thank you."

The dowager watched her a moment, her expression unreadable. At last she said, "I am glad you are here, Arabella. I so hope you will be happy at the Park."

"I know I will be. I know it."

The dowager nodded. "I will leave you to your unpacking. If you feel up to it, I would appreciate you joining us for our planning session. I could use some extra eyes and hands in the final arrangements for this party."

"Of course."

She stepped inside her temporary bedchamber, intent on hanging up her gowns and placing her smallclothes in the clothespress as quickly as she could so as not to be late. The room was, as the dowager had pointed out, rather masculine, with heavy fabrics and darker colors, but it was also very pleasant. The large window let in a great deal of light, brightening the space.

She would be very happy here for the interim. She also intended to remain busy enough that her time in this corner of the house would be limited.

"Whatever you are asked to do, you consider it a command," her aunt had said on the drive over.

Arabella would consider it a privilege. She was at last part of the earl's household; she would not allow this long-awaited dream to die.

She had not been permitted to bring much with her, though even had she brought everything she'd owned, it would have looked sparse in this bedchamber. Laying out her things required little more than a moment. Last of all, she pulled a glove from the bottom of her portmanteau. Hidden inside the thumb was her gold chain and glass bead.

She held it a moment, comforted by it as she always was, before clasping it around her neck. She set her open palm against the bead, where it hung over the bodice of her gray gown. Her pulse pounded beneath her fingers, echoing her nervousness.

"I am here at last," she whispered. She would not squander this opportunity.

She found the dowager in the sitting room but only after wandering a bit in search of it. Philip and his wife had not joined her there. The dowager patted the seat beside her on the sofa.

"Is there anything I can do for you, Lady Lampton?" Arabella asked.

"You really are going to have to stop calling me that. The title also belongs to my daughter-in-law. You will confuse everyone when she is also present."

Arabella acknowledged the truthfulness of that but didn't know what would be proper.

The dowager absentmindedly twisted her black-bead necklace around her finger while she thought. "My mother-in-law had everyone call her 'Old Lady Lampton' after her husband died. She thought it was hilarious. To her credit, it was."

Arabella could smile at that. "Is that where your son gets his sense of humor?"

"Most likely. His father was quite entertaining too."

Entertaining was not the word Arabella most associated with the late earl, but it still fit. She had seen him join in his sons' antics many times, and he had always been quick with a jest or a laugh or an irresistible smile.

"I think, Arabella, you must call me Mater, just as the boys and their wives do," the dowager said. "In public and amongst guests, of course, I will have to be Lady Lampton or the dowager or some variation on that. But amongst family, and especially when only the two of us are present, Mater will do nicely."

Arabella could hardly imagine such a thing. "That is a very personal term for one who is here as little more than a servant."

"Arabella." The dowager set her hand atop hers. "You have always been and always will be far more than a servant."

A sudden ache clutched her heart. "More than a servant" was a far cry from "part of the family," but it sent an almost painful surge of hope through her, a desperate, aching hope. But optimism had proven ill-advised before. "Are you certain?"

"Quite. If need be, I will declare it an order, like a cantankerous old matron."

Arabella smiled at the exaggerated tone. "Very well, *Mater*, though it will take some getting used to." And yet, happiness bubbled inside at the prospect of being on such personal terms with a lady she had so long loved and admired.

The clanking of watch fobs announced Philip's approach. "I have news, Mater." He sauntered over to where they sat. "The Duke and Duchess of Kielder have accepted your invitation, with the caveat that they be permitted to bring little Lord Falstone."

Mater—thinking of her by that endearment, let alone speaking it, would take time to feel at all natural—nodded. "Of course. Do the Windovers mean to bring their children as well?"

Philip expertly lobbed his quizzing glass into the small pocket on his shirtwaist designed specifically for holding it. "It is my understanding the little Windovers will be visiting an aunt for the next few weeks."

"And the duchess's brother and sister?" Mater pressed.

"Both coming." Philip made a minute adjustment to his intricately tied cravat. "That was the last of your guest list. This party of yours has all the makings of a roaring success."

Far from appearing triumphant, Mater's expression grew immediately concerned. "If Sorrel does not choose to participate though . . ."

Sorrel was Philip's wife and, lately, something of a recluse.

"I believe she will," he said. "She has never been one to neglect what she sees as her duty and obligations, no matter her current preference for solitude."

"And if she doesn't?" Mater sounded genuinely worried at the possibility.

Arabella kept her gaze lowered, not wishing to intrude on what had become a rather personal topic. She may have been granted the right to address Mater by her boys' name for her, but she knew hers was not that close of a connection to them.

"Let us worry over that if it proves necessary." Most of the ridiculous-ness had left Philip's tone. "I refuse to believe we have lost her so entirely."

Arabella didn't know what had sent the new countess into seclusion, but all the neighborhood had noticed how withdrawn she had grown. She had not attended any of the assemblies before the family had gone to London for the Season. She had returned before her husband, long before the social whirl would have ended in Town, and hadn't been seen much since. Though she still attended church on Sundays, she did so with a distant and heavy expression permanently affixed. It was discussed often, but no one had answers. The Jonquil family, unshakably loyal to one another, had refused to indulge anyone's curiosity.

"I do worry a little about the wisdom of inviting the Duke of Kielder," Mater said. "He can be harsh. Sorrel might not respond well to his abrasiveness."

Philip took a deep, uneasy breath. "It is a calculated risk, to be sure. But I have seen the fire in her rise when faced with a difficult person. I am hopeful that His Grace's presence will prick her into action."

"And I am hopeful"—Mater didn't sound entirely hopeful—"that you will be proven correct."

This was not at all the direction Arabella had anticipated the house party planning to take. She had come to the sitting room ready to accept any number of tasks, to carefully ascertain her place in this household. Finding herself awkwardly pretending to not overhear so personal a conversation was decidedly uncomfortable, a firm reminder that she was very much an outsider despite a lifetime of daydreams.

"You will be pleased to know"—Philip's voice had regained its ridic-ulousness—"that my tailor intends to deliver to me a newly made jacket in an extraordinary shade of blue."

"The duke will hate it," Mater warned.

"I know," Lord Lampton answered with a laugh. "I look forward to it."

Mater shook her head. "Inviting his displeasure is dangerous."

"Which is what makes it so very entertaining."

Mater laughed quietly, real pleasure in her expression. She took up the topic of the coming party and the needed preparations. Arabella was given several small tasks, which she eagerly accepted. The family would find her to be a welcome addition to their household. She would find a place among them and a purpose; she was absolutely determined to.

She would make the late earl proud, and she would, at last, not be alone.

Chapter Three

"I DON'T UNDERSTAND WHY HIGHWAYMEN never attacked our carriage." Artemis, Linus's nineteen-year-old sister, had lodged a great many complaints over the course of their journey to Nottinghamshire. Most had involved adventurous experiences she felt herself deprived of. "Adam makes no effort to hide the fact that this conveyance likely contains items of value, or at the very least people who might be held for ransom. His coat of arms is on the door, and the Kielder heraldry flies from every corner."

"And thus, your mystery is solved," Adam said as he turned a page in his newspaper.

After a moment's thought, Artemis looked to their oldest sister for an explanation. Persephone paused long enough to tuck a blanket more firmly around the shoulders of the child sleeping on her lap. Three-year-old boys did not generally keep still during long drives, but this one had tired himself out.

"The crest and the heraldry are not advertisements of wealth," Persephone explained. "They are a warning."

Artemis crossed her arms over her chest and sank low on the squabs. "Adam ruins all of my adventures."

"You're welcome," Adam said without looking up.

"Someday," Artemis said, "a dashing and daring rogue will whisk me away, probably to Scotland"—she emphasized the scandalous nature of her hypothetical destination with both volume and a tone of intrigue—"and you won't be able to stop him."

"*Stop* him?" Adam's mouth twisted in dark amusement. "On the contrary, I will fund the excursion."

"You are the very worst sort of guardian." Artemis clearly meant the observation to wound him.

"I have heard it said that a guardian becomes what his ward requires." Adam tipped his paper to allow more of it to be illuminated by the light from the carriage window. "Or perhaps that was 'what his ward *deserves*.'"

"I was a rousing success this Season." Artemis had, in fact, been quite the diamond of Society. She had been so in demand that Linus had hardly seen her or Persephone, or his sister Athena, for that matter, she being just as involved in their youngest sister's debut.

"I consider myself to have been successful as well," Adam said a bit darkly.

"Yes," Artemis muttered. "I know."

Persephone, ever the mediator, entered the fray. "Adam was right to dampen the pretensions of the young gentlemen as he did. You are yet too young, as were all of them. A few were known to be cads. To have accepted a courtship—"

"I wasn't looking for a courtship," Artemis insisted. "I simply wanted a crowd."

As far as mottoes went, it was a remarkably good one for Artemis Lancaster.

Persephone's little bundle opened a single eye, blinking a few times. A moment later, he began to squirm.

"Why could Adam not go back to the Castle while we attend this party?" Artemis asked. "It would be vastly more enjoyable for all of us."

Persephone's armful grew more uncooperative as she attempted to soothe her sister and her husband.

Linus wasn't particularly necessary to their discussion—he very seldom was—so he held his arms out to his nephew. "Come sit with me, Oliver," he said.

The child complied, moving gladly from his mother to his uncle. Oliver had taken to Linus straight off. Linus adored the little boy and cherished his nephew's attachment to him. Too many years away from his family had rendered him a bit distant from them. But not this boy. Oliver loved him.

"Did you sleep well?" he asked his bleary-eyed companion and received a slow nod in return. "Did you have any dreams?"

"Papa fought the wolf." Oliver didn't seem frightened by the recollection.

"Did your papa win the fight?"

Oliver's tiny black brows shot up in offended surprise, the perfect mimic of one of his father's signature expressions. "'Course he did."

"I should never have doubted," Linus said.

Oliver raised his dimpled chin and very nearly looked down his nose at his uncle. "Papa is the duke."

"*The* duke?" Linus hazarded a glance at Adam.

Nothing in the set of Adam's features had noticeably changed, and yet there was no mistaking the amused pride he felt.

"What else does your papa do?" Linus asked his little lapful.

"Everything." Oliver popped up his little fingers and counted them off as he listed his father's impressive achievements. "He has a castle. He has a cage on a chain."

"Yes, the infamous gibbet."

Oliver's eyes opened wide, and he whispered, "Papa let me go in the cage."

Persephone was apparently listening in. "He did what?"

"I am *the* duke," Adam answered. "I can put children in gibbets if I wish."

"Well, I am *the* duchess. And we will be having a discussion about this later."

Oliver leaned closer to Linus and whispered, "We weren't s'pposed to tell Mama."

"I suspect not." Then, in a conspiratorial whisper, he asked, "Did you have fun in the cage?"

Oliver nodded emphatically. Across the carriage, Adam unrepentantly grinned. A mere moment later, Persephone was fighting a smile of her own. Linus did not doubt she would make Adam fully aware of her opinion on the matter of their three-year-old son being placed inside a medieval torture device, but she knew her husband well enough to find humor in the situation.

Linus had known few couples better suited than they. Truth be told, he had known few couples *at all*. Life aboard ship did not provide ample opportunity for interacting with families. Still, having spent every shore leave with them from the time Adam and Persephone had married, he had seen their connection grow and deepen. He had watched as they'd become more comfortable with each other, more understanding, more integral to one another. He'd seen the same in his sister Athena and her husband, Harry. Sister number three, Daphne, and her husband, James, had not been married as long, but the beginning of that same enduring connection was clear between the two of them as well.

His family had grown up and left. When he returned to the Shropshire estate, only he would be there. He thought often of the gaping loneliness of the place, the empty corridors, the vacant rooms. His every footstep would echo into the silence. Only the sound of his heart beating would interrupt the memories he knew would plague him there. His mother. His father. Both gone now. And Evander. His brother's memory never wandered far, but in their childhood home, in the bedchamber they had shared, Evander would haunt him. There would be no escaping that loss.

Adam's gruff voice interrupted Linus's musings. "Come sit with your papa, Oliver."

The little boy eagerly obeyed. Few people truly liked Adam—he worked very hard to make certain of that—but Oliver adored his father, idolized him. Society would have been confused and amazed to see such affection.

Oliver sat on his father's lap, gazing up into his eyes. Adam, his paper set aside, locked his hands behind his son.

"Show me your very best smile," Adam instructed. Oliver must have complied, because Adam nodded with approval. "Now, cast that smile toward your mother. Look as adorable as you can manage."

"Do not use our child to get out of my black books," Persephone said. "It won't work."

"Smile cuter, Oliver," Adam whispered loudly.

The little boy set both his fists beneath his chin and looked directly up at his mother. She didn't smile back, but the laughter in her eyes was evident. Even Artemis looked amused despite her continued determination to be put out with her brother-in-law.

"You always have fought dirty, Adam Boyce," Persephone said, shaking her head.

"I will thoroughly apologize to you later, my dear." Adam's tone grew noticeably warmer.

The corners of Persephone's mouth tipped upward ever so slightly. Her eyes twinkled. "Do you promise?"

Artemis groaned. "Please, stop."

"Would you rather Adam whisk me off to Scotland?" Persephone asked.

"Yes." Artemis turned her head toward the window, her posture speaking of continued discontent. "One of us needs to be in Scotland. If it can't be me, it might as well be him."

Linus met Adam's eye. It was sometimes hard to know if he was more amused by Artemis or thoroughly annoyed. Likely a bit of both.

"Am I meant to prevent you from 'torturing or maiming' this one as well?" he asked Adam, motioning to Artemis.

"That depends on how much you like her," he said.

"I do like her quite a lot."

Adam nodded. "Then you have your task."

Artemis slid the rest of the way to Linus and slipped her arm through his. "I like you too."

Though she was often overly dramatic and sometimes gave the impression of flightiness, Linus had seen in her a foundation of kindness he didn't suspect many were privy to. Indeed, over the past few months he had come to suspect that she purposely presented only one aspect of her character to the world. What he did not know was why.

"Let us see if we can't find a young gentleman at this house party who likes you enough to *not* whisk you off to Scotland," he said. "I have missed all of our sisters' weddings. I would very much like to be present for yours."

She smiled at him. "And I would like to attend yours."

"Mine?" He laughed out loud. "What makes you think I am getting married?"

She shrugged and set her head of golden curls on his shoulder. "What else do you have to do?"

That very question had hung heavy in his thoughts since his arrival in London. Once this party was over and he returned to Shropshire, he hoped to find something to fill his days that appealed at least a little. Long lists of tasks for his staff and tenants to undertake, hours spent sitting by a fire, balancing a ledger . . . He could not imagine feeling much enthusiasm for the undertaking.

Evander would have been far better suited to this life had he survived the war. Linus would have happily continued on as the younger son, visiting on occasion but leaving the tedium of gentlemanly living to his brother.

He pushed away thoughts of Evander. That pain was still too raw, even after eleven years. His family had begun to change while he'd been away. They had become more a part of Adam's life than his.

Three of his sisters were married. Two of them now possessed titles. All were important and influential in their spheres. He was a one-time lieutenant, a mere "mister," late of the Royal Navy—late of his own family, it often seemed.

For a time, he'd had his brother to keep him connected to someone, to something. When his brother died, Linus had lost far more than his very best friend. He had lost the strongest, most enduring connection he'd felt to the life and family he'd left behind when poverty had sent him to sea. Nothing had been the same since. It likely never would be.

Chapter Four

Arabella's heart picked up pace at the sound of a servant's voice echoing down the corridors of Lampton Park. "The Dangerous Duke's here! The Dangerous Duke's here!"

Mater turned to Arabella. "Would you be so good as to slip upstairs to see if Sorrel intends to join us in greeting the arrivals?"

Arabella had been given few responsibilities since taking up the job of companion, which worried her. She would not last long in this household if she had no purpose. She was grateful every time someone asked her to do something. Yet she hesitated at this latest assignment.

"I do not wish to impose upon her privacy." Arabella was hardly in a position to invade Lady Lampton's isolation. "I would not want her to be upset with me."

"As you come to know Sorrel better, you will find her less overwhelming," Mater said. "But I assure you she is good-hearted. You need not worry."

It was not reassurance enough. "Perhaps if a member of the family—"

"You are not exactly a stranger, Arabella. Simply peek down the corridor and see if she is on her way."

Not exactly a stranger. More than a servant. The brief phrases were encouraging.

Arabella made a quick curtsey and left the sitting room. Footmen and maids were gathering in the front entry in anticipation of the guests stepping inside. She quietly tiptoed around them and up the stairs. Knowing time was short, she took the stairs at a fast clip, rendering herself more than a touch breathless.

No sooner had she reached the landing of the floor on which the family bedchambers lay than she spotted Lady Lampton only a few paces away.

Her eyes met the countess's. How could she explain her presence without admitting she had been sent to check on her? Such a thing would hardly be welcome, nor would it be loyal to Mater. Navigating this family was proving more complicated than she had anticipated.

An explanation was not necessary; Lady Lampton spoke first. "Have they sent you as a spy?" She spoke in tones not entirely devoid of humor, which seemed to Arabella to be a good sign. "If it is my husband for whom you are spying, feel free to tell him I have my walking stick handy, and I am not averse to using it." Lady Lampton continued on with head held high and a wave of dignity rolling in her wake.

Arabella hadn't the least idea what that message meant nor whether or not she was truly expected to deliver it. Amongst the Jonquils, she lived in a constant state of uncertainty, not knowing if she was proving disappointingly unhelpful or simply a nuisance.

The countess paused at the head of the stairs and looked back at her. "I do not move swiftly, as you have no doubt observed, so you have ample time to make your report before my arrival." It was both an observation and an instruction.

"Yes, my lady." Arabella descended as quickly as she had ascended.

At least she had a task.

She glanced at the entryway below as she made her way down the last portion of the front staircase. The servants stood at petrified attention as a couple, who could have been none other than the duke and duchess, stepped inside. Directly on their heels came a young lady, beautiful, poised, with ringlets of gold that most women would have given nearly anything to claim.

Arabella slipped around the gathered servants and moved toward the spot where Mater and Philip stood awaiting the opportunity to greet their guests.

"Is Sorrel coming?" Philip asked her in hushed tones.

She nodded. "She told me to tell you that she has her walking stick and is not averse to using it." Arabella shrugged a little. "She did not elaborate."

He smiled, though not broadly and not with true amusement. "She is displeased with me, apparently."

"I did get that impression," Arabella admitted.

"Lud, I hope this works," Philip muttered under his breath.

Philip sauntered in the direction of the new arrivals. Arabella stayed back—*Do not draw attention to yourself*—and kept to the shadowed corner at the side of the stairs.

Mater joined her son. A moment later, Lady Lampton arrived as well. Greetings were exchanged, with pomp and grandiosity on Philip's part and barely concealed annoyance on the duke's. Lady Lampton's expression remained as impassive as ever. Where her husband was all bright colors and overt displays, she was the very picture of ironclad composure. Though Arabella was yet disappointed at the notion of living at the dower house and not at the Park, where she felt so close to her long-lost earl, she felt some degree of relief at knowing she would not be under the same roof as Lady Lampton. There was an unreachableness to her that Arabella found intimidating.

The servants were seeing to the guests' trunks and portmanteaus. Her Grace, Lady Lampton, and Mater were all exchanging the expected warm greetings. Philip was waxing long about the joys of a well-sprung carriage, while the duke appeared to barely tolerate the uninterrupted flow of words. By His Grace's side, the golden-haired beauty waited in polite impatience.

Arabella leaned her shoulder against the side of the staircase, waiting to see if she would be needed. The scene playing out before her was fascinating. She was not overly familiar with fine visitors and the requirements of a host in greeting newly arrived guests. The late earl had visited her uncle's house now and then, always on some business or another. His arrival had inspired much the same awe-filled formality in her uncle as the duke's arrival was even now creating in the servants. The earl, however, hadn't appeared to require nor appreciate the grandiosity. Philip looked as though he were thoroughly entertained by the current display.

As the Jonquils and the duke's party made their way up the stairs, Arabella caught sight of someone she hadn't yet noticed at the back: a gentleman, younger than the duke. He held his back ramrod straight and broad shoulders squared, as if ready to face an enemy, yet he carried what appeared to be a case for some kind of musical instrument. He must have been related to the young lady in the group; he had the same golden curls. He was beautiful, if such a thing could be said of a man. That beauty was tempered, however, by an aura of command and a fearsomeness she sensed in him.

He looked in her direction as he passed, the only member of the group to do so. She doubted he could make out much more than her silhouette, tucked as she was in the shadows. Yet his emerald-eyed gaze lingered as he took the first step.

She pulled back further into the shadows. No words were exchanged. He didn't smile or dip his head as one would in acknowledgement of seeing her there. Yet he had noticed her, something few people ever did.

∞

Linus followed the Lampton Park housekeeper down the corridor of guest rooms, but his thoughts remained in the entryway and with the lady who'd stood tucked into the shadows. The faintest shaft of light had illuminated her face. She'd not said a word, but she'd watched him. Amongst his illustrious relations, he seldom drew anyone's notice, but she'd seen him. She'd studied him.

He could not explain why, but her impression of him mattered. It mattered greatly. They'd not exchanged a single word—he didn't even know her name—but his thoughts remained on her. He'd never felt such an immediate draw to any lady before. It both intrigued and unnerved him.

The housekeeper indicated the bedchamber that would be his for the duration of the party. He offered a thank-you and stepped inside.

He set the case he carried inside on the bed. The latches opened a little too easily. He would need to tighten them. His lyre sat securely inside, whole and unmarred. Of course, the instrument had sailed between continents during wartime. An uneventful and comparatively short jaunt between counties ought not destroy it. Linus ran his fingers over the strings, setting them humming. The familiar sound had accompanied him through countless journeys. After the voices of his family had grown vague in his memory, those strings and the tunes he'd played with them had become the sounds of home to him.

He snapped the case shut once more. These memories would find him the moment he returned to Shropshire. He need not face them yet.

With a quick breath and a firming of his posture, Linus moved to the window. He told himself he meant only to survey the view beyond. If he were completely honest, he would have to admit that he hoped to catch even a fleeting glimpse of the mysterious lady he'd seen below.

The prospect offered views of a copse of trees and a bit of a side lawn. Alas, no intriguing, if unnamed lady. It was a beautiful vista though. Green and lush and alive. He did like that about being on land. The sea offered its own sort of beauty, but the English countryside held a charm not to be found anywhere else. His own family home boasted many lovely vistas. He only hoped his ignorance of estate matters did not prove truly detrimental. Perhaps Lord Lampton had a book or two in his library that Linus could peruse during the quieter moments of this gathering, assuming there were any. If he was to be an active member of the landed gentry, he'd do well to figure out what that meant.

A quick question to a passing maid afforded him directions to the library. Lord Lampton's frivolity had led Linus to expect a somewhat neglected space, it being dedicated to more serious pursuits. That, however, was not the case. The large desk showed every indication of being regularly used. Several shelves' worth of treatises on estate management sat near the desk without a trace of dust to indicate disuse.

He had likely best ask his host before removing any books, as they appeared to be regularly consulted. Perhaps during one of his rescue missions, he could turn the topic from fashion or gossip or whatever a dandy chose to expound upon to the possibility of borrowing a volume or two.

A young gentleman stepped inside the library. Though Linus did not know the new arrival, he had little trouble placing him. He was tall and slender, with light eyes and fair hair. He was in many ways the very image of Lord Lampton, though likely at least a decade younger. Linus felt certain this young gentleman was the earl's brother.

"I didn't realize anyone was in here." The young Mr. Jonquil stepped back as if to leave.

"I do not require solitude," Linus assured him. "I was looking for reading material."

"Are you anticipating being bored at this house party?" A smile lay in the question.

"As I suspect you are brother to my host, I had best be very diplomatic in my answer."

"Don't lie on my account." The young Mr. Jonquil stepped farther inside once more. "I am planning to be bored myself."

Interesting. "Do you not enjoy house parties?"

"Did you at my age?"

He would guess the young man to be somewhere near eighteen or nineteen. "At your age, I was on board a ship."

"You're in the navy?" He stepped closer, clearly intrigued.

"Retired."

"What do you plan to do now?"

Take up a position that ought to have been my brother's. But he did not intend to delve into that matter again, even silently. "I will spend my time fending off boredom at house parties. That is my only concrete plan."

That earned him a laugh, just as he'd hoped. His retreat from life's unpleasantries had always been to a place of lightheartedness and jests. It had saved his sanity more than once.

"There is no one here to make a formal introduction," Linus said. "Still, I think we can be forgiven for undertaking it ourselves. I am Linus Lancaster."

"Charlie Jonquil," he responded.

Jonquil. "You're one of the earl's siblings?"

Charlie nodded. "One of many."

"Brothers *and* sisters?"

"No. Just brothers."

The lady in the entryway was not the earl's sister, then. A cousin, perhaps. She'd not held herself like a servant.

Charlie sat near the fireplace. Linus did the same. The young gentleman took a small figurine from the end table and tossed it from hand to hand.

"Are you down from Cambridge?" Linus asked.

Charlie nodded. "Summer holiday."

Linus had assumed most students were overjoyed to be away from school for a time. Charlie, however, seemed to be anything but. "Would you rather be there?"

"Ask me again at the end of holiday, and I might say yes."

The young gentleman didn't want to be at school, but neither did he seem to want to be home, yet he also expected his preferences to change. There were few things Linus found more diverting than a mystery.

"What does your family have planned for the next fortnight?"

"I don't know," he said, still tossing the porcelain milkmaid. "They don't really talk to me."

That helped explain Charlie's assumption that he would be eager to return to school after a little time spent with his family. Feeling overlooked at home would certainly do that.

"I, for one, am hoping for some kind of excursion to the river," Linus said. "A navy man never can resist the pull of the water."

"The Trent can't be as interesting as the ocean." Charlie tossed the figurine again, but it fumbled as he attempted to catch it. Several grabs didn't save it, and an unpromising crack announced its arrival on the floor below.

"Ah, tare an' hounds," Charlie muttered. He bent down and picked it up. The milkmaid had lost both arms. He met Linus's eye. "Don't tell my mother."

"I've never been a taleteller," he assured the young gentleman.

"She'll probably sort it out anyway," Charlie said. "This kind of thing always happens to me."

"Perhaps it's a good thing for the dons that you aren't returning immediately."

Charlie tucked the broken figurine in a drawer. "It only happens at home."

That was decidedly intriguing. It certainly added to the mystery young Charlie presented.

His host's odd behavior, his brother-in-law and youngest sister's animosity toward each other, and now this conflicted member of the Jonquil family. And, of course, the unidentified lady who refused to leave his thoughts.

Perhaps this house party would prove a better distraction from his own troubles than he had at first anticipated.

Chapter Five

ARABELLA SAT IN THE DRAWING room, a little apart from the ladies, wishing she knew if she would be welcome among them. She wanted to be. She wanted to join them and be part of the gathering. But she was a companion, a poor neighbor far beneath these exalted guests. She was meant to be helpful, not equal.

An elegant and graceful lady entered the room, another Lancaster if the golden curls and green eyes were any indication. Was the duchess the only one of her siblings not in possession of that striking combination?

The duchess rose and greeted her sister with a fond embrace. Miss Lancaster did the same. The newest arrival offered a curtsey to Mater and received one in return.

"I am so pleased you could be with us, Mrs. Windover," Mater said. "I trust your journey was an uneventful one."

"Blessedly," Mrs. Windover said, sitting beside the others. "Any journey undertaken without our children is destined to be far less eventful than those we undertake with them."

Mater grinned in amused acknowledgment. The duchess offered a vocal, "Indeed."

Mrs. Windover met her older sister's eye once more. "Your little Oliver is no doubt here. His father never can bear to be separated from him."

"Or he from his father," the duchess replied. "I fully expect them both to descend into an irreversible decline when Oliver begins his schooling."

Were all fathers so tenderly attached to their children? Her earl had certainly been. She had so little experience with fathers that she wasn't entirely certain which was the rule and which was the exception.

How she wished she were in a position to ask. But these ladies were far enough above her touch to be utterly intimidating.

"I seem to remember you fell apart when the boys left home," Mrs. Windover said to the duchess. "You can hardly fault Adam for feeling the same way."

"Our brothers were not simply going to school," the duchess said. "They were going to war. The two are hardly comparable."

"From what Harry has told me of Adam's experience at school, he very much viewed it as a battle."

The duchess sighed. "For Oliver's sake, I hope his experience is a better one."

Mrs. Windover faced her younger sister. "And what mischief do you have planned to keep yourself entertained during this house party?"

Miss Lancaster rose in palpable dignity, clearly offended by the implication. "Why would you assume I mean to make trouble?"

"Perhaps because you always do," Mrs. Windover replied.

"You shall see. I will be a pattern card of respectability."

Whatever response the youngest sister had been expecting, Arabella would wager it wasn't the laughter she received. All offended sensibility, Miss Lancaster sat once more.

"While Artemis decides what dire revenge she means to enact upon us," Mrs. Windover said, "I have a matter of family business I find far more pressing."

The duchess appeared intrigued. "This sounds urgent."

"Quite." Mrs. Windover looked to her youngest sister, then once more back to her elder. "We simply must find Linus a wife."

Linus? Who was Linus?

All three sisters turned eager eyes on Mater. Their hostess was not even the tiniest bit confused. "A number of eligible young ladies will be joining us for various entertainments over the course of this party. I can't imagine your brother wouldn't find at least one of them interesting enough to wish to know better."

"Perfect." Mrs. Windover seemed the most excited, though all three sisters clearly meant to participate.

Linus was their brother, the gentleman from the entryway. Her heart fluttered at the memory of him. Those beautiful curls. His handsome features. *Linus Lancaster.* She would certainly see him again. Would he speak to her? Offer a greeting?

He was brother to a duchess, a member of a fine family. He had likely already forgotten her.

"Does your brother know he is destined to make a match at this party?" Mater asked.

"He does not need to know," Mrs. Windover said. "He has three sisters here who will make absolutely certain he finds himself in the perfect situation for falling desperately in love."

Though they spoke with obvious mischievousness, tenderness filled their words. Arabella would have liked to have had sisters who cared about her that way.

"Once we have decided on the most likely candidates," Miss Lancaster said, "perhaps I could take turns about the room or the grounds with them and make certain to cross Linus's path whenever possible. I could 'accidentally' bump into the lady I'm walking with, sending her falling into his arms."

Mrs. Windover laughed openly. "If we find ourselves in need of dramatic intervention, we will make certain to employ your services."

Their laughter filled the room, the joyful sound of family. It pricked at Arabella's heart. She was grateful that Mater's party was going well and hoped she would have ample opportunity to prove herself useful, but she also felt . . . alone. She ought to have been accustomed to the feeling, yet at times, it settled as a weight in her chest.

Mrs. Windover held her hand out to her younger sister. "I have been dying to see your new yellow gown ever since you told me of it. Let us go have a look." The two of them left, deeply discussing fashion.

"Do you mean to tell your brother that his sisters are plotting his future?" Mater asked the duchess.

Her gentle smile grew to an unrepentant grin. "Where would be the fun in that?"

"I will enjoy watching this," Mater said.

Arabella would enjoy it as well. People could be endlessly diverting, and she suspected the Lancaster siblings' antics would prove vastly entertaining. And just as she had all those years ago when the earl was alive and his boys were making mischief of their own, she would watch this loving family and imagine what it would be like to be part of one at last.

❦

Linus reached the drawing room to await the promenade into dinner that evening and was immediately accosted by his sister Athena. He had not seen her in a few weeks.

"I have yet to grow accustomed to seeing you out of your naval uniform," she said after a lingering embrace.

He was not entirely accustomed to his change in clothing either. "Is my civilian attire an improvement or a disappointment?"

"There is no need to dig for compliments, Lieutenant Lancaster." She swatted at him playfully. "You have always been handsome."

"With all these curls?" He motioned at his hair. He'd not had it cut recently, and the result was a touch riotous.

"Tread carefully, brother. I have those same curls."

"Something applauded in a lady but not particularly praised in a gentleman."

She patted his cheek, something she and Persephone had done regularly when he was a very young boy. "You give yourself too little credit."

Harry approached in the next instant, slipping his arm through Athena's. "Did Adam behave himself in the brief time before our arrival?"

"He made very abrupt introductions, eyed Lord Lampton with unconcealed annoyance, and, no doubt, sent a tremor of terror through all the staff."

Harry grinned. "There may be bloodshed before day's end."

"You seem excited at the possibility," Linus said.

"I missed the Battle Against Lord Techney the two of you undertook during Daphne's Season. I'm owed a bit of bloodshed."

"Persephone assisted with that effort; she has forbidden this one."

Harry turned to his wife once more. "You'd protect me from your sister, wouldn't you?"

"No," she said flatly. She slipped her arm free of Harry's and through Linus's instead. "There is someone to whom I simply must introduce you."

With a degree of force that would have quailed many a hardy seaman, Athena led him directly to a small grouping of people. Linus surveyed them quickly. None was his mystery lady.

"Linus," Athena said, "this is the Earl of Marsden." She indicated a rotund man with a narrow circle of silver hair. "His wife, the Countess of Marsden." Her hair was the same shade as her husband's, but that was where the resemblance ended. "And this"—something in Athena's tone grew more pointed, though subtly so—"is Lady Belinda Hudnall." After a moment's pause, Athena addressed the group. "This is my brother, Linus Lancaster, late a lieutenant in the Royal Navy."

The expected bows and curtsies were exchanged. As conversation became general once more, Lady Belinda kept her gaze on him, assessing him with no effort to hide her perusal. He wasn't overly concerned with her evaluation.

After a moment, her studying gaze lost some of its pointed edge, replaced instead by the casual disinterest a young lady was expected to show to the world. Her unreadable smile gave no hint as to her final assessment of him.

Athena jumped in. "Lady Belinda, I believe your family has an estate in Shropshire."

"Yes, though not the principal one." Her voice was far higher than Linus would have expected. It was not unpleasant, simply a little startling. "I do like Shropshire. It is a fine county."

"Though not one of the principal ones," Linus said.

Lady Belinda's brow creased. "There are no *principal* counties." She had not, it seemed, recognized the reply as a teasing one, a bit of word play.

He offered an apology as he knew was expected. "An ill-executed attempt at humor, Lady Belinda."

"Ah." Her slight laugh was clearly obligatory.

An uncomfortable silence fell between them. Linus searched around for something to say. A remark on the weather, perhaps. A general observation. Anything.

Then he saw *her*. The lady he'd been watching for. All thoughts of forcing a friendly conversation with Lady Belinda fled. The same pull he'd felt earlier for this stranger returned.

Again, she was a bit apart from everyone else, watching. Perhaps if he found Charlie, they could be introduced. Why did the thought cause him such immediate nervousness? He'd been introduced to countless people during the past Season alone. He'd not been nervous then.

The lady sat in silence, looking out the window. He couldn't explain the strength of the draw he felt. Was it the mystery she presented? Was it that she seemed as out of place as he felt?

She looked away from the window. Their eyes met.

Her position, posture, and appearance spoke of one who was bashful, humbled, likely by circumstances, yet her expression held something different—an eagerness, a hopefulness. And to his surprise, he sensed laughter beneath the surface. What did she find so funny? The guests? Him? Something to which he was not privy?

He held her gaze, indicating with the smallest tilt of his head and raise of his eyebrows that he had noticed her watching him. She looked away again, her lips pressed together with effort, though it did nothing to hide her amusement. She was, it seemed, laughing, at least in part, *at him*. But why? He had dressed with care. He'd not cut himself shaving nor did he think he had any smudges on his face or person. She was too far distant to have overheard anything he'd said.

The arrival of Lord Lampton pulled him away from the mystery she still presented. Even if he hadn't met the earl earlier, he would have had no difficulty guessing the identity of the gentleman currently clad in a deep-purple jacket, bright-yellow waistcoat, trousers of so brilliant a shade of gray as to be almost silver, and a cravat knot more extravagant than those generally seen outside of the finest ballrooms and gatherings of Society's most elite.

Lady Lampton walked at his side with the same difficulty she'd displayed earlier. She leaned on her walking stick and moved with obvious pain. Though Linus had not directly interacted with her, he felt certain she was the very opposite of her husband in disposition: subdued, pragmatic, and rational.

A hand slapped down on Linus's shoulder. Harry had arrived at his side. "I believe Adam's archenemy has arrived."

Archenemy was doing it a bit brown, but that was the general idea. They'd been brought to protect Lord Lampton from the Dangerous Duke and the Dangerous Duke from his wife's wrath. Linus was bound for battle once more. Here was something he knew how to undertake.

"Shall we go earn our pay?" Harry asked.

"Are we being paid for our services?"

"No." Harry tapped his chin, his brow pulled in thought. "Why are we doing this if we aren't being paid?"

Linus matched his theatrical expression of pondering. "Because we are remarkable human beings?"

Harry shook his head. "Can't be that."

"Because we're afraid of Adam?"

Harry actually snorted. "Definitely not that."

"Because we're afraid of *Persephone*."

Harry nodded firmly. "That's it."

Linus made a show of straightening his jacket and cuffs. "Once more into the breach, my good man. Once more."

Lord Lampton jangled as he and his wife crossed directly toward Adam. Linus spared a quick glance for the mystery lady. She had returned her gaze to the windows. She did not, it seemed, feel the same pull he did.

Harry and Linus moved to where Adam stood, reaching him as the Lamptons did. Acknowledgments were made all around and the required bows and curtsies exchanged. Lampton's, Linus noticed, was deeper and grander than was generally seen, almost to the point of being laughable.

Adam's expression hardened, annoyance clear in every angle of his face. His eyes slowly shifted from Lampton to Harry. There was no mistaking the command inherent in Adam's expression: intervention.

"A pleasure to see you again, my lord," Harry said. "I understand your youngest brother is home on holiday."

"Indeed. He wishes to experience the unparalleled delight of watching his eldest brother do the pretty." Lord Lampton spun his quizzing glass on its chain. "I could not deny him the opportunity."

"And in the process, inflict me with it," Adam grumbled.

"It is pronounced 'favor,'" Lord Lampton said. "*Favor* you with it."

"No. It's not."

Lord Lampton turned to his wife and, in an overly loud whisper, one clearly meant to be overheard, said, "He must be accustomed to the French pronunciation."

"Perhaps you were not warned," Adam said, "but I do not endure ridiculousness."

Lampton nodded. "I was warned, but clearly"—he motioned to his attire—"that will not be a problem."

"It is already a problem."

Lampton turned toward Harry with a look that held just the tiniest bit too much theatricality for Linus to be certain it was sincere. "Jealousy?"

Adam appeared ever more annoyed.

"As much as I am enjoying this," Harry said, "I suspect we would be well-advised to mingle elsewhere." Harry took full custody of Lord and Lady Lampton, the former of whom looked delighted by the prospect of socializing, and the latter of whom appeared to want nothing more than to return to the quiet of her own room. They made an odd pair.

"I suppose I had best go offer my apologies to Persephone," Linus said.

"Apologies for what?" Adam asked.

"For the inevitability of you landing Lampton a facer."

"Land him facer?" Adam shook his head. "Harry has you using cant, now, does he?"

Linus chuckled. "I spent more than half my life on board a ship. I hardly need Harry to teach me lower-class expressions."

Adam's gaze shifted to something just beyond Linus's shoulder. Looking back, Linus realized Lampton still held Adam's attention.

"What are the chances," Adam asked, "that someone will set fire to the Castle and I will be forced to leave this party early to look over the smoldering heap of stones?"

"Not very good, I'd wager."

Something very near a growl escaped the duke's throat. "Sounds like you and Harry have your work cut out for you, then."

On that foreboding pronouncement, Adam made his way to Persephone's side across the room. Adam would not make trouble, Linus felt certain of that. But he had no doubt his brother-in-law would be miserable, and that was not an enjoyable experience for anyone.

Chapter Six

WHEN ARABELLA HAD STILL BEEN quite small, she had frequently retreated to a quiet corner of her uncle's back garden and pretended to take part in elaborate meals with very fine and fancy people. They, of course, had all been thrilled with her company, and she had been everything lauded in a young lady of distinction. Her conversation had been witty and her manners above reproach.

Sitting at Lampton Park's formal dining table that night, living the actual embodiment of those long-ago daydreams, Arabella found she was not so well equipped for the experience as she had once imagined herself to be. She was too overawed, too afraid of proving an embarrassment to the Jonquil family to be anything but silent. No witty repartee occurred to her, let alone emerged from her trembling lips. She, instead, kept very still, allowing all the others to speak while she did her utmost not to draw any attention to herself.

She did take particular delight in watching the machinations of the Lancaster sisters as they slyly made every effort to force their brother to interact with Lady Belinda. He, as near as Arabella could tell, did not fully realize their designs; neither did he have any real interest in their current choice.

She also kept her eyes and ears perked for any opportunity to be of assistance to Mater. Of the two Lady Lamptons, the younger seemed most in need of . . . something. She didn't entirely refuse to participate in conversations, but she didn't show any real enthusiasm either. Arabella would have been willing to help if only she knew how.

When the ladies retreated to the drawing room after the meal, Arabella placed herself at enough of a distance to be unobtrusive but near enough to be easily summoned if Mater needed her.

After only a brief interval, the gentlemen joined them. Despite herself, Arabella's eyes fell first on Mr. Lancaster. She couldn't help herself.

"Mr. Lancaster." Mater waved him over. "Will you settle a disagreement?"

"I will do my best." Mr. Lancaster stepped toward the gathering of ladies. He really was very handsome.

"We are trying to decide what entertainment we ought to undertake tomorrow afternoon," Mater said. "My second son and his wife will be joining us, as will a family of some importance—they have two daughters of socializing age—and I wish to find something we can all do that will not be too chaotic."

They have two daughters. A barely withheld look of conspiratorial excitement crossed the Lancaster sisters' faces. They were certainly trying their best to find their brother a wife. If Arabella's long-held impossible dream of joining the Jonquil family had come true, she would likely have been a matchmaking "sister" as well. She cared about them so much; she would have done anything to help them find their happiness.

"Since the activities are in the afternoon," Mr. Lancaster said, "I would suggest lawn games. That would entertain a large number with little effort. If further entertainments are needed, perhaps a musical evening?"

Mater looked intrigued. "Surely enough of the guests possess musical talents. Arabella plays the pianoforte quite well."

"Who is Arabella?"

"Oh heavens." Mater turned in her direction. Arabella's heart lurched. "I have neglected introductions."

"Do not fret over it, my lady. You may simply do so now. I am certain the joy of meeting this elusive Arabella of yours will more than compensate for the delay."

A silver-tongued gentleman, this one. His sisters might find that their efforts were unnecessary. Between his handsome looks and honeyed words, Mr. Lancaster could claim the notice of nearly any lady.

Mater walked with him to where Arabella sat. She knew what was expected of her in a formal introduction yet had very little actual experience. How she hoped she would not embarrass Mater by managing the thing poorly.

She rose and attempted to look at ease. For his part, Mr. Lancaster looked more aloof than anything else. A man with his connections likely found an introduction to a lady's companion something of a bother one must endure for the sake of being polite.

"Arabella, this is Mr. Lancaster, who has served as a lieutenant in the Royal Navy."

A navy man. It was little wonder he exuded an aura of command.

"Mr. Lancaster," Mater continued, "this is Miss Hampton. She is a friend of the family, having grown up in the neighborhood, and now we have the joy of her living here, she having agreed to come be a help to me."

That was a generous way to describe her role.

"A pleasure to meet you, Miss Hampton," Mr. Lancaster said.

"And I you." The three words emerged whole, which was an improvement over what she'd expected to happen.

"I was telling Mr. Lancaster of your talent on the pianoforte," Mater said. "We may have a musical entertainment tomorrow evening. I certainly hope you will play for us."

"Of course." Again, she managed whole words. "I will do my best."

Mater waved that off and turned to Mr. Lancaster. "Do not let her modesty fool you. She is very talented."

Arabella's face heated, though she was beyond pleased by the praise. She had taken great pains over the years to improve her abilities on the instrument. It was a source of both pleasure and pride.

Philip called his mother over in the next moment. Arabella lowered herself once more to her chair, fully expecting to return to her isolation. Mr. Lancaster quite unexpectedly remained there.

"This promises to be a fine house party," he said.

Though she was not particularly adept at conversation, this was a topic she felt relatively equal to discussing, having spent many days helping Mater with the final arrangements. "With such an impressive guest list, I cannot imagine the fortnight will be anything but an inarguable success."

Amusement filled his expressive green eyes. "It is still quite odd to hear my family described as 'impressive.' I well remember them as little girls climbing trees and chasing each other around the house in a very undignified manner. Now one of those sisters is a duchess. It is difficult to reconcile."

Arabella could appreciate that. "I knew the Jonquil brothers when they were young and endlessly mischievous. Now one of them is an earl."

"I have met the earl," he said. "I do not think *mischievous* is a descriptor that belongs exclusively to his past."

Mr. Lancaster was more insightful than most people were. Philip's antics were generally regarded as the entirety of his character rather than a single piece of a complicated puzzle.

"If you think the oldest brother is impish, you should meet the youngest. I've never known anyone with his knack for finding himself in one scrape after another."

Mr. Lancaster laughed softly. "Younger brothers often have that talent."

Arabella couldn't remember the last time she'd made someone laugh. She rather liked the experience.

"May I ask you something, Miss Hampton?"

"Yes, of course." She couldn't imagine what he meant to ask.

He stood framed by the window. "Something about me thoroughly amused you during the wait for dinner and, if I am not mistaken, during the meal itself. I cannot for the life of me sort out what though."

She had not, then, kept her amusement hidden as she'd hoped.

"I do not believe anything is terribly amiss in my appearance," he said. "We had not yet been introduced, so you could not have been reacting to my odd name."

"'Lancaster' is not so strange."

He acknowledged that with a brief nod. "But 'Linus' is not particularly common."

"I suppose it isn't." She was managing a full conversation. That was unusual for her when faced with a stranger. She wasn't shy; she had simply been rebuffed too often to approach conversations without trepidation. Stranger still, she was enjoying the undertaking.

Mr. Lancaster leaned a shoulder against the window frame, watching her with every appearance of casual curiosity, yet something subtle in his posture spoke of discomfort. "Why were you laughing at me before dinner?" To her relief, he did not sound offended.

"I was not laughing *at* you, Mr. Lanc—Lieutenant Lancaster."

He sighed a little, the sound one of weariness and resignation. "I have been Lieutenant Lancaster for nearly a decade, but I'm now retired and must accustom myself to being a mere mister."

"You prefer lieutenant?"

"I confess I do." The admission seemed to embarrass him. "I don't know if that makes me prideful or simply stubborn."

"Why not both?"

A laugh lit his eyes. "You have neatly avoided my question, Miss Hampton. What were you laughing about? I know it had something to do with me." He crossed one arm over his chest while the other hooked upward so his finger could tap his chin. The pose and gesture contained a lavish measure of theatricality. "Every time I saw you holding back a laugh, someone was talking to me." His gaze narrowed. "Always one of my sisters, if I am not mistaken."

She couldn't deny the truth of that.

"Ah. My sisters *are* involved. I should have known." He nodded firmly. "They are scheming again; I can sense it in the air."

His overblown tone and mannerisms pulled a smile to her lips. He reminded her a little of Philip as he had been before his father's passing: friendly, humorous, but not ridiculous in the way he often was now.

"Their schemes must have something to do with me," Mr. Lancaster said. "Surely you heard more detail."

Was he as entertained by this very odd conversation as she was? "I do not know that I am at liberty to divulge all that I heard."

"*All* that you heard? This conspiracy runs deep, does it?" He smiled a little as well. "And it involves me . . ." His eyes pulled wide. "Oh, lud. They are matchmaking, aren't they? Or attempting it, at least."

She didn't confirm his guess but suspected he didn't need her to.

"I shouldn't be surprised. The first thing Athena said to me when I stepped on dry land was, 'We need to get you married.'"

She was conversing so easily with this gentleman who claimed a status so much higher than hers. She wasn't at all certain what to think of the unexpected situation.

"Sisters can be a sore trial," he said.

"They would likely say the same thing about brothers. *Unmarried* brothers, at least."

He tipped his head, eying her ponderously. "What is the consensus on unmarried brothers who are vastly outnumbered?" He sighed as if enduring a very great ordeal.

"While they are to be pitied," Arabella said in tones of deep regret, "they are also quite fortunate; they have sisters who wish to see them happy."

"I, for one, wish to see those sisters squirm a little bit." His smile twisted asymmetrically. "Now, if you will excuse me, I suspect one or more of my sisters is eying me impatiently."

Arabella leaned forward, enough to check the current focus of his sisters' attention. As predicted, Mrs. Windover was watching him while the youngest sister was crossing the room toward him.

He had turned to fully face Miss Lancaster by the time she arrived.

"Linus, I need you to intervene," she said at his side. "Mr. Jonquil is not flirting with me."

"And you want him to be?"

Miss Lancaster threaded her arm through her brother's. "I never said *I* wanted him to; I simply want *him* to want to."

"Does Adam have any idea how much trouble you are going to be?"

Miss Lancaster laughed low. "What he doesn't know is that I haven't even begun giving him trouble."

Arabella turned her gaze to the window to keep her amusement hidden. Once the party truly got underway and Mr. Lancaster was provided with ample diversions, he would forget that he'd spent a few moments speaking with her. But she would think on it for days. She seldom spoke easily with strangers. She seldom spoke *at all*.

"You have so very much to say today," the earl had once remarked after she'd chattered incessantly about one subject after another.

She had apologized, assuming he was offering a rebuke. Her uncle and the woman who at that time had been her aunt had complained without fail whenever she'd rambled on too long.

But he had taken her little hand in his, just as he'd so often done. "No gentleman of sense would ever be anything but delighted to have you choose to share your thoughts with him."

"You are not angry?" she had pressed.

"I am honored."

She pressed her hand over the single bead hanging from her neck. Years had passed since any gentleman had shown an interest in her conversation. But Mr. Lancaster had. And she had enjoyed herself, none of her usual nervousness encroaching on their interaction. She had always imagined that living at the Park would change her for the better, that the influence of the earl would buoy and support her. Perhaps she had been right after all.

That sent a wave of hope over her. Perhaps she was not destined to be as lonely as she had so long feared.

Chapter Seven

"My boat is sinking, Uncle Linus!" Oliver made the observation with all the panic one would expect if an actual ship were succumbing to the waves and not merely a folded section of the *Times*. "Help the people!"

"Which one is the captain?" Linus asked in his most solemn voice.

Oliver pointed at one of their handmade twig sailors.

Linus nodded. "You can save the rest, my boy, but the captain goes down with his ship."

Horror filled his sweet little face. "He drowns?" Oliver's characteristic use of the *w* sound in place of his *r*s rendered the question all the more heart-tugging.

"He does," Linus answered.

Oliver's brow puckered in thought. "You were a captain."

"I was going to be." *I was going to be a lot of things.* "Being a captain is a fine thing."

"Not if you die." Oliver had a knack for making observations in the same tone of questioning the hearer's intelligence that his father had perfected. He watched as Linus removed all but the ill-fated twig captain from the sinking boat. "Why does the captain die?"

Heavens, this was proving a grim topic. "Because he doesn't abandon his duties. He is brave no matter what."

Oliver seemed to accept that answer. "My papa is brave."

"Yes, he is." Linus had long ago lost track of how often Oliver spoke of Adam's bravery. Something about that aspect of his character was a source of pride and, if Linus didn't miss his mark, reassurance to the little boy.

"But he isn't a captain," Oliver added with an earnestness that bordered on a desperately asked question.

Linus pulled his nephew into an embrace, recognizing the declaration for what it was. "I don't believe he has any plans to pursue a captaincy."

"And you aren't a captain," Oliver said. "So you won't die."

Oliver clearly had full faith that Linus would have the fortitude to go down with his ship were he a captain. "I appreciate your confidence in my bravery. I am not always courageous."

"You're scared?"

"Sometimes. Just last evening, I had a conversation with someone who made me very nervous." Looking back on his brief exchange with Miss Hampton, Linus was at a loss to explain why she rendered him so unaccountably ruffled. He was absolutely certain he'd rambled and generally made himself a little ridiculous. He'd had conversations with admirals and dukes. He'd even spoken with the Prince Regent once. None of them had upended him the way Miss Hampton did.

"Was the person mean?" Oliver asked.

"No." She had been rather charming in her quiet way. Still, he had turned into something resembling a molded jelly inside. That never happened to him. He hoped he'd hidden his inner struggles.

"You shouldn't be scared of someone who isn't mean. I'm not." Oliver spoke with all the dignity of a future duke. He was, Linus imagined, very much like his father had been at this age but softened by Persephone's influence.

The last bits of their ill-fated ship disappeared beneath the water, illuminated by the midmorning sun. Oliver turned his heartbroken gaze on Linus. "Make another one?"

"Do you remember how?"

Linus had spent some time with Harry and Athena's children, who were unfailingly energetic and enthusiastic and highly prone to gleeful outbursts of excitement. Oliver was so very different from them. He had enough of both his parents in him to make him quietly observant but a force to be reckoned with when he so chose.

"I don't remember." Oliver made the admission with all adorable *w*s for *r*s and with such an unnecessary tone of disappointment in himself.

"You have only watched me do it twice," Linus reminded him. "Most people don't learn the trick of it that quickly."

"We'll make boats every day?" Oliver asked.

"Every day that I am able." He, after all, was at the mercy of Adam's dictates as well as the dowager countess's scheduled diversions.

While Linus set himself to the task of folding a new boat, Oliver poked at the water with a stick. Footsteps sounded nearby, pulling Linus's gaze away from his task. Charlie Jonquil was walking up the bank in their direction, a girl of likely five or six at his side. For a moment, Linus could only stare. The little one bore a striking resemblance to Artemis at that age: eyes eagerly taking in every detail, perfect golden ringlets held back by a ribbon tied in a bow.

Artemis had been this small when Linus had been pulled from her life. She was all but grown now; he'd missed everything in between.

Charlie offered an apologetic dip of his head as he and his little companion arrived near them. "We hadn't intended to interrupt. We were merely out for a walk."

"You are welcome to join us," Linus said. "We are folding paper boats and sailing the seven seas." He met the little girl's eye. "Do you know how to fold paper boats?"

Her gaze drifted lower, away from his, her cheeks heating on the instant. Linus's sister Daphne had always been bashful. He had long since learned to recognize the look of timidity.

He turned his attention to Charlie. "I didn't mean to embarrass her."

Charlie bumped the little girl with his hip. "You haven't been bashful in months and months, Caroline. What has come over you?"

"Does she not care for strangers?" Linus guessed.

"She warms to people very quickly."

The little girl's gaze rose once more, meeting his for the briefest of moments. There was no fear in her expression but something more like hesitant hope. If he did not miss his mark, she wanted to make his acquaintance but felt a little overwhelmed. Her physical resemblance to Artemis and the closeness of her expression and mannerisms to Daphne gave her immediate place in his heart, and he would grant her all the time she needed to decide if she meant to accept him or not.

"You are welcome to sit with us if you'd like," he said. "If you do not know how to make boats, your—" He shot a look at Charlie, unsure what his connection to the child was.

"Uncle," Charlie supplied.

"Your uncle will show you how." A little under his breath, he asked Charlie, "You do know how, don't you?"

Charlie smiled, his countenance lighter than Linus had yet seen it. "I've made a good number of paper ships in my time. My brothers and I used to set them afloat very near this spot."

Linus eyed the little eddies in the current. "It is proving a difficult harbor to launch from. The water is a bit rough."

"Yes, well, we lost a lot of ships." He sat near the stack of newspapers. Little Caroline sat on his lap and watched as he began folding.

"Do you live nearby, Caroline?" Linus asked.

She nodded. Linus smiled at her, and she reddened further but did not shy away.

Linus had learned a little of the Jonquil family during his nearly twenty-four hours at Lampton Park. There were seven brothers, the oldest five being married already. Like Linus, Charlie must have had a good number of nieces and nephews.

Linus watched him as he folded his ship and explained to Caroline what he was doing. He was patient with her whispered questions and didn't balk at the childish undertaking. There was little on the surface to indicate that he was anything but perfectly content, but Linus suspected that was not entirely true. He'd seen frustration in the young man's face as they'd sat in the library.

Charlie turned his attention to Oliver. "Do you not make paper boats?"

"I'm too little." It was not a statement of fact but a clear and obvious complaint.

Charlie nodded gravely. "I was always the littlest. I didn't get to do a lot of things."

"I'll be big. Like Papa. Then I can do anything I want." Oh yes, he had a great deal of Adam in him.

"I could make you a boat," Charlie offered. "I'll even launch it for you."

Oliver nodded eagerly. He looked up at Linus. "We'll make the stick people?"

"Of course." Linus set aside his unfinished paper boat. "Should we also make the captain?"

"We have to. Someone has to die."

Linus laughed right out loud, unable to help himself. Oliver was a joy, an unmitigated joy.

As the morning passed, Caroline moved to sit closer to Linus, while Oliver very nearly adopted Charlie as another uncle. Linus sensed a deep and abiding goodness in Charlie Jonquil as well as a loneliness that he himself knew all too well.

"If you've no other plans, I had intended to go for a ride in the morning," Linus said, hoping the invitation might be welcome. He'd appreciate the company. "Being on ship for most of the last thirteen years of my life, I've missed riding."

His offer clearly surprised Charlie. "You're inviting me?"

Linus watched him closely. "Is there some reason why I shouldn't?"

Charlie shrugged. "I'm not usually the one who gets asked."

Hmm. "One of the perils of having so many brothers, no doubt."

A chuckle. "One of many perils." With a grin, Charlie asked, "Do you have brothers?"

That was not a topic up for discussion. "I have a plethora of sisters, which comes with its own set of dangers."

"I would imagine so."

They returned to the task at hand, the subject of families left where it was.

After they had used up all their paper and sunk a great many ships in the depths of their substitute sea, they walked back to the house, Linus carrying a very nearly asleep Oliver and Charlie walking hand in hand with Caroline.

They had taken only a few steps inside when Artemis accosted them. "Where have you been, Linus?"

"Seeing to matters of great naval importance." He spoke in his lieu-tenant's voice.

Artemis released a puff of exasperated air. "You have missed everything."

"Everything?" Linus attempted to match her aura of theatricality.

"Today's guests are due to arrive in only a few hours, and Persephone refuses to tell me what activities have been decided upon. How am I to arrange for the proper partner if I don't know what that partner will be undertaking?"

"Did it occur to you, dear sister, that your partner might be chosen for you?"

"Oh, pish." Artemis waved that off like so much smoke. "I am not so helpless as all that."

Out of the corner of his eye, Linus caught sight of Charlie's bewildered expression. Artemis could be a bit overwhelming to those who did not know her well. Linus turned and, with utmost solemnity, said, "You had best make a hasty retreat, Mr. Jonquil, lest you find yourself one of her unwitting minions."

Charlie executed a very brief bow. "I thank you most sincerely for the warning and will make good my escape."

He, with Caroline still in tow, had only just disappeared down the corridor when Artemis spoke again. "He is not taking the least interest in me. It is very frustrating."

"You can't expect all the young gentlemen to fall head over heels in love with you."

She rolled her eyes. "I said nothing of love. He is handsome and seems charming, even if he is a little young."

"I would wager he is the same age as you are," Linus said.

Artemis didn't acknowledge the truth of that. "It is very odd that he won't flirt even a little bit."

"He is not the only one." Linus indicated his now-sleeping armful. "Lord Falstone here is so unimpressed that you've bored him into a state of slumber."

She smiled at her little nephew. "Is it not rather amazing that Adam, of all people, should have a son who is so very darling and sweet?"

"He is his mother's child as well, you will recall."

"That is true enough. After all, it does not do to place too much emphasis on a father's influence." She spun and walked away with an air of dignity so overblown no one would have believed it.

Though it pained Linus to think ill of their father, he had been neglectful of them all. Father had, at first, been paralyzed by grief, then by the fear of stepping out of his self-imposed exile. Before he'd found any degree of healing after Mother's death, Father's mind had begun to deteriorate. Linus had memories of him as the thoughtful and kind father he had once been, but Artemis never knew that part of him. More devastating still, she had never experienced the love of a parent, their mother having died shortly after Artemis's birth.

Oh, Artemis. Are you hurting more than you let on?

Linus slowly made his way up the stairs. He worried for Artemis, just as he had all his sisters over the years. He was every bit as helpless in her case as he had been in theirs. He was a rather pointless brother.

He'd only just reached the second-story landing when Miss Hampton appeared there.

"Mr. Lancaster." She appeared pleased to see him.

"Miss Hampton," he returned. "I apologize for not offering the expected bow. Little Lord Falstone's mother would likely wring my neck if I woke him."

Wring my neck. That was hardly a gentle turn of phrase. He was making a mull of this. Why was he so nervous in her company?

Miss Hampton's gaze settled on Oliver. "You appear to have exhausted him quite thoroughly, which should please your apparently violent sister."

With that quip, offered in unmistakable but subtle levity, she eased a degree of his inexplicable discomfort.

"I do all I can to keep my oldest sister happy, I assure you. She has access to a gibbet, you know."

She made a show of being impressed. "Her husband allows her to borrow it?"

He shook his head. "*She* allows *him* to borrow it."

"Sisters truly are a sore trial," she said.

"The sorest."

A soft smile touched her lips, gentle amusement in her eyes. For a moment, he couldn't breathe. His brain turned to useless mush even as his tongue tied itself in knots.

His reaction to her was wholly ridiculous. He hardly knew her, after all. "I should allow my nephew to rest." He moved past her. "A good day to you, Miss Hampton."

"And to you," she returned.

With determined steps, he strode down the corridor. After a moment, he paused and looked back. She was gone.

Chapter Eight

THE DOWAGER HAD TAKEN LINUS'S suggestion regarding the afternoon's activities. The east lawn of Lampton Park was set up for lawn games. Tables and chairs had been placed around the area with awnings erected to provide shade. In addition to Linus's family, that afternoon's gathering included a few neighbors. The family who had been mentioned earlier, who boasted two socializing-aged daughters, had arrived, as had the second of the Jonquil brothers. The local curate, whom Linus had not yet met but suspected, based on the tall, slender build and golden hair, was a relative of the Jonquils, attended as well.

He did not spy Miss Hampton. Did she not care for lawn games? Perhaps she simply didn't care for crowds. During their brief conversations, he'd come to suspect she preferred quieter, more personal interactions. Truth be told, he rather did as well. But his place amongst his family was trivial enough without making himself socially pointless. He would do well to see to it he was friendly.

He made his way to where Mr. Layton Jonquil and his wife, a lady with a head of shockingly red hair and a brilliant smile, were talking with the dowager. Layton's wife held a young child in her arms, one likely not yet a full year old. Little Caroline stood with her hand in Layton's, and the mystery of her place in the broader Jonquil family was solved.

"Good afternoon, Miss Caroline," Linus said, offering a bow.

She blushed and smiled. "Good afternoon."

"Have you come to play lawn games with us?" he asked.

She nodded. "Papa said I could. He said Olive would be here too."

Olive? "Do you mean Oli*ver*?"

She nodded again.

Linus hadn't heard that his nephew would be taking part. He hoped it was true. Oliver's quiet disposition coupled with the intimidating nature he had inherited from his father would make friendships more difficult to come by down the road if he were not afforded opportunities to practice interacting with others. Beginning that practice early seemed a good idea.

"Do you have a favorite lawn game?" he asked little Caroline.

"I like bowls." She faced him fully, though with her hand still in her father's.

"I am quite good at bowls," he said. "I enjoy it very much."

"As much as making paper boats?"

He thought on it a moment. "Probably, provided I have a fun partner."

Her eyes dropped, and her mouth pressed closed. Bless her dear little heart.

"Would you be my partner?" he asked.

Her head immediately snapped up. "Really?"

Linus met Caroline's father's eye. "Mr. Jonquil," he said very formally, "might I beg the honor of partnering with your daughter for a game of bowls?"

Layton matched his staid tone. "Are you a reliable gentleman? I do not allow my daughter to play bowls with just anyone."

"He made boats with me, Papa. And he told Charming they could ride horses together. And he kept Olive from falling in the water by telling him he couldn't go in the water. And he talked to me even though I was shy when I first saw him."

Tenderness filled her father's expression when he looked at her. "Would you like to play bowls with Mr. Lancaster?"

"Yes, please."

Layton looked at Linus once more. He mouthed the words "Thank you."

Linus smiled back.

Caroline's mother entered the discussion. "Should Caroline grow tired"— dropping her voice almost to silent, she added—"or should you"—then returned to her normal volume—"simply bring her back."

"I will." He offered a quick bow to the both of them, then held his hand out to Caroline. They walked toward the spot where the bowls equipment was set out, their arms swinging between them. "I should warn you in case we are teamed against my youngest sister, she cheats."

Caroline skipped alongside him, her hand still in his. "Flip cheats too."

"Who is Flip?"

"One of Papa's boys. He lives here. He's an earl, but he's still funny."

Flip, then, was her name for Lord Lampton, whose Christian name was, if Linus remembered correctly, Philip. And Caroline had referred to Charlie as Charming. Oliver was Olive. Did she have odd names for everyone?

"That gentleman just over there," he motioned to the gentleman he had been told was the curate. "Is he one of your father's brothers as well?"

She nodded. "That is Holy Harry."

Holy Harry. Linus had to bite back the snort of amusement that arose at that name. What a horridly perfect moniker for a man of the church.

"He is not a vicar yet," Caroline continued. "But Flip calls him the vicar because it makes his face turn red, and that makes Flip laugh. And when Flip laughs, all of Papa's boys laugh. Except Chasin'. Flip makes him roll his eyes, though not as much as he used to. Chasin's butterfly makes him very happy, so he does not get frustrated like he did before."

Most of that made little to no sense. But hearing the little girl speak so eagerly and with such animation did his heart a world of good. Her earlier quietness had reminded him so strongly of his dear sister Daphne, whom he'd worried about for so many years. Sharing a friendly moment with this golden-haired version of her felt almost like stepping back into his own childhood and being part of his family again.

They had not yet reached the bowls section of the lawn when Athena, accompanied by two young ladies likely somewhere near Artemis's age, approached. His older sister wore the same intent expression she had the night before when introducing him to Lady Belinda. Apparently her one-at-a-time strategy hadn't inflicted quite enough misery.

"Linus," she said, "I do not believe you have yet made the acquaintance of Miss Romrell and Miss Jane Romrell."

"I have not." He offered the expected bow. "And I do not know if the three of you have had the pleasure of being introduced to Miss Jonquil." He set his hand on Caroline's shoulder and tucked her up against his leg, knowing she was a little bashful at meeting strangers. "She is one of my favorite people and has agreed to be my partner for lawn bowls."

The two Misses Romrell looked to Athena, surprise and alarm in their expression. Had his troublemaking sister promised them his attention? He didn't know whether to be annoyed at her efforts or amused at how very diverting it was to thwart them.

"If you will excuse us," he said, "Miss Jonquil and I are eager to begin our game."

Keeping Caroline at his side, Linus stepped away, moving toward their original destination.

"Am I really one of your favorite people?" Caroline asked quietly.

"You absolutely are."

She smiled up at him, the brilliance of her expression warming him through. "My mama says that too. She says she liked me from the very beginning."

"I am certain she did."

Artemis, practically dragging Charlie Jonquil behind her, arrived at the designated location for bowls just as Linus and Caroline did. Telling his tiny partner about Artemis's questionable history with bowls had likely fated them to this arrangement.

"Are we to be opponents?" Linus asked.

"How fun." Artemis's enthusiasm was as apparent as Charlie's lack thereof. Poor lad. "I hope you are good at bowls, Mr. Jonquil."

"I'm not."

Artemis was not discouraged. "My brother is not very good either, so it should even out."

"He *is* good," Caroline insisted.

Artemis looked down at her, smiling and friendly. "Who is? My brother or your uncle?"

Caroline thought about it a moment. "Both."

Artemis tossed Charlie a saucy look. "Have you been downplaying your talents?"

To his credit, he set aside his annoyance enough to join in the banter. "A gentleman does not brag."

"Is it also a violation of the gentlemen's code to heartlessly trounce one's competition?" she asked.

"It is when that competition is my favorite six-year-old niece." He winked at Caroline, and she giggled.

"I believe we can all agree," Linus said, "that Caroline is the one in charge here."

Her giggle turned to a full laugh.

Artemis smiled broadly. "Shall you and I set up the game?" she asked the little girl.

Caroline eagerly joined her, leaving Linus and Charlie behind.

"How did my sister force your hand?" Linus asked.

"She asked in front of my mother, who is still put out with me over the milkmaid figurine."

"Ah."

Charlie shrugged. He clearly didn't find the arrangement entirely to his liking, but he was being obliging. "I was only standing there because I had hoped to spy Arabella and ask her to be my partner. We've known each other forever. I wouldn't have been under any pressure to be impressive."

"Do you often feel that pressure?"

"Jonquils are supposed to be exceptional," Charlie said. "It wouldn't do to be the only one who turned out ordinary."

There was a piece of the puzzle this young gentleman presented. Though his contradictory thoughts that first day had been focused on his schooling, it seemed at least part of his struggles were familial.

Linus could appreciate that worry. His brother had been extraordinary. Stepping into the role meant to have been Evander's was only serving to highlight his own shortcomings. His inadequacy would be obvious once he returned to Shropshire and took up the reins of the estate. Everyone would see it, and he would have to face it all himself: how ill-suited he was, how empty the estate now sat, how irrevocably and painfully lost to him Evander truly was.

"I should warn you," Charlie said, "if Arabella returns from her walk earlier than usual, I intend to abandon your sister."

One glance at Charlie's face told Linus he was jesting. He had manners enough not to rudely leave, even if he'd been strong-armed into being present.

"Does Miss Hampton often go for walks?"

Charlie nodded. "Every day. She always has, sometimes for hours on end. She's known in the neighborhood for it."

It was an odd hobby. Linus didn't know that he'd ever met anyone who walked long enough and frequently enough for the entire neighborhood to associate her with it. She grew more intriguing the more he learned of her.

Caroline skipped back over to them. She looked up into both their faces. "Miss Lancaster says I am delightful."

"She is absolutely correct," Linus said.

Charlie chucked her under the chin. "Have you made another friend, sweetie?"

She nodded.

Good for Artemis. Though his sister had her difficulties and some aspects of her behavior worried him, moments such as these gave Linus hope.

She returned to where they stood, tossing and catching a bowl. "Are you gentlemen ready?"

A commotion nearby pulled all their attention. A swirl of activity had erupted. Adam was barking orders that Linus couldn't quite make out. Persephone looked utterly frantic.

Linus caught a servant rushing past. "What's happened?"

"Lord Falstone's gone missing," she said.

Merciful heavens.

He turned to Charlie. "Return Miss Caroline to her parents."

"Of course." Charlie scooped his niece up into his arms.

Artemis moved swiftly, doing her utmost to keep pace with Linus. He assessed the situation as they approached and knew, without question, Adam was the one to ask for an assignment and not Persephone. She was distraught, while he was in battle mode.

"Give me my orders," Linus said.

"You and Harry search the copse of trees to the east."

"Aye aye." Linus spun and, meeting Harry's eye, motioned with his head for them to move in the direction they'd been assigned.

"How long has Oliver been missing?" he asked his brother-in-law.

Harry shook his head. "No one is certain."

Linus swept his gaze over the area as they moved closer to the trees. "How did this happen?"

"Again, no one is certain."

Adam and Persephone would sort the *how* of it later. "You head south," Linus said. "I'll sweep northward."

Harry nodded, and they stepped into the trees, each going in their own direction. Oliver was a small boy. He couldn't have gone far. That was Linus's one source of consolation. He could not have gone far.

Arabella was at a loss. There was absolutely nothing for her to do despite the extensive entertainments planned for the day. The servants were more than capable of setting up lawn games and tables of food. Mater had directed their efforts with no show of fatigue. The one time she had found herself wishing for her shawl, one of the maids had rushed to fetch it before Arabella had had a chance.

She did not seem to be needed the way a companion usually was, nor did anyone seem to expect her to truly fill that role. What, then, was her purpose among the Jonquils?

Seeking permission to undertake her daily walk whilst the afternoon's games were underway had proven her best option. She would not be in the way, nor would she be left in the uncomfortable position of standing about, wishing she knew how to claim a place among them.

She could not remember when she had first begun walking, but it had become a daily part of her life. She knew every inch of the area around her uncle's home, everything from the town of Collingham to the narrow cart path at the far end of the Sarvol estate. Walking was her escape, her most reliable means of survival.

That day's excursion she limited to the grounds of Lampton Park nearest where the guests' activities were taking place. She didn't allow herself to think too closely on her reasons for staying so near them all, knowing the decision spoke clearly of desperation.

The river Trent ran through the Park grounds. She wandered in that direction. The sound of the running water had often been soothing. She'd sometimes found the earl there, walking as well, his head bent in contemplation, his hands clasped behind his back.

Arabella clutched her fingers around the bead he'd given her and ran it back and forth on its chain. Had the earl also found solace in walking? Or was it the solitude that he'd benefited from? Either way, it had endeared him to her even more. They had had this in common.

She clasped her hands behind her as she walked on, but a sound stopped her in her tracks. She listened more closely. Someone was crying. A very small someone, she would guess.

"Who is there?" She looked around but didn't immediately spot the source of the cries.

No answer was forthcoming. She stepped off the riverside footpath and farther into the brush. After a moment, she found the child, the same little boy Mr. Lancaster had carried in his arms earlier that day: little Lord Falstone.

Why in heaven's name was he here? And all alone? The child could not have been more than two or three years old.

Arabella knelt in front of him. "Are you lost, dear?"

He nodded, even as his tears picked up. His hands clutched one of his shins. A closer inspection showed three rivulets of blood seeping down his leg.

"Did you hurt yourself?"

Another nod.

"May I see, please?"

He hesitantly pulled back his hands. A deep gash ran nearly the length of his lower leg. Dirt and tiny bits of rock had lodged inside.

"Is there anyone here with you?" she asked.

He shook his head no. His family was likely frantic, then.

"Let's get you back to your father and mother." She lifted him into her arms, careful of his leg. She had no desire to cause him more pain.

The boy leaned heavily against her. "Will Papa be angry?" he asked between shaky breaths.

As far as Arabella knew, the Duke of Kielder was *always* angry. How she hoped that did not prove true this time. "I believe he will be very happy that you have been found." She held him a little closer as she navigated through the narrow gaps between bushes; her larger frame did not fit into the same small spaces his tiny one had. "When I was young, I became terribly lost once. Not far from here, in fact."

"Were you scared?" he asked.

"A little."

"Did your papa find you?"

Explaining to the already worried little boy that her father had been long dead by the time this particular story had taken place did not seem at all necessary. And the gentleman who had found her had been enough like a father that she didn't feel guilty answering as she did. "Yes. He found me, and he wasn't angry or scolding. He was simply happy to have me with him again." What she wouldn't have given to be with him now.

"Oliver!" A voice echoed among the trees.

The little boy perked up. Oliver was likely his Christian name.

"Does that sound like your papa?" she asked.

He shook his head no.

"Oliver! Where are you?"

She paused her navigating of the copse of trees. "I am going to bellow quite loudly, Oliver." She didn't want to startle the already overset child. "We are over here!" she called out.

A moment later, Mr. Lancaster came stomping through the under-brush, his expression and demeanor exactly what one would expect of a military man on campaign. There was a fearsomeness in his expression she'd not seen before. He eyed her, then Oliver. His aura of determination increased, and he reached them far faster than she would have expected.

"Where did you—?" His gaze froze on the boy's leg. "What happened?"

"I don't know any details," Arabella said. "But the cut is deep and will need a thorough cleaning."

"I falled," Oliver said.

Mr. Lancaster's focus did not lessen. "Has he any other injuries?"

"None that I know of."

He nodded crisply. He was Lieutenant Lancaster through and through. Firm, commanding, all because his family needed him to be. Little Oliver likely had no idea how fortunate he was to be so deeply cared for.

"You disappeared," the lieutenant said to his nephew. His fearsome expression softened. He brushed his hand over the little boy's mud-splattered hair. "We've been worried about you, little one."

"I wanted to see the boats."

Boats?

Mr. Lancaster paled a little. "You were going to the river?" He turned worried eyes on her.

"He did not get that far," she said.

"Thank heavens," Mr. Lancaster whispered. "Let's get him back to his parents."

Mr. Lancaster moved with singular purpose. Arabella kept pace with him. They made their way to the edge of the tree line and stepped out onto the lawn where the games, now abandoned, had been set up.

Mr. Lancaster cupped his hands around his mouth and shouted to a servant standing at the edge of the back terrace, no doubt watching for the return of anyone sent out to search, "He's been found!"

The maid waved back and rushed into the house.

Arabella leaned her head a bit closer to Mr. Lancaster and lowered her voice. "Oliver is nervous that his father will be angry with him. I think it might be best if you return him to his parents, as you know them better than I do and will know best how to stave off any storms."

"The duke will not be angry," Mr. Lancaster said. "But he can be frightening when he is worried."

That might very well be interpreted the same way by the anxious little boy. "Oliver," she said, "would you mind terribly if your uncle carried you the rest of the way to the house?"

He nodded without hesitation or uncertainty. The transfer was made easily and quickly.

"You were very brave," she told him. "And I know your family will take very good care of you."

"Were you brave when your papa found you?"

She smiled. He had been paying attention. "I was."

Oliver squared his tiny shoulders, a firmness to the movement that spoke of resolution. "I'll be brave some more, even if Papa is angry."

"I know you will be." She turned back to Mr. Lancaster. "You'd best hurry. His parents are likely beside themselves."

She watched as Mr. Lancaster, moving so fast that his short curls bounced against the nape of his neck, carried his nephew to the house.

Were you brave? the sweet boy had asked. While the earl had been alive, she had always been brave. She'd leaned on his strength when her own courage had faltered. She felt as though she'd been struggling ever since.

Chapter Nine

Linus eyed that evening's gathering, wondering which of the guests his sisters meant to foist upon him this time. Lady Belinda had been pleasant enough, but she hadn't so much as smiled at a single jest—of his or anyone else's—and she'd not seemed any more interested in him than he had been in her. The Misses Romrell were yet a mystery, his encounter with them being exceptionally brief. None of the three was included in that evening's festivities.

A young widow, Mrs. Blackbourne, had joined the party for the evening. Linus firmly suspected he would find himself in her company often. His sisters would see to it.

Mr. Stroud, a gentleman likely near Linus's age, numbered amongst the new guests as well. Thus far, Stroud was innocuous, although he had taken an interest in Artemis that would bear watching.

Miss Hampton, Linus had noted straightaway, was not in the drawing room. He felt the oddest mixture of relief and disappointment. He wished to know her better, if for no other reason than to discover why she made him nervous. Despite that discomfort, he enjoyed her company. He sensed there were hidden depths in Miss Hampton that few were permitted to see, and that was endlessly intriguing. Beyond the pull he personally felt, there remained the need to thank her properly for the service she had rendered Oliver that afternoon.

Lud, if she hadn't found the boy before he'd reached the river, the results might have been disastrous. Linus had sworn to Adam and Persephone that he would personally teach Oliver how to swim, a skill he'd learned in the navy.

The dowager stood before the group, having already welcomed the guests to the evening's entertainment. "Her Grace and I have decided upon a game of tableau vivant for this evening."

A murmur of enthusiasm rolled over the gathering.

"You will be divided into two teams," the dowager continued. "Each team will be assigned a scene to portray. His Grace and I will be acting as judges when the tableaux are staged."

Though the dowager presented Adam's role as a magnanimous thing, Linus suspected the assignment was actually the result of Adam flatly refusing to participate in the staged scenes.

"The team that is deemed the winner will receive a prize."

"What is the prize?" Artemis asked, never one to worry over being demure.

"The duke will agree not to throttle you," Harry suggested.

"Capital," Lord Lampton declared, earning Adam's obvious annoyance.

The dowager waited with obvious enjoyment for the amusement to die down. "The teams will be a little uneven, I am afraid. Lady Lampton is not feeling well enough this evening to join us."

That was unfortunate. Linus suspected Lady Lampton was a calming influence on her husband, something that would have made keeping Adam's temper in check far easier.

"Our first team will consist of Her Grace, Mr. and Mrs. Windover, Mr. Stroud, and Lord Lampton."

Heads turned about as the team already named began searching each other out.

"Our second team will be Mr. Jonquil, Mrs. Blackbourne, Miss Lancaster, and Mr. Lancaster."

Mr. Stroud spoke immediately. "That is not so very uneven. Only a difference of one participant. I don't see any reason why the other team should lodge a complaint."

No one had lodged a complaint. Indeed, Mr. Stroud had come the closest with his veiled implication that the dowager's acknowledgment of the uneven numbers had been so unnecessary. Linus knew enough of civility to recognize the faux pax for what it was. One simply did not insult one's hostess.

The dowager, ever gracious, ignored the criticism and moved along. "I am designating Lord Lampton and Mr. Lancaster as the heads of their respective teams and will give them their assigned scenes."

She gave a paper to her son, then crossed to where Linus stood.

"If it will set your mind at ease," he said, "I am fully confident we will trounce the competition despite our smaller number."

The dowager, in a voice the tiniest bit dry, said, "Oh, but the sides are not so very uneven. Only a difference of one participant."

An exact recounting of Mr. Stroud's observation. The dowager had a sharp wit; there was no denying that.

"It is a shame Miss Hampton did not join us this evening." Could the dowager tell he was fishing about for information?

"Oh heavens." She held her hands up in a show of sudden realization. "Of course Arabella should be here." The sigh that followed was one of frustration. "I often forget how likely she is to assume she is not included in an activity if I haven't very specifically insisted otherwise. Of all my boys, only Corbin ever needed that reminder. It seems I am out of practice with one who is so very quiet and keeps to herself."

"She is perhaps a little reserved, but when we have spoken she has not struck me as shy."

The dowager's brows drew upward. "She spoke with you?"

He nodded. "A couple of times."

"More than once?" That was clearly unexpected. "I have not known her to be very open, even with those she knows well. She must feel some degree of ease with you."

How odd that she, by the dowager's account, was apprehensive in nearly everyone's company except his, while he was hesitant only in hers.

"I will send word to Arabella," the dowager said. "She will enjoy the evening's entertainment, and we will be the better for having her here." She slipped a folded paper in his hand. "Your tableau," she explained, then made her way quickly but with a very countess-like degree of dignity to a maid sitting diligently near the door.

She was sending for Miss Hampton. The nervousness he felt was, this time, mingled with a growing hint of excitement.

"What is our assignment?" Artemis said.

He unfolded the paper. "It says, 'Linus.'" He flipped it over, wondering if he'd missed something. Had the dowager forgotten to include the assignment in addition to the name of the team's leader?

Artemis moved closer, pulling Mrs. Blackbourne along with her. The dark-haired beauty was deposited—there was no other word for Artemis's almost forceful placement of her—at Linus's side.

Both ladies eyed the paper in his hand.

"That really is all it says." Artemis sounded rather put out.

Mrs. Blackbourne maintained her calm far better. "It is odd, I will acknowledge. We cannot truly proceed without an assignment."

"Perhaps 'Linus' *is* our assignment," Charlie said. "He was the subject of a myth, was he not?"

"He was, indeed," Linus said. All the Lancaster siblings were named for figures in Greek mythology, himself included.

Mrs. Blackbourne laid her hand lightly atop his arm. It was an unexpectedly forward gesture, considering they did not know each other at all. Linus moved his arm free but did so subtly in order to not draw undue attention. He did not wish to embarrass either of them.

"At the risk of making something of a spectacle of myself," Mrs. Blackbourne said, "I will confess I am not familiar with the details of Linus of old."

Artemis took up the explanation before Linus had a chance. "He was the creator of melody and rhythm, and he was murdered with his own musical instrument in an act of petty revenge. What it lacks in visibility, Linus's myth more than makes up for with excitement. Art. Intrigue. Even death. It is absolutely perfect for a game of tableau vivant."

Mrs. Blackbourne met Linus's gaze and offered what could only be interpreted as a look of conspiratorial amusement. She, it seemed, had taken Artemis's measure quickly. Did she also realize that Artemis was part of his sisters' conspiracy to find him a match? If so, she did not seem to object.

"Oh, Linus." Artemis took hold of his arm, excitement rendering her noticeably giddy. "Do let me plan our tableau. Please. I am ever so much better at these things than you are. We will be victorious for certain if I am in charge."

Linus didn't particularly want to undertake the arrangements. He nodded his agreement. "Although I reserve the right to put a stop to anything I feel needs stopping."

Artemis rolled her eyes. "I am not a child anymore."

"No, but you are still Artemis." He dared her to contradict him.

Despite her show of displeasure, Artemis's lips twitched. "If I promise to behave, will you allow me to plan our tableau?"

"With supervision."

She sighed, her shoulders rising and falling. "Older brothers are such a burden."

"Yes, they are." Charlie couldn't possibly have sounded more empathetic.

"Well, then," Linus said, "let us give the planning of this endeavor to Artemis and do our utmost to trounce young Mr. Jonquil's older brother. He is heading the other team, you will remember."

Artemis stepped directly to where Linus stood, forcing him to move aside, which necessitated Mrs. Blackbourne's moving as well. She did not return to her previous place but rather kept near him. The young widow certainly didn't want for boldness.

He offered what he hoped would be interpreted as an innocuous smile and placed some distance between them.

"Linus will, of course, be assigned the role of Linus," Artemis declared. "We will also need to fill the part of his parents and choose someone to portray Heracles."

Miss Hampton stepped inside the drawing room. A bubble of excitement formed in Linus's chest. She paused at the doorway. Her expression was not one of ease and pleasure but of uncertainty and worry. She sought out the dowager, who smiled at her and motioned to the side of the room where Linus's group stood. Miss Hampton pushed out a breath, not looking the least bit eager to join in the evening's diversion. She crossed the room toward him.

He had been the one to suggest she be included. Seeing her discomfort made him doubt the wisdom of that idea. Maybe she really was shier than he had realized.

"I see the dowager convinced you to join us," he said.

She nodded minutely. "She can be very persuasive."

"Would you have preferred not to come down?" He hoped not.

"Actually, I was pleased to be invited." A hesitant contentment entered her expression. "I want to participate, but . . . I'm not family or a guest or anyone of significance. I never can be certain where I fit in this gathering."

How well he understood that uncertainty. "I *am* family to a significant portion of this gathering, and I don't truly know where I fit."

"We are the misfits of this house party, are we?" She laughed lightly.

He pointedly squared his shoulders. "I believe I am equal to the challenge."

"I have you bested there," she said. "I was born for this challenge."

He held back a grin. "You were born a misfit?"

She nodded solemnly. "Do try not to be consumed by jealousy."

"I will make a valiant effort."

She looked toward the others, and her nervous demeanor returned. "I feel so out of place."

"We misfits must stick together," he said.

"Are you proposing we form a club?" How easily he could bring a smile to her face. It made a man feel less pointless to be a source of joy in another person's life.

Artemis interrupted. "Miss Hampton, are you joining us?"

"Yes. The dowager asked me if I would." She spoke more quietly than she had only a moment earlier.

"Perfect," Artemis said. "You can be Calliope."

Miss Hampton looked to Linus once more. "It seems I am missing some crucial information."

"Tableau vivant," he said. "We are portraying the myth of Linus."

"I am to be your mother?" She laughed almost silently. "This is proving to be an odd sort of club."

Linus was impressed. Few people knew the details of his namesake's myth outside of scholars and mythological enthusiasts. Did she share that interest with him?

"I was not charged with assigning roles," he told her.

She tipped her head, barely concealing her amusement. "Do you doubt my ability to portray the illustrious muse?"

He grinned; he couldn't help himself. Though she still rendered him a bit jelly-like, he found he enjoyed her company more every time he was granted it. Her conversation, though he'd had only the briefest moments of it, had proven more diverting than most of what he had encountered in the months since leaving the navy. And she'd shown herself to be in possession of a wonderfully subtle sense of humor.

"I was not able this afternoon to offer you a sufficient expression of gratitude for the service you rendered Oliver."

"I simply found myself in a position to help." Her tone was one of dismissal, as if her actions did not warrant acknowledgment.

"You showed him such patience and kindness," Linus said. "He needed that tenderness likely more than you realized. I thank you for that."

Embarrassed color touched her cheeks. "I have been in need of tenderness many times in my life. I am grateful to have offered that to someone else when he needed it."

Artemis interrupted their conversation. Again. "Linus, you are not paying attention. How are we supposed to have a deep reservoir of theatricality if our most essential role is taken on by someone who isn't even listening?"

He turned to fully face her and bowed quite deeply. "My most sincere apologies."

Artemis addressed Miss Hampton. "Calliope needs to be standing with Oeagrus."

Miss Hampton nodded. "Who is Oeagrus?"

She had known that Calliope was the mother of Linus of myth, and therefore, it stood to reason she knew perfectly well that Oeagrus was ancient Linus's father. Still, he couldn't resist teasing her a little. "He is the mythological king of—"

She leveled him a look of such pretended offense that he laughed out loud. Artemis eyed him as if he had lost his mind. Her gaze slowly slid back to Miss Hampton, something very like worry entering her expression. If he didn't know better, he would think his usually unflappable sister was distressed. Did she not care for Miss Hampton? That seemed unlikely.

"Mr. Jonquil." Artemis pointed toward Charlie. "He is Oeagrus. You should go stand with him."

Miss Hampton did so without comment. If she noticed the tactlessness with which Artemis sent her away, she did not let it show.

"You were rude," he told his sister in hushed tones.

True to form, she took the criticism far too much to heart. "I'm simply trying to organize. We haven't very much time for arranging our tableau, and I want to do my best. You were not helping."

The final accusation emerged too watery for him to do anything but put his arm around her shoulders. "I know you grow impatient when you are enjoying yourself and you feel others aren't contributing." His words of intended reassurance missed the mark. Artemis's chin quivered. *Good grief.* "I promise to be very cooperative."

She nodded, though she still looked a little hurt. "I should hope so."

"What role do you mean to take on?"

Artemis rallied with alarming speed, as always. Linus was not certain if she was one who recovered quickly or if she made a greater show of offended sensibilities than was truly accurate.

"I will be music personified." The declaration emerged a bit breathless.

Music personified. There really was no sensible response to that. It was little wonder the very staid Duke of Kielder found his youngest sister-in-law so exasperating.

"That, however, will mean Mrs. Blackbourne will have to be Heracles, which would not have been my first choice." She gave the young widow a look of commiseration. "You are simply not convincing as a musical murderer."

"I do not know whether to be proud or disappointed in myself." Mrs. Blackbourne tossed Linus a look that felt a bit too personal for two people who'd not had a single conversation.

"Do your best," Artemis instructed. "And stand next to Linus; that is where you are meant to be."

Far from objecting, Mrs. Blackbourne's gaze grew warm. Ah, yes. His sisters had definitely settled upon Mrs. Blackbourne for that night's matchmaking efforts. She seemed to have embraced the role quite enthusiastically. Linus was both flattered and a little annoyed. He'd been the recipient of a few flirtatious gazes, especially when he'd been in uniform. He'd not wanted for dance partners on the few occasions when Persephone had convinced him to attend a ball, but this was far closer quarters than he was accustomed to. Did the widow know the conspiracy amongst the Lancaster women, or was she merely enthusiastic for his company?

Miss Hampton, blast the lady, was biting back a smile. Her amusement relieved some of his discomfort. The situation was a little funny, though only a very little.

The dowager returned to their corner of the drawing room. "There is a trunk just over to the side with various possible costume pieces and items. You are welcome to look through them as you design your tableau."

"Is the trunk large enough to lock a certain recalcitrant sister of mine inside?" Linus asked, sensing the dowager would appreciate his struggle, having raised a large family of her own.

She nodded. "If necessary."

"I heard that," Artemis said.

"Do not fear, Miss Lancaster," the dowager said. "The trunk does not lock."

"A shame." Linus let his shoulders rise and fall with a feigned sigh. "I suppose 'music personified' will have to be let free after all."

The dowager offered a warning. "You have only thirty minutes remaining."

That sent Artemis into a panic, her offended sensibilities entirely forgotten. She rattled off instructions to everyone, telling them where to be and what to do.

They were all forthwith provided with various oddities to complete their costumes, none of which bore the slightest resemblance to anything that had existed in ancient Greece. No one seemed to particularly mind. Miss Hampton and Charlie were enjoying themselves, though Linus could not overhear enough of their conversation to know what they were saying. Mrs. Blackbourne continually whispered observations, the low volume of her voice rendering the conversation far more intimate than was warranted.

Sensing escape was necessary, Linus made a hasty observation to the group. "This tableau needs a lyre, else what am I to be strangled with?"

Artemis pressed a hand to her heart. "I hadn't thought of that."

Linus took a step away from Mrs. Blackbourne. "I will return with one shortly."

"You know where one is?" Miss Hampton asked, her attention on him for the first time in nearly twenty minutes.

"I happen to play the lyre," he said.

Her lips twitched. "Do you not fear that history might repeat itself? This tableau ought to serve as something of a warning."

He assumed his most roguish expression. "I like to live dangerously."

Chapter Ten

"Miss Lancaster might very well hunt her brother down if he does not return soon," Charlie said.

Artemis—Arabella struggled to think of the young lady in more formal terms when she stood so clearly on the verge of a tantrum—glared at the drawing room doors through which her brother had disappeared nearly ten minutes earlier. "Where is he?"

Mater had wandered over to their group as that question was asked. "Arabella, would you be so good as to see if you can ascertain Mr. Lancaster's whereabouts?"

"Of course." She took up the assignment eagerly, grateful to be of help.

"But then we will not have our Calliope," Artemis protested.

"I will return directly." While she was every bit the misfit in this gathering that she had told Mr. Lancaster she was, she had been enjoying herself. She had been included in the activities. And she had found a kinship with the kind and handsome former lieutenant, something she very much wanted to continue.

Upon reaching the corridor containing the guest bedchambers, she glanced in all directions. There was no sign of anyone there. Where might he have gone? Perhaps his lyre was in the music room. Except, if he'd gone only two doors down from the drawing room, he would not have been away so long. Where else could he be?

Twice that day, she had seen Mr. Lancaster with his nephew. Perhaps he had chosen to look in on the little boy. If she didn't find him there, she would simply have to return and face Artemis's wrath.

He was, indeed, in the nursery, holding tiny Lord Falstone, rocking the whimpering child in his arms.

"Has something happened?" she asked.

"He's feverish," Mr. Lancaster said. "The nursemaid couldn't comfort him enough to calm his cries."

Arabella moved to his side. Mr. Lancaster smelled of cinnamon. She didn't think she'd ever known another gentleman who did. It was unique but not at all unpleasant.

She set her hand gently on the boy's flushed cheeks. "He is *quite* feverish. Have his parents been sent for?"

"Not yet. I was hoping I could get him to sleep. His parents have been worried enough about him today." A heartbreaking little cry pulled Mr. Lancaster's attention back to his bundle. "Perhaps worrying them can't be helped. Would you feel better, Oliver, if you had your mother here?"

The boy simply continued whimpering.

Mr. Lancaster turned to the nursemaid, who was pulling the curtains around the room. "Janey, will you please fetch Their Graces?"

The nursemaid slipped quickly out of the room.

"Uncle Linus." The little boy's tender words were soft and pleading.

"I know," was the gentle reply. "Feeling unwell is a misery."

Mr. Lancaster was such a contradiction. He had the unmistakable bearing of a military man, yet he laughed easily and readily and was as at home in the nursery as the drawing room. He belonged to a family of tremendous importance yet had spoken to Janey without any of the pomposity so common in the aristocracy. He had full access to the stables, the grounds, the carriages but had chosen to spend his morning with a little boy and now his evening tending to the same child. And he had reached out to her, offering kindness and the first trace of friendship.

"I can't say that I know very much about treating ill children," Mr. Lancaster said. "My sister Daphne, on the other hand, would know precisely what is to be done."

"He is not throwing any spots," she observed. "That is a good sign. And while he is clearly uncomfortable, he is still alert."

The boy rested with such trust against his uncle's shoulder.

"Perhaps we should invite him to join our club," Mr. Lancaster said. "That should cheer him up quickly."

It had certainly lifted Arabella's spirits. "I doubt his parents would consider him an outcast."

"They certainly would not." He rocked the boy gently in his arms.

Arabella had known only one gentleman in all her life who had emanated such kindness. The reminder of the caring man she had lost so long ago clogged her throat and rendered her thoughts heavy. How she missed him. How she wished he were there.

The duke and duchess arrived, both crossing directly to where Mr. Lancaster held their son. The duke wore such a fierce look that Arabella, on pure instinct, moved to intervene. In the next instant, however, little Lord Falstone reached for his father without a hint of trepidation. The duke held him protectively, gently, the very picture of compassion.

"You might as well have my effects moved in here, Persephone," His Grace said. "I will not be leaving."

Emotion built ever stronger in Arabella's heart. She had expected to confront memories of the earl in this house but had not anticipated the reminders coming from guests who were little more than strangers to her.

Mr. Lancaster stood beside the duchess. "I ought to have known he'd be more comforted by his father's presence than mine."

She gave him a look of empathy. "That child is more comforted by his father's presence than by *mine.*" The observation was not made bitterly. "Perhaps this next child will be equally fond of its mother."

Mr. Lancaster turned wide eyes on his sister. "Persephone, are you—?"

She laughed nearly silently. "That was meant to remain a secret for a time."

"Never fear. Uncle Linus can be trusted to keep mum." He put an arm around her shoulders. "I'm happy for you."

Arabella felt entirely *de trop*. That happened so often. So very often.

She quietly slipped toward the door.

"Miss Hampton." The duke's voice was quiet but every bit as authoritative as ever.

She turned to face him, quaking a little inside.

"Have the dowager or Lord Lampton send for the physician forthwith."

"Adam," Her Grace said in tones of light scolding.

"Please," he added.

Arabella offered a brief dip of her head.

"And, Miss Hampton." The duke held her gaze with a firm and unwavering one of his own. "Thank you again for finding my son this afternoon."

"I am grateful to have helped," she said and, feeling a surge of discomfort, slipped out of the room.

She'd not yet reached the ground floor when Mr. Lancaster caught up with her. The speed of his descent sent a wave of fresh worry over her. "Has Lord Falstone worsened so quickly?"

"No. His father has." Mr. Lancaster had a way of saying things quite seriously but with undertones of humor. Arabella liked it very much. "He sent me to make doubly certain Lord Lampton isn't 'blinded by his own pantaloons and rendered incapable of responsible action.'" His impression of the duke was uncanny.

"Perhaps we should wait to deliver the request until after the earl's valet has undressed him." The moment she spoke the words, she realized how uncouth they were. Heat filled her face. "That was inappropriate."

"But funny." Indeed, he looked far more entertained than offended.

"You won't tell the dowager how improperly I spoke just now?"

He nodded solemnly. "I will guard your secret with my life."

"That is very good of you," she said.

"Anything for a fellow club member."

He meant to continue with their jest? He had family, despite his insistence otherwise. Yet he still felt a kinship with her and empathy for her situation.

"We really should deliver the duke's request," he said.

"For what it's worth," she replied, "I do not actually doubt Lord Lampton's reliability."

Mr. Lancaster walked alongside her, matching her pace. "I don't think the duke doubts it either. His grumpiness simply grows when he is concerned, and few things concern him more deeply than his family's well-being."

Arabella shook her head. "That surprises me."

"It is meant to," Mr. Lancaster said. "His Grace works very hard to be intimidating. He is also genuinely fearsome. Yet those who know him best love him. I am not certain how he manages it." He leaned a little closer, lowering his voice as if about to share a great secret. "Should you sort out the mystery of my brother-in-law's behavior, feel free to pass along your discovery."

"You must have great confidence in my ability to solve mysteries."

He shrugged. "You *did* figure out what mischief my sisters were undertaking."

"I did manage that, didn't I?" He was surprisingly easy to talk with. "I spend a great deal of time explaining your family to you."

He smiled broadly, the expression bringing light and cheerfulness to his green eyes. Heavens, he was even more handsome when he smiled that way. "What can I say? I have a very mysterious family."

"Mine is not so difficult to sort out. Only two are still living, other than myself, and they are not overly friendly."

"I am sorry to hear that." He spoke to her without even a hint of dismissal. It warmed her heart.

They had reached the drawing room. Mater met them only a few steps inside. "How is the little one?"

"His Grace has requested that Dr. Scorseby be sent for," Arabella said, delivering the message she had been charged with.

"I will send one of the stable hands." Mater left to deliver her request.

The other guests quickly gathered around, inquiring after Lord Falstone's health and well-being. The comfort Arabella had felt in Mr. Lancaster's presence dissipated. She had never been overly fond of crowds. He, on the other hand, seemed entirely at ease surrounded by people as he answered their questions.

She slipped away, skirting the other guests as she made her way toward the window that had become her place in the room.

"Are we canceling the tableaux?" Artemis asked her brother.

"Your nephew will be fine," Mr. Lancaster said drily. "I am certain you are relieved."

She looked immediately chagrined. "I hadn't meant to be insensitive. I simply—I wanted—" Her chin quivered. In the next instant, Artemis fled the room.

Mr. Stroud moved to follow her, but Mr. Lancaster was faster. His concern for his nephew extended to his youngest sister as well. Arabella liked him all the better for it.

She sat, knowing she would be unobtrusive in her little corner.

Charlie, however, did not permit it. He joined her there. "Was Lord Falstone very ill?"

"He did not appear to be." Arabella, of course, was no expert. "I imagine we will hear about it if that does not prove to be the case."

Charlie stood a moment, eying the room from this vantage point. "Why do you always sit over here?"

"It is quiet. And it seems more appropriate." It was also more familiar. In her uncle's home, she had kept to corners and out of the way. This was not such a change. "I am, after all, a companion, not a guest nor a member of the family."

He shot her a look of patent disbelief. "Did Mater say you had to keep to the corner?"

"No. But sometimes finding one's place, no matter how humble, is the best that can be made of a situation."

His brow creased even as his gaze turned to his brother in conversation with Mr. Windover across the room. "What if there isn't really a 'best' to be made? What if everything is just . . ." He ended the sentence on a shrug, apparently not having the right word.

"Has something happened?" she asked.

"I'm trying to sort some things out, is all. It's a bit of a mess in my head just now."

"Have you tried talking with your brother?" Philip had enough of his father in him that he would be the very best person for Charlie to confide in.

"My brothers are always busy."

"Is there no one else you could turn to?" She felt odd even asking the question. The closeness and loyalty of the Jonquil family was legendary.

He shook his head, his gaze wandering to the window. After a moment, he said, "Mr. Lancaster invited me to ride with him in the morning. He might—he might have time for me." Years' worth of hurt lay beneath those words.

"At the very least, he will be a captive audience."

Charlie laughed, and the sound did her heart good. She had always been fond of him. And her dear earl had adored his littlest one. She still remembered the way he had lit up whenever Charlie had run across the lawn to greet him. She had sat in the shadows of the back wall, usually unnoticed, and imagined that had she been a Jonquil, the earl would have loved her that deeply and openly.

"Speaking of captive audiences," he said, "I do wish we could have seen my brother's portrayal of Hades. The other team was assigned the myth of Persephone. From what I hear, Philip's performance alone would have won the competition for them, though he likely would have been strangled by the duke for it."

"Truly?" Arabella couldn't imagine why it would matter so much. "Does His Grace dislike the tale?"

"That myth, as I understand it, strikes a bit close to home," Charlie said. "Philip does know how to be entertaining. And without Sorrel here, there is no one to keep him out of trouble."

"A difficult task, I would imagine."

Charlie shook his head. "Yet my family insists I am the one always landing in scrapes."

"You do have a rather extensive history of precisely that," she reminded him.

"It doesn't happen as often as it used to," he insisted.

She chose not to point out that he had found himself in one predicament after another only the summer before.

"Do you think Mr. Lancaster would listen to me?" He sounded so hesitant yet so very close to being hopeful.

"I do," she said.

Mr. Lancaster understood the struggle of being lost amongst a gathering, amongst family. He would not dismiss Charlie's feelings. He would reach out to him as he had reached out to her.

It was little wonder she was coming to like Mr. Lancaster so much. She had not known much true benevolence in her uncle's home but had clung to the belief that it did, indeed, exist elsewhere.

Chapter Eleven

DURING HIS RIDE WITH CHARLIE the next morning, Linus discovered he had a lot in common with the young gentleman. Neither of them had spent much time in London, a place they both found more than a bit tedious. Though Charlie had benefited from extensive schooling and Linus had spent those years at sea, they shared similar academic curiosity. Linus spoke of the myths his father had loved so much and that he had learned to love as well. Charlie told him about his study of mathematical theories. Much of what he said was beyond Linus's comprehension, yet the young man's enthusiasm was contagious.

"Our navigator on board ship used a tremendous amount of mathematics," Linus said. "I spent the better part of a year studying with him. It was fascinating, though in the end, I preferred other responsibilities. You might consider that. Nineteen is a little old to begin in the navy, but it is not unheard of."

Charlie shook his head. "My interests tend to the more theoretical. More academic."

"I suspect you and my father would have appreciated one another. He thoroughly enjoyed the academic aspect of his studies."

They had been riding for an hour, and the horses were tired and moving at a slow, meandering pace. The stables had come into view, but they had a little distance yet to cover before ending their morning excursion.

"How did your father support his family on the income of an academic?" Charlie, it seemed, knew something about the challenges of that particular career choice.

"Are you considering pursuing academics?"

"A little." He shrugged as if it didn't matter, but the lines in his face said otherwise. This was a topic of some importance to him. Charlie might have been a bit tossed about, but it seemed he wasn't as lacking in direction as he had at first appeared to be.

"Our family was certainly not wealthy," Linus said. "But we did have a small stipend from my grandfather's estate."

"At the risk of commenting where I'm not welcome, it is rather well known that your family was in far worse straits than being merely 'not wealthy.'"

That was fair. "Our poverty was not the result of our father's career choice but rather his decline. Had he been able to continue his speaking engagements and publications, our circumstances would have been much improved."

No more was spoken on the matter. Linus didn't push for further confidences. Evander had often allowed Linus to express his worries and frustrations, patiently listening, not pressing the discussion. Being in that role now was unfamiliar but not as ill-fitting as he would have guessed. Evander's influence could still be felt, even after more than ten years. But he had never known his brother in the role of master of the estate. He would not have that example to lean on when he returned home. He would be as lost as ever.

A stable hand greeted them as they approached. Linus pulled his thoughts back to the present, where they belonged.

They dismounted, handing their reins to the stable staff. No sooner had they begun walking the path toward the terrace doors at the back of the house then Linus spotted Miss Hampton just stepping out. She wore a shawl and a pair of heavy walking shoes. He was more than pleased to see her; he was eager.

"It seems Miss Hampton means to take a stroll," he said. "Does she really walk as often as you said yesterday?"

"All the time." Charlie brushed some dust off the front of his jacket. "Even when we were all little, she was forever wandering the neighborhood. Philip told me once that she was probably escaping."

"Escaping what?" Linus asked.

"Home."

She had told Linus the evening before that she had only two family members and they were not kind people. Charlie's description of her painted those relatives in an even less flattering light. What must her life have been like if she had avoided home as much as Charlie's memories indicated?

"Good morning, Arabella," Charlie greeted her when she came near.

Christian names were not generally permitted between a young lady and a gentleman who were not related. The dowager's description of Miss Hampton as a friend of the family had clearly not been an exaggeration.

"A good morning to both of you," she returned. "Did you enjoy your ride?"

"I did," Charlie said. "Mr. Lancaster let me talk at length about things that could not possibly have interested him. I can't remember the last time that happened."

"I have seen Mater listen to you for hours on end, Charlie Jonquil. Do not dismiss that."

Why that hadn't occurred to Linus, he couldn't say. Charlie thought his brothers too busy for his concerns and questions, but surely he felt his mother would listen.

"Why don't you go offer your mother a good morning," Linus suggested. "I'm certain she would appreciate it." And perhaps Charlie would think to turn to her with more of his worries.

"I likely should." Charlie whistled as he made his way farther up the path.

"That was well done of you, sir." Though she spoke seriously, a hint of humor touched her words. "I do believe he was going to attempt to infiltrate our club."

"And what is the point of a club if it is not *very* exclusive?" His attempt at appearing grave dissolved into something that felt an awful lot like embarrassment. "I am glad you were willing to endure my ridiculousness last evening."

"I think we all need a bit of ridiculousness now and then," she said.

Linus didn't think he'd met anyone who so fully shared his view of things. He was eager to discover in what other ways they were similar.

"How much younger is Charlie than you?" She asked the question with confused curiosity. She didn't seem to be certain of his own age. That, no doubt, was the result of long days out at sea in the sun and harsh winds that had aged him quickly.

Did she think him haggard and aged? Lud, he hoped not.

"I am twenty-four." He watched for any signs of shock but, blessedly, didn't see any. "Half a lifetime spent at sea no doubt makes me seem like forty-two."

She shook her head. "I would not have guessed forty-anything. And if you know what is best for you, you won't guess my age near there either."

His grin only grew. "I know better than to guess at all."

She pulled her shawl more snugly around her shoulders. "Twenty-three," she said. "Though a lifetime spent walking this neighborhood in all weather no doubt makes me seem like one hundred twenty-three."

"That was my next guess," he said.

She shook her head in clear amusement. "I suspect, sir, that you are something of a handful."

"Guilty."

"I will have you know, *I* have never been difficult a day in my life." She was teasing, yet there was truth in the declaration.

"I believe you," he said. "I cannot imagine you being anything but an absolute delight."

She blushed deeply and immediately. Did the color rise out of embarrassment or because she liked knowing that he enjoyed her company?

"May I join you as you walk?" he asked.

She looked at him once more. "Going for drawn-out walks will make you an oddity in this neighborhood."

"This seems a fitting course of action for a misfit."

"Who am I to deny a fellow outcast?" Her smile tugged at him fiercely. She began walking. He moved alongside her. "Did Charlie speak with you during your ride?"

"No. He was silent the entire time. Not a single word."

She eyed him doubtfully. "There is only one Jonquil who can remain silent for any length of time, and it's not Charlie."

"You know the family well."

"I have spent my life among them."

Something in her use of *among* belied the word, as if she had been with them but not truly *with* them. Heavens, he knew that feeling. He lived among his family but still felt in many ways like an outsider.

"Charlie was feeling a bit down last evening," Miss Hampton said. "I had hoped he would confide in you."

"He did a little."

She looked genuinely relieved. "I know it is none of my affair, but I do worry for him, just as I worry for the dowager and for Lady Lampton."

"Is Lady Lampton often unwell?" He held his hand up in an attempt to dismiss the question. "Forgive me. I realize that is more prying than I ought to be doing."

"The two of us missed our calling," she said. "We ought to have been gossipy matrons."

"Yes." He nodded emphatically. "I have been trying to decide what to do with the remainder of my life. I believe you have hit upon it." She likely thought him inexcusably nosey.

"I *am* a problem solver."

She seemed truly at ease with him, laughing and jesting. The dowager had indicated that such openness on her part was unusual. They'd known each other two days. Two. Yet they spoke as easily as if they were longtime friends.

"You've lived in the neighborhood all your life, then?" he asked.

She nodded. "The estate that now belongs to my uncle was my father's. My parents passed away when I was six years old."

He knew the pain of losing one's parents. "We lost my mother when I was five. My father died while I was at sea."

"I am sorry for your losses."

The mournful empathy in her tone and expression brought a tightness to his throat and a twinge to his heart. He pushed his reaction down fiercely and immediately. Losing his family was not a weight he allowed his mind to carry for more than a moment.

"You must have known the current Lord Lampton while you were young." An abrupt change of topic but a necessary one. "Was he always so . . . unique?"

A flash of something resembling regret crossed her features. That was wholly unexpected. What in his question had caused her grief, however momentary?

"He was always entertaining," she said hesitantly. "The brother just younger than he, Layton, enjoyed larks every bit as much but had a more somber mien. The neighborhood often remarked on the oddity of the younger of the two being better suited to the role of heir. Of course, Layton was heir to his own estate through his mother. And Ph—Lord Lampton— grew into his role, as unique as his approach to it has proven."

How was it that this conversation, focused as it was on other people, continually struck at the heart of his own experiences and uncertainties? "The son best suited to a role is not always the one to assume it."

That brought her searching gaze to his face once more. "Do you not consider yourself 'the son best suited' to the role you have assumed?"

"I was the younger son. The part I have been given should never have been mine." He could hear that his voice and tone had grown more tense, more clipped. That always happened when he spoke of Evander. He didn't seem able to prevent it.

She turned her focus to the flowers they walked past, not speaking or looking at him any longer. Had his tense response wounded her? He'd not been unkind in his words, but it was entirely possible she had taken his change in tone as a rebuke, as an indication that her conversation was not welcome. Nothing could be further from the truth. They simply needed to choose a different topic, return to the light banter they'd been enjoying.

"Miss Hampton." A man's voice echoed from up the path.

Her attention shifted in that direction. She didn't speak but seemed pleased to see the new arrival.

The man reached her side and offered a quick bow. "I have come to check on the children. Those from Farland Meadows are also here, both having developed fevers. Having all three in the same place simplifies their care."

Miss Hampton didn't respond verbally but did indicate with a quick dip of her head that she approved of the arrangement.

"Their location is also very fortunate for me as I have the opportunity of seeing you."

She blushed. Linus did not like that at all.

The man eyed Linus. He thrust out his hand. "Dr. Scorseby."

Doctor. A physician. Linus grasped the offered hand firmly. "Lieutenant Lancaster." He was retired now, so "lieutenant" was not entirely appropriate, but it was the only impressive claim he could make for himself.

"Army or navy?" Dr. Scorseby asked.

"Navy."

"What has you on dry land?"

Linus glanced at Miss Hampton. Quietly, he said, "The company."

"I wish I had more time for such pleasant pursuits," Dr. Scorseby said. "I have too many patients depending on me." He spoke with palpable self-importance.

"Don't let us keep you from your patients," Linus said.

Dr. Scorseby turned once more to Miss Hampton. "Am I asking too much to hope you might accompany me to the house?"

He spoke properly but with a hint of less exalted beginnings. Linus had heard that a lot during his years at sea. Those who'd started in the navy young and who'd come from lowered circumstances but had had eyes on advancement and opportunities had often practiced speaking more properly.

What were Scorseby's origins? Physicians were considered gentlemen.

Miss Hampton spoke for the first time. "I am taking a turn about the gardens with Mr. Lancaster."

Her reference to their excursion sounded far more like a confession of obligation than a joyful experience. He had been enjoying their time together. Had she not?

"Do not reject the invitation on my account," he said. "By all means, accompany Dr. Scorseby to the nursery."

For the length of a breath, she didn't answer. She didn't look at him or move. Was she hesitant? Anxious to remain? But the moment passed, and she turned fully to the doctor. She gave a quick nod.

Dr. Scorseby offered his arm. She accepted and, arm-in-arm, walked beside him back up the garden path and out of sight.

That hadn't ended at all the way he'd hoped. He'd suggested their club of outcasts as a jest, but there'd been some truth to it.

He did feel like the misfit at society gatherings and the member of his family least likely to be missed should he wander back to sea. With Miss Hampton, though, much of this misery and loneliness disappeared. She made him a little nervous, yes, but she also made him feel as though he had a place once more.

She had shown him real concern and kindness. She had teased and jested and lightened his mood. He missed her company already. Reluctantly, he returned to the house.

Voices drifted out of the sitting room as he passed. One, he was certain, belonged to Athena. He would enjoy some time with his sister; he'd had little enough of it the past thirteen years. However, like Miss Hampton, she had company of her own: a room full of ladies. Though he would have preferred to make good his escape, he'd come too far inside to go unnoticed.

The expected bows and curtsies were exchanged. Athena eagerly urged him to sit near her, which placed him very near Lady Belinda, who was visiting with her mother. Nearer his youngest sister was Mrs. Blackbourne, who eyed him with the same look of suffocating familiarity she had worn the evening before.

The dowager was among the group as well. While Linus's sisters were watching him with earnestness and Lady Belinda's mother eyed him with curiosity, it was pure, unmistakable amusement he saw in the dowager's eyes. Did she know of his sisters' plotting as well?

"Aren't you so pleased Lady Belinda has returned?" Athena asked him.

Lady Belinda was pleasant enough, but he had no desire to raise expectations in that quarter. "A house party is always more enjoyable with lovely ladies present."

Athena's smile remained, but she eyed him a bit more narrowly. His verbal dodging, it seemed, had not met entirely with her approval.

Their youngest sister entered the fray. "And we have Mrs. Blackbourne here. I am certain you are particularly pleased to see her."

Subtlety never had been Artemis's strong suit.

Fortunately, Linus was a dab hand at maneuvering around shoals. "As she was the Heracles to my ancient Linus only last evening, I find myself a little trepidatious at seeing her again."

Mrs. Blackbourne laughed.

Artemis rolled her eyes. "She didn't actually portray Heracles. We were interrupted."

"Perhaps she has arrived today to finish the job." Linus only hoped a jesting approach would communicate his lack of romantic interest in the widow. Or Lady Belinda. Or whoever else they brought around to toss at him.

The dowager spoke next. "I'm certain you will be equally pleased to meet two more of our guests who will be joining us this evening."

He met her eye. Her expression was far too innocent and far too full of laughter. She did know of the Lancaster sisters' efforts, and she, like Miss Hampton, was laughing at him.

"I am certain I will be," he said. "I have enjoyed all of the people you have invited to the party thus far."

Athena and Artemis eyed him with frustration. They had chosen their favorites in the "Find Linus a Wife" scheme and clearly did not like that he'd offered such a general compliment and hadn't shown any preference for their picks.

Was Persephone participating as well? Although he trusted her judgment more than either Artemis or Athena, having spent more time with her during his shore leaves, he didn't particularly care for three-against-one odds.

The dowager tapped the seat beside her. He recognized the invitation and sat.

"How was your ride this morning?" she asked.

"Very pleasant. Your youngest is excellent company."

She smiled fondly. "He is a good boy, though I say it myself."

"And I spoke again with Miss Hampton. Despite your insistence that she is painfully quiet, we conversed quite easily. Indeed, I was more nervous than she seemed to be."

She studied him. "What is it about you that has set her so uncharacteristically at ease?"

"I am nothing special." He didn't care to admit that, yet it was true.

"On the contrary, Mr. Lancaster." She studied him.

Artemis and Athena were watching him, as were Lady Belinda and Mrs. Blackbourne.

Beating a hasty retreat proved quite simple. A bow. A word of excuse. A barely dignified flight from the room. He had insisted to Miss Hampton that he could withstand his sisters' machinations. He was beginning to fear he had been overconfident.

Chapter Twelve

ARABELLA HAD SEEN DR. SCORSEBY treat patients before. Her aunt had required his expertise to clear up a purification of the lungs a few months earlier. Uncle had sought the young physician's evaluation of what proved to be gout. Dr. Scorseby had looked after a small child who had managed somehow to cut her finger during church services the week before.

He had a very pleasant way about him. Even little Lord Falstone, who had been very reluctant to leave his father's arms, allowed the physician to examine him after a mere moment's interaction. Caroline and Henry Jonquil accepted the necessity as well without fuss or concern. Henry, of course, was not yet a year old and knew nothing of what was happening, but he had been quite fussy right until Dr. Scorseby had held and soothed him.

Arabella liked that about their local man of medicine. Gentle kindness was tremendously important to her.

Lady Marion Jonquil, who had been rather fretful herself, calmed as she watched the physician care for her children. The duke, however, never stopped looking thunderous. At first glance, Arabella had thought he was angry. As she watched him, his gaze never leaving his son, she realized his look of anger was not anger at all but the strain of worry over someone he loved.

She looked away, the old, familiar ache resurfacing at seeing such affection. She'd wished for that all her life, to know with such certainty that she was loved.

She had stepped out for her walk that morning earlier than she usually did on account of Philip and Layton, the second brother, both being in the house. The weight of her memories had proven difficult, and she'd sought her customary escape.

She had been quite pleased to encounter Mr. Lancaster as she'd stepped outside. His company lifted her spirits. She felt different with him, as though she were truly welcome and wanted. But he had dismissed her company so easily, so quickly. *Do not reject the invitation on my account.* He'd not seemed to regret her departure. Perhaps there was less enjoyment and more pity in his attentions than she'd allowed herself to acknowledge.

Arabella pulled her mind back to the present just as Dr. Scorseby returned to the small writing table where she stood. He sat and began writing out instructions, no doubt for the worried parents as well as the nursery maids.

"Do you know if the dowager has been taking the powders I left for her a fortnight ago?" he asked, apparently, her.

"I was not aware that she was meant to be taking powders," Arabella said.

He glanced up at her. "You are acting as her companion, are you not?"

"I am, but I have not been privy to the more private aspects of her life." It was a very circumspect way of saying "I serve no real purpose in this household."

He was still writing, somehow managing to keep his written words and his spoken ones from interrupting each other. "I sensed when I suggested the treatment that she was not fully convinced of the necessity."

Arabella grew alarmed. "Is her health in danger?"

"It is nothing truly serious, but she will feel better if she uses the powders. That, in turn, will give her a better quality of life and greater longevity."

This did not sound like a simple thing. "What is the matter with her?"

He shook his head. "I make a point of not divulging personal information about my patients. I would not have mentioned the powders if I hadn't assumed you, as her companion, were aware of them."

How ridiculous she must seem, a companion who knew nothing of the lady she served. Her embarrassment was not the most pressing matter in that moment, however. "Does her son know?"

Dr. Scorseby smiled, a sight that likely sent a lot of female hearts in Collingham aflutter. He was a handsome man, that was certain. "Which son?" he asked.

A fair question. Mater had quite a few. "The earl."

The doctor nodded. "I did suggest she tell him, though I do not know if she has."

This non-dangerous ailment was significant enough that he thought Philip ought to know. The more Arabella heard, and it was minimal information, she admitted, the more convinced she was that this was an important matter after all.

The late earl had passed so quickly, so unexpectedly. Only after his death had anyone seen the symptoms of his quickly declining health. She could not bear to think of Mater slipping away as well from poor health that had gone unaddressed.

"I will see if I can ascertain whether or not she is taking the powders."

"I would appreciate that. And, please, encourage her to send for me if she is ever in need." He finished his writing and stood once more. "I have a difficult enough time convincing the younger Lady Lampton to do as much. Two stubborn ladies in the same house is quite an obstacle to overcome."

The arrival of Lord and Lady Lampton shifted Dr. Scorseby's attention to the countess. His was the evaluating and studying gaze of a man devoted to medicine. Arabella fully expected him to begin asking any number of questions of Lady Lampton, but he did not. He simply watched.

To Arabella's untrained eye, Lady Lampton appeared more pale than usual, which was something of a feat. She walked with a more pronounced limp and a heavier dependence on her walking stick.

Philip was his usual frippery self. *Usual*, though, did not feel like the correct word. He had not always been this way. And over the past few days, she had been privy to a few instances when he had been anything but the mindless, fashion-focused dandy. The one thing that could be counted upon to secure his more responsible side was his wife's health. If he was prancing and preening, Lady Lampton could not have been as ill as her appearance would suggest.

"How are your children?" Lady Lampton asked both Lady Marion and the duchess.

"Still miserable," Lady Marion said, holding little Caroline's hand. "But Dr. Scorseby tells us they are not in danger."

"He can be depended upon." Lady Lampton spoke with conviction but little emotion. That was her way. Arabella didn't think she lacked feeling or was careless of others' concerns. Hers was simply a very frank manner. She made such a contrast to her husband.

"Caroline." Philip approached the red-cheeked little girl, swinging his quizzing glass as he so often did. "Have you been up at all hours dancing again? I am always very tired after a night of dancing."

She offered a feeble smile in answer.

"The trick, you must understand, is to find a very fine pair of slippers." Philip assumed a pose every bit as arrogant and self-important as the Prince Regent himself could possibly manage. "Inferior footwear is the very bane of our country at present—renders far too many people worn and weary."

"I wasn't dancing, Uncle Flip." The little girl's weary voice held a bit of amusement.

Lady Marion looked instantly relieved.

"Weren't you?" Philip shook his head in an overblown show of disbelief. "I thought for certain you must have been, the whole lot of you."

"Even Henry?" Caroline asked, weakly but with obvious enjoyment.

"Especially Henry. All the Jonquil men are dancers from birth."

Arabella's eyes shifted of their own accord to the Duke of Kielder, and she had to covertly cover her mouth with her hand to hide her grin. His annoyance had increased significantly. Only with great effort, which he appeared to resent, did he keep himself silent and in his seat while Philip waxed long about the joys of dancing.

Caroline, despite her obvious discomfort, giggled a little, and more startling still, the very staid, intimidating Lady Lampton smiled at her husband. It was a sigh and a laugh all contained in the small upturn of her mouth.

"Perhaps Lord Falstone is also worn thin by a night of revelry," Lord Lampton said, turning to the small boy in his father's arms. "Did—"

"If you fill his head with your nonsense, I will—"

"Adam." The duchess cut off whatever no-doubt violent threat the duke meant to level at his host.

"He is accusing my son of dancing, Persephone. I will not stand for it."

"Someday he will be dancing," Her Grace said. "What do you mean to do then?"

"I'll disown him." The duke was in a sour mood, even for him.

Philip either didn't notice or didn't worry about it overly much. "If he finds himself in need of a few bits of dancing advice, I would be happy to—"

"Do not try his temper, Lampton." Her Grace sounded remarkably like her husband in that moment, who offered his host a look of satisfaction. "I will not rescue you if you push him too far."

"Everyone is pulled rather thin at the moment." Lady Lampton apparently recognized the need to intervene. "Philip, focus your efforts on entertaining your niece so Marion can tend to Henry and so His Grace can be spared the necessity of shredding your tongue with a rusty garden rake."

Whether or not that was the threat the duke had originally thought of, he appeared to embrace it, nodding firmly in response to Philip's curious gaze.

"Dr. Scorseby, thank you for your efforts here," Lady Lampton said. "Do let me know if anything else is needed."

"I will, my lady."

Lady Lampton's commanding gaze fell on Arabella. "Will you walk with me a moment?"

She dipped a curtsy even as her heart jumped to her throat. Was she in trouble? Had she neglected something she'd not known was required of her? Of all the members of the Lampton Park household, Lady Lampton intimidated her the most.

Dr. Scorseby stopped her with a light touch of his hand, then, in a low voice, said, "I hope I might come by and see you again."

She didn't know entirely how to respond. She would like to have a visitor, especially after the party was over and she and Mater were relegated to the dower house with only one another for company. Yet the idea of a visitor made her inarguably nervous. A nod was all she could manage. He took the agreement as encouragement and smiled warmly.

Arabella met Lady Lampton in the corridor outside the nursery. The countess did not wait even a moment before speaking.

"Though you are Mater's companion, I hoped *I* might ask a favor of you, one personal to me." There was both authority and uncertainty in her voice. It was an odd combination but one that rendered her less overwhelming. "You appear to be on friendly terms with Dr. Scorseby."

Arabella nodded. That was generally true.

"Would you ask him if there is a time in the next few days when I might make a call on him at his house?"

Physicians generally went to their patients and not the other way around. "Could you not ask him yourself?" She hoped the question sounded less impertinent than she feared it did.

"I could, but my husband would likely overhear, and I would rather he not know."

She was being asked to keep this a secret from Philip? "Is this also meant to be hidden from the dowager?"

"It is." Lady Lampton must have sensed her growing uncertainty; she quickly spoke again. "It is nothing untoward, I promise you. I simply need

Dr. Scorseby's medical evaluation of a difficulty I am having. However, being very familiar with my husband's tendency to fret, I do not wish him to be aware of it until I know if this is really anything worth being concerned about. And Mater cannot keep a secret from her son."

That, Arabella now knew, was not entirely true. She suspected not even Philip was aware that Dr. Scorseby had prescribed his mother powders for some mystery ailment.

"I will relay your request to Dr. Scorseby when he has completed his efforts in the nursery," Arabella said.

Lady Lampton dipped her head and continued her belabored walk down the corridor. After a moment, Arabella absentmindedly wandered away as well.

Philip was inciting a clash with the duke in the hope that his wife would rouse from her isolation to defend him. Lady Lampton was hiding something from her husband. Mater was hiding something from everyone else. Charlie felt abandoned and left out.

Arabella might not have truly been a part of this family, but she was finding herself privy to more and more of their secrets.

With her head down and her thoughts fully preoccupied, she walked directly into something. The force of the collision sent her lurching backward. Something stopped her, keeping her upright. The collision occurred so quickly she hadn't a chance to piece together exactly what had happened, what she'd run into, what had saved her.

"I am so sorry, Miss Hampton." *Mr. Lancaster.* "I was not paying the least heed to where I was going."

She looked up into his startlingly handsome face, his sparkling green eyes, the rebellious golden curl falling across his forehead. He stood so close she could smell the hint of cinnamon that clung to him. His arm was wrapped around her, no doubt the reason she hadn't fallen over. Warmth radiated from that simple touch. Her mind emptied, then filled with little beyond the sound of her own pounding heart.

"Miss Hampton?" He watched her with confused concern. "Are you hurt?"

She shook her head.

"Unwell?"

Again, she shook her head. He hadn't relinquished his hold on her. She felt an unexpected, undeniable urge to lean in to the one-armed embrace, to rest her head against his shoulder. Confused and a little alarmed, she stepped back. His arm dropped to his side.

"It seems I should traverse corridors with a bit more care," she managed to say it lightly despite her spinning thoughts.

"Gothic novels do warn us of dangers lurking around corners."

How grateful she was for a bit of banter. "Do you read a great many gothic novels?"

"I read them exclusively. All sailors do." He was teasing, as he so often did. Yet there was a tension in his posture, in his words, and filling the air between them. "You are certain you were not injured when we collided?"

"I was merely startled," she said.

"I was a little startled myself." His quiet admission set her pulse racing once more.

"I should—I should see if the dowager is in need of anything."

"Of course." He offered a quick, somewhat awkward bow.

She executed an extremely brief curtsy and hurried down the corridor. Her feet took her not to the sitting room, where she felt certain Mater was, but to her own bedchamber. She closed the door and, heart still drumming in her head, crossed to the chair by the window.

She sat, and for the first time since finding herself so unexpectedly in Linus Lancaster's arms . . . she breathed.

Chapter Thirteen

LINUS'S MIND WAS FULLY SPINNING. That very morning he had congratulated himself on having shed much of the nervousness he'd felt in Miss Hampton's company. Standing so close to her just now, with his arm around her, that nervousness had returned in full force, accompanied by something new and unexpected: sometime in the last few days, he'd developed a small fancy for her. Although, judging by how hard his pulse was still pounding long after she'd left, he had to admit that fancy might not be so small.

How had that happened? *When* had it happened?

He needed a quiet place to think.

The back terrace proved the wrong choice. Artemis and Charlie were already there. She was prattling on while he sat in silent and obvious disinterest. Linus stopped only a few steps onto the terrace, trying to decide if he should stay or keep searching for solitude.

"Perhaps you will be in London next Season," Artemis said to Charlie. "You should be old enough by then."

"Which would make you *more* than old enough, wouldn't it?" Charlie muttered, slouching down in his chair.

Artemis bristled a little. "I am the same age you are."

"Bad form, my man," Linus said, pulling their attention to him. "Never cast aspersions upon a lady's age."

"She was casting aspersions on mine," Charlie said.

"It is for a gentleman to endure, not reciprocate."

Charlie rolled his eyes. "Believe me, nothing about this exchange is reciprocated."

Artemis's eyes widened. "You are not enjoying talking with me?"

"Talking *with* you? There is no *with*. I am being talked *at*. I am not even certain you ever stop for air, let alone a reply."

She tipped her chin up confidently. "I will have you know there are any number of gentlemen who enjoy my conversation, seek it out even. They arrive in droves, hoping for even a moment's exchange of words."

Charlie dropped his head against his upturned hand. "Could you not find one of them to talk at? I am getting a headache."

Artemis's lips pursed, and she leaned menacingly forward on her chair. "I don't like you, Charles Jonquil."

"I don't care," he replied. "And do not call me Charles."

All the haughty assurance returned to Artemis's posture and tone. "You prefer Charlie? That is a child's nickname. It is ridiculous for you to cling to it."

Charlie looked across at her, not with anger or challenge but with a growing weariness. "Do you truly want to engage in a competition over whose name is more ridiculous, *Artemis?*"

She stood, the very picture of offended dignity.

"Artemis, do calm yourself." Linus's attempt to rein her in was ignored.

"My name is dignified and important," she said. "You have a forgettable name because you are a forgettable person. Your own family overlooks you."

Charlie stood as well, matching her challenging posture. "And I have seen how your family looks at you. They don't forget you're present; they simply wish you weren't."

"Enough." Adam's bark likely echoed across the entire back lawn. Though Linus had heard it many times before, even he felt a chill enter the air at that commanding and threatening tone. Adam crossed the terrace to where the combatants stood, his bearing that of the Dangerous Duke all of Society feared. "Artemis, apologize."

She turned a sickeningly sweet smile on Charlie. "I am sorry to have told you something you likely already know."

"Again," Adam said.

Artemis's jaw tightened, and her hands curled in fists. Still speaking to Charlie, she said, "I apologize for speaking rudely."

"Again. You'll keep at it until you do it right."

Linus had wondered if Adam was equal to the task of dealing with their often-difficult youngest sister. He was beginning to realize that an unbending guardian who was not easily distracted and who cared very little for how he was perceived was likely the best thing for her. Artemis could not bend him to her will the way she did so many others.

After a breath so deep it flared her nostrils, Artemis made a third attempt. "Mr. Jonquil, I apologize for the things I said. They were uncalled for and inappropriate."

"Better," Adam said. His steely gaze fell on Charlie. "Your turn."

That he had offered Charlie the opportunity to apologize rather than calling him out or skinning him alive was a stroke of tremendous fortune, whether or not Charlie realized it. To the young gentleman's credit, he wasn't quaking in his boots, though some of his bluster had died away.

"No matter the provocation, my remarks were inexcusable," he said. "I hope that you will accept my apology for any pain I may have inflicted."

Both young people offered very stiff, very abbreviated motions of acceptance, though neither looked at the other nor gave any indication of being truly abject.

"Come with me, Artemis," Adam said. "We need to have a discussion."

"I do not wish to," she said, quite on her dignity.

"I did not ask you what you wished; I told you what needed to happen."

She set her fists on her hip. "I am not a child."

"Yes, you are," he said. "And that is precisely the problem. Now, come with me before I lose patience with you."

She followed her brother-in-law back inside with her chin notched upward and her self-importance wrapped firmly around her. Linus hoped Adam and Persephone could help her mature in the ways she needed but without entirely dousing her spirit. The undertaking would have to fall to them; he simply didn't know her well enough.

His own sister, and he only vaguely knew her. Evander would never have allowed himself to grow so distant from his own family.

Charlie dropped into his chair again. "I'm sorry about that," he muttered. "I know she's your sister, but I really don't like her."

"Would it surprise you if I told you that you are likely the only person who feels that way?"

Charlie shot him a look of such disbelief that Linus had little choice but to laugh. "How could anyone endure her mindless prattle and self-aggrandizing conversation? It drives me mad."

Linus thought on that a moment. "Mindless prattle is common in Society, expected of a young lady. That is what her conversation leans toward most of the time. The haughtiness I don't see often."

"It is grating," Charlie said.

"Grating or not, you do have to be kinder when speaking to ladies. That is part of being a gentleman."

Charlie leaned his head back against the chair. "Apparently my father used to say things like that a lot, about treating girls and women and ladies the right way. My brothers have mentioned it often."

"Did you not know him?"

"I did." Charlie's voice lost much of its edge and a good amount of its volume. "I just don't remember him well. If he were here, I could ask him what to do with my life and how to act when I don't know and . . ." The sentence dangled a minute. "He would have had time for me. I know he would have. And he wouldn't forget about me."

Did Artemis have any idea how tragically precise her aim had been with that verbal barb? Linus knew what it was to be lonely, what it was to not feel a part of one's family.

"Perhaps"—how he hoped the offer he was about to make would prove a welcome one—"when you next have a school holiday, you might come visit me in Shropshire rather than come here. Mine is not a large estate, and it's comparatively humble, but it is pleasant and peaceful."

"Are you in earnest?" Charlie eyed him doubtfully. "You would wish me to visit?"

"I would enjoy it immensely."

For the first time since his sparring match with Artemis, Charlie looked encouraged. Just as quickly, his expression darkened again. "Will Miss Top Lofty be there?"

Linus shook his head. "She lives in Northumberland with the duke and duchess. I live alone."

Charlie laughed humorlessly. "Sometimes, so do I."

"I hope you will come." He meant it. "We could both use the company."

They talked for some time about the things they could do during this hypothetical visit. And the longer they discussed the possibility, the more eager Linus became. A feeling of camaraderie and brotherhood he'd not experienced since before Evander's death began to tiptoe over him.

Lord Lampton stepped out onto the terrace. His gaze fell immediately on his brother. "I passed His Grace in the corridor."

Charlie groaned quietly. "I'm in the suds now."

"I thought you were past your troublemaking stage," Lampton said.

"It's not a stage; it's a talent." A heavy dose of sarcasm hung in the declaration.

Lampton crossed to where they sat and loomed over his brother. "When Mater hears of this latest mischief, she'll have your neck." Lampton shook his head. "You spend an awful lot of time ruffling her."

"We all have our role in this family," Charlie muttered.

Lampton turned to Linus. "Your brother-in-law doesn't mean to call him out. Do you?"

"No," Linus said. "The young people have sorted it out between them."

Lampton glanced at Charlie. He sighed as he turned away. "What are we going to do with you?"

"Same thing you always do," Charlie muttered as his brother returned to the house. "Walk away."

The evening's entertainments were limited to mingling and a game of whist at a corner table. The guest list, however, was longer than it had been on previous nights. Lord and Lady Marsden and Lady Belinda were present, as were Mr. Stroud and Mrs. Blackbourne. A Mr. and Mrs. Widdleston and their daughter were in attendance. A young Mr. Carter and his sister were as well.

The guests mingled but not with Miss Hampton. Linus couldn't make sense of it. He would have spent the entire evening with her if he'd been permitted to. As it was, his evening passed in the far less pleasant pursuit of avoiding his sisters and the glint of determination in their eyes.

Persephone still managed to corner him.

"How is Oliver?" he asked, keeping to safe topics.

"Resting," she said. "His father, on the other hand, is still something of a mess."

Linus smiled at the seeming absurdity of that. "The man whose mere arrival at an event brings all of Society to its knees and who can, with a single look, send all of Lords into a fit of horror-fueled hysterics has been rendered 'a mess' by a three-year-old boy."

"Adam lost his father when he was quite young," she said. "He still cannot speak of him without growing emotional. He has lived his life since his father's death so terrified of losing the people he loves that he works very hard not to love anyone. Yet, he has a good heart, and when he does love, he loves fiercely."

"That is why you love him so much."

She nodded slowly, thoughtfully. "One of many reasons."

"What does he think of Artemis?"

"She drives him a bit mad." Persephone's laugh changed to a sigh. "I think he will be more than a little sad to see her go when she eventually has a home and family of her own. He cried after Daphne left, though don't you dare tell him I told you that."

"You have my word, though I am keeping a lot of your secrets just now."

"I hope this next child is a girl," she said, her voice low. "I would dearly love to watch Adam raise a daughter."

"He'll lock her in the tower once she's old enough to have a Season."

Persephone wiggled an eyebrow. "Won't that be diverting?"

"You are happy together." Linus had known as much since the first day he'd met his brother-in-law, but he was grateful to see that it was still true.

"What of you, Linus?" Persephone asked. "Is there anyone you think you might be happy with?"

"Do not act innocent with me," he said. "I know you, Athena, and Artemis have been acting the part of matchmaker. The only reason Daphne is not in my black books like the rest of you is she is not here and is, therefore, not participating."

"I have watched you tonight. You are doing your best to not fall in line with our efforts."

He only hoped that was all she'd noticed. "There will be time enough for courtship. Eventually."

"You mean, for example, once Dr. Scorseby vacates his seat?"

The physician was, in that moment, sitting beside Miss Hampton. "Whatever do you mean?"

"I am not blind, Linus. She has captured your attention, perhaps a bit of your affection."

How had his sister already seen what he himself had only just realized?

Persephone hooked her arm through his and walked with him along the edge of the room. "Don't fret over Artemis and Athena. They've been too distracted by their own ideas to notice what is right in front of them, and I don't intend to say a word to either one."

There was little point denying the truth of Persephone's conjecture, but any idea she might have beyond that needed squelching. "I've only known her a few days," he reminded his sister. "I have enjoyed talking with her and laughing with her."

"You've been laughing?"

"We both are uncertain of where we fit in this gathering, so we formulated a plan for creating a club of outcasts." Spoken plainly, it sounded a bit juvenile, yet he thoroughly enjoyed jesting with Arabella about it. "I know it's ridiculous, but as preposterous as the jest is, it's been comforting to have someone understand how I feel."

"That is a fine thing, Linus," she said. "You do not jest and tease as often as you once did."

"I have found a *friend*, Persephone. Do not infer more than that."

"I'm not sending Adam for a special license. I'm simply saying she seems a pleasant lady."

"I have found her to be," he said.

"Then I wish you luck and something even better."

His curiosity was piqued. "What is that?"

She slipped her arm free of his. "Courage." She gave him a firm but gentle shove, placing him directly in front of Miss Hampton, then walked away.

"Lieutenant Lancaster." Dr. Scorseby stood and offered his hand. Linus shook it firmly.

"How are your young patients?" Linus asked.

"Improving."

They hadn't ended their handshake.

"I'm glad to hear it," Linus said. "I'm certain the children's parents are as well."

The doctor's grip tightened. "I hope that they are. I do all I can for the people in my care."

Linus pulled his hand away from the physician's. After a quick nod, he turned to the person he actually wanted to spend a moment with.

"Miss Hampton." He offered a bow. "I've not yet had the opportunity to speak with you this evening. How are you?"

"I am well. And you? Have you enjoyed any gothic novels lately?"

He grinned, ignoring Dr. Scorseby's surprised expression. "What else would I be doing with my time?"

"Making paper boats with a tiny child," she said. "Choosing a tender-hearted little girl as your bowls partner. Befriending a struggling young gentleman." The soft look she gave him sent a wave of warmth over him. "I suspect you spend your time very wisely and very kindly."

"That is praise, indeed, Miss Hampton."

Her gaze dropped to her clasped hands resting on her lap.

"You've put her to the blush." Dr. Scorseby censured. "That was not well done of you."

He hadn't meant to embarrass her. He was grateful for her words. Few things hung heavier on his mind than the worry that he didn't make a difference in anyone's life, that he did very little that mattered. Knowing that she felt otherwise meant a great deal to him. He ought not repay her kindness by making her uncomfortable.

"I will not take up more of your time," he said. "I do have my collection of Minerva Press offerings to return to."

Her eyes sparkled, and all was right in the world once more. "Enjoy your reading," she said. "I will be working on the bylaws for our club."

"Include a provision excluding three-year-old boys, because I am certain Oliver will be our downfall otherwise."

"I will consider it." She laughed.

She never laughed with Scorseby. She seldom smiled. Did he not at least try to bring some sparkle to her eyes, some joy to her countenance? She deserved to be happy. The doctor ought to be doing everything he could to bring her a bit of cheer.

"A good evening to you, Miss Hampton."

"And to you."

A quick bow. A brief glance at Scorseby. Then he moved along, but his thoughts remained with her. He needed to find a way to spend more time with her in the days and evenings to come. He could bring her a smile or two, and she would lift his spirits as well.

He longed for her company. Did she long for his?

Chapter Fourteen

Arabella accompanied Lady Lampton to Dr. Scorseby's house two days after he had come to the Park to look in on the children. She didn't know why she had been chosen to take the short journey and not Lady Lampton's abigail. Perhaps the countess feared the servants' loyalties to the Jonquil family would mean none of them would keep her secret.

Was this the future Arabella had to look forward to? Being the repository of the family secrets, dancing around the things they didn't tell each other. It was not what she had imagined all those years ago when she had told the earl how desperately she'd wanted to be part of his home and family. This was not belonging. Perhaps someday she would find her elusive dream.

She waited in the front sitting room of Dr. Scorseby's home while Lady Lampton spoke in the next room with him about whatever was ailing her. The sitting room overlooked the street beyond. The house did not sit near the market cross but was close enough for many people to pass by. Arabella knew any number of them from her many long walks to and from town and about the neighborhood. The earl had even occasionally taken her up alongside him in his curricle. During those drives, she had allowed herself to pretend she was his daughter passing an afternoon with her father. She would imagine them returning to the Park and receiving the enthusiastic welcome home he always received from his family.

Sometimes when watching the people in Collingham, as she was doing then, she would catch herself looking for him only to have to remind herself again that he was gone.

Two gentlemen walked past Dr. Scorseby's front window, both of whom she knew on sight. Charlie Jonquil was as easy to recognize as all his brothers were: tall, lean, golden haired, though his was almost a bit ginger. Beside him was Mr. Lancaster, whom she could have picked out in a crowd, with his authoritative, military gait, golden curls, broad shoulders, and heart-fluttering smile. She watched him as he walked, easily picturing him at the prow of a ship.

How quickly and often her thoughts returned to him. He made her laugh. He set her instantly at ease, something few people did. She looked forward to his company, laughed at the memory of his jesting and banter. And she could not fully put from her mind that moment in the corridor.

He'd held her in his arms for a fleeting moment. Her heart pounded at the recollection. How often she had relived that moment, imagined it happening again, then scolded herself for being ridiculous. It had been an accident. Nothing more.

Yet his repeated return to her side, their pleasant conversations, had not been unintentional. He sought her out. With him, she didn't feel alone.

Outside on the walk, Mr. Lancaster said something to Charlie. He grinned. Charlie laughed. On they walked, their camaraderie clear. He was so kind to Charlie. He was kind to everyone. And quick-witted. And funny. Thoughtful.

Watching him disappear up the street, she had to admit to herself that she was a little bit in love with him. She wasn't pining or wasting away, but her heart was pricked with a whisper of likely unrequited affection, and there was little to be done about it.

She was a poor relation with a pity-gained position as an unneeded lady's companion. He was a navy man with his own estate and the highest of connections. *You must be reasonable*, she reminded herself.

A door opened out of sight down the corridor, followed by footsteps. Lady Lampton returned to the sitting room, Dr. Scorseby arriving directly behind her. Arabella rose and brought the countess her spencer and gloves. She was thanked in a very off-hand manner. Lady Lampton's focus was clearly elsewhere. Indeed, she wandered to the window and stood there a moment in distraction.

Dr. Scorseby approached and addressed Arabella. "Did you have an opportunity to ask the dowager if she has been taking her powders?"

"I did not," she confessed. "When the opportunity arose, I could not convince myself that it truly was my place to ask after a personal concern she has not chosen to share with me."

He nodded his understanding. "I will ask her myself tonight. Lady Lampton has been kind enough to invite me to join in the evening's diversions."

She was happy to hear it. He would be a fine addition to the gathering, and he would be granted the opportunity to make certain Mater was well.

"I hope I will see you there," he said.

"I will be there."

That answer appeared to disappoint him. Still, he nodded and indicated that he looked forward to socializing that evening. For her part, Arabella's enthusiasm was waning. She had enjoyed watching the gathering of people and families the past evenings, and she had been grateful that Mater had included her. Yet she longed for things to be quiet and peaceful.

The efforts of the Lancaster sisters to find their brother a bride had long since lost their diverting quality. She did not doubt that Linus Lancaster would, at some point, make a match.

"We should be on our way, Arabella," Lady Lampton said.

"Of course."

Dr. Scorseby accompanied them to the door. A Lampton Park footman handed them up into the carriage. A moment later, the carriage rolled down the lane.

"Dr. Scorseby seems very fond of you," Lady Lampton said. It was by far the most personal remark the countess had ever said to her, yet it didn't feel prying. It was friendly.

"He is a good man."

Lady Lampton didn't balk or laugh at her simple answer. "One cannot underestimate the importance of a good man, and a kind one. Far too many ladies are not treated with tenderness by the men in their lives."

That was all too true. "Forgive me if this is too personal, but having known him all my life, I can with confidence say that your husband quite easily falls into the category of good and kind men." All of the Jonquils matched that description, just as their father had.

A softness entered her expression that Arabella had never before seen. "He is the very best of men."

One who was enduring ridicule and the temper of a dangerous man in the hope of helping his wife. "His Grace does not seem to share your opinion."

Lady Lampton's shoulders squared, and her chin lifted. Her mouth tensed in a fearsome line. "He does not know my Philip as well as I do."

"Perhaps Lord Lampton does not know *himself* as well as you do. I think he—" She cut off the remark before wading any deeper into forbidden territory.

Lady Lampton did not let the sentence end as it had. "What is it you think?"

Arabella shook her head, not wishing to cause difficulty.

"I would like to know, and I vow not to grow angry with you."

She took a breath and rallied her courage. "I think he wonders sometimes if you are unhappy, not in general terms but *with him* in particular, with the life you are building together."

Lady Lampton's color dropped off a little. "Surely, he does not doubt that," she said quietly.

Arabella suspected Philip's antics had grown more pointed of late because His Grace's insults and annoyance hadn't inspired any reaction whatsoever in his wife. While Arabella interpreted Lady Lampton's composure as a matter of not particularly caring what a near stranger thought of her, she could see that the neutrality was being interpreted differently by Philip.

"I have known the Jonquils all my life," she said. "They love deeply, but that means they can be deeply wounded as well. A heart is a vulnerable thing."

Lady Lampton did not answer. She sat in heavy silence, her brows pulled low. Arabella's mind was no less at ease. *They love deeply.* She had seen that again and again as she'd watched the family interacting. She slipped her fingers around the bead hanging from her neck. No one could have blamed her for begging the earl to make her part of his family. All she'd ever wanted was to be loved.

As soon as Linus had the opportunity, he was going to throttle Artemis. Leave it to his youngest sister to choose a contender in his family's matchmaking efforts who was unrelenting in her determination. Mrs. Blackbourne had kept a very close eye on him all evening. She was . . . aggressive to the point of being a little frightening.

Linus did not have a preference for mousy women or ladies who possessed no backbone. Far from it. This, however, was something different. He felt almost like he was being hunted.

Keeping to the edges of the music room whilst the evening's musical performances were underway did not prevent him from drawing Mrs. Blackbourne's attention. Even when she wasn't looking at him, he felt certain she was aware of where he was. Their conversations and time together had not been such that this degree of attachment made any sense. She was in pursuit, not acting upon a true fondness.

The one lady at this party he truly wished to see was nowhere to be found. He wondered about Arabella. Worried a little, truth be told. Life had not dealt her a particularly fair hand. But though her situation was not ideal, she was not broken by it. He admired that. He felt a kinship with her, an unexpected connection, one that tugged at him when she was away.

Mrs. Blackbourne, sitting not nearly far enough across the room for his peace of mind, adjusted her position on her chair. The movement spoke of preparation to rise.

Linus was a man of the military; he knew when a retreat was called for. With speed that likely robbed his flight of any grace or subtlety, he made directly for the music room door and walked quickly down the corridor. He slipped around the corner, then the next, quickly taking the stairs two at a time and reaching the landing above without a pause. The library was on this floor. He could slip in there, grab the book on land management that Lord Lampton had recommended, and retreat to his bedchamber, where he could lock the door, perhaps even push a chair under the handle. An overreaction, likely, but any prey that wished to survive understood the importance of hindering its assailant.

He'd only just stepped inside when his ears perked at the sound of a cough. He turned in that direction, moving toward the fireplace and the sofa set in front of it. Another cough told him he'd not imagined the first.

Stepping around the sofa, his stomach sank. Arabella was lying there, curled in a ball. He might have thought she was sleeping if she weren't coughing so much.

He knelt on the floor beside her. "Arabella?"

He lightly touched her hand. It was quite warm. A quick check of her cheek and forehead revealed the same. Was this the same fever the children had?

"Arabella." He gently moved her damp hair away from her face. She was clammy and sweating and, upon closer look, he realized, shivering a bit.

Her eyelids fluttered open. He offered a reassuring smile; awakening in an unexpected place could be worrying and disorienting. She coughed again but didn't speak.

"Are you feeling poorly?" Only after posing the question did he realize how obvious the answer was.

"Quite." Her voice was not hoarse, neither was her response nonsensical. That was a good sign.

She wrapped the fingers of one hand around the bead on her necklace. It was such a simple adornment yet clearly held particular importance to her. She wore it every day without fail.

"My lungs hurt when I breathe," she said.

"Dr. Scorseby is here this evening. I think perhaps he'd best check on you."

A rattling cough. "I haven't anything to pay him with."

Linus slipped his hand around her free one. "Lord Lampton will not require that of you."

"I don't want to be a burden." Her fingers wrapped around his, and he felt the gesture clear to his heart.

"I doubt you could be a burden even if you tried." He rubbed her hand between his. "Though I would enjoy watching you make the effort."

Her smile was weak but genuine.

"I am sorry you are ill," he said. "I wish there were more I could do."

"What is this?" Mrs. Blackbourne arrived on the scene, eyes taking in everything on the instant.

Linus did not permit even a moment's speculation on her part. "Miss Hampton is quite ill. Will you ring for a servant? Quickly?"

To her credit, the widow changed course without objection. She tugged on the bellpull while Linus kept his position.

"Dr. Scorseby will be here soon," he reassured Arabella. "He'll have you feeling well again."

"If only I'd felt this way earlier," she said quietly. "He could have made his diagnosis while I was at his home."

"You were at his home?" Mrs. Blackbourne asked the question on Linus's mind.

"On an errand for Lady Lampton," she said.

Relief surged through him. For just a moment, he'd thought she had visited the doctor for personal reasons—Dr. Scorseby had not exactly made his interest a secret—and the possibility had not sat well at all.

Into the momentary silence, a fourth voice sounded. Lord Lampton. "What errand were you seeing to on my wife's behalf?"

He stood at the foot of the sofa, having somehow silently entered the room. One would never expect the flamboyant Earl of Lampton to arrive anywhere without drawing attention.

Arabella's eyes were closed once more. Her coloring had worsened in the last few moments, and she'd begun to shiver more.

"Is there a blanket or a shawl or something nearby?" Linus asked Lampton.

The earl nodded and crossed to a small trunk in the corner. He pulled out a light throw and returned, handing it to Linus, who had stood in anticipation of receiving it. Carefully, he spread the blanket over Arabella, hoping to alleviate some of her misery.

"I saw you running for your life," Lampton said in a barely audible whisper, "and then Mrs. Blackbourne following close on your heels. I thought I'd come and save you from her." Lampton's amusement dissipated when his gaze returned to Arabella. "She does not look well, does she?"

Linus shook his head. "She felt feverish."

"Mater has been worried about her," Lampton said. "We all have been."

Had Arabella shown signs of illness before this? Linus hadn't noticed any.

One of the maids stepped inside. Lampton took charge, not a hint of his dandified mannerisms in evidence. "Send word to the dowager and Dr. Scorseby that they are both needed forthwith here in the library."

The maid dipped a curtsey and hurried from the room.

The earl was not yet finished. "Mrs. Blackbourne, I believe you can return to the music room to enjoy the remainder of the evening."

Linus had all but forgotten about the other lady present.

"I would not wish to leave Miss Hampton unattended." Mrs. Blackbourne moved a bit closer.

"She is in no danger of being abandoned or mistreated." Lampton spoke sternly, something that seemed to surprise the widow as much as it did Linus. "This family has cared about her all her life. I will not give you leave to doubt our loyalty to her."

"I hadn't intended to imply that you would neglect her." Mrs. Blackbourne had, in fact, heavily implied exactly that.

Lampton dipped his head. "I should hope not."

"I will see if I can help locate your mother or the physician." Mrs. Blackbourne shot Linus a look that was far more uncertain than the ones he was accustomed to receiving from her. Had their frivolous host managed to quell the unquellable?

"You were nearly as fearsome just now as my brother-in-law," Linus said once the lady had slipped from the room.

"I am absolutely certain no one is that fearsome. Not even him."

Linus studied him out of the corner of his eye. "You doubt the dangerousness of the duke?"

Lampton laughed. "I am not so foolish as that. Still, we all have roles to play."

Linus had come to Nottinghamshire expecting to find the shallowest of gentlemen acting as host of this gathering. He was discovering, instead, a man every bit as complicated, nuanced, and, he suspected, misunderstood as the brother-in-law from whom Linus was charged with protecting him.

Arabella coughed again. Linus knelt once more, taking her hand in his. Still warm. She was no longer shivering though. The light blanket seemed to have helped.

"I wish she had told us she was feeling poorly," Lampton said. "Mater would have had her bundled up in bed, resting, with all the teas and tisanes she could possibly need to feel better."

It was a reassuring declaration. "Not all companions benefit from such concern."

"Arabella is far more than a companion. We grew up together. She was, in many ways, like a little sister to us. My father, in particular, adored her. We all did, really."

"Did?" Linus knew Arabella felt left out of the Jonquil family. What explanation did Lampton have for it?

"We didn't see much of her after Father died. I don't know if she pulled away or we did. Or both. But it's been good having her back again."

The dowager arrived, her expression showing curiosity more than alarm. Until she spotted Arabella. "What's happened?"

"She is feverish," Linus said. "And she is coughing. I came in here to fetch a book and found her here. She's been dozing, but fretfully."

The dowager touched the back of her hand to Arabella's forehead. "Was Dr. Scorseby sent for?"

"He was," Lampton said.

The dowager nodded. "He will know what is best to be done. In the meantime, though, I can say with certainty that Arabella would be mortified at the thought of being in such a vulnerable state whilst in full view of any- and everyone."

That was most certainly true.

"Philip, you remain here so you can direct Dr. Scorseby to Arabella's room. Mr. Lancaster, would you be so good as to carry her. I will, of course, accompany you."

Linus lifted the blanket from Arabella and gave it to the dowager. He slipped one arm under Arabella's back and the other under her legs. He carefully lifted her from the sofa, holding her close to him.

She stirred.

"Rest, dear," he said quietly.

Without a word of protest, she laid her head on his shoulder. The dowager tucked the blanket around his feverish armful. The warmth radiating from Arabella was not his greatest concern. She was far too light.

"Is she eating properly?" he asked the dowager in quiet tones as they made their way toward the family wing.

"She is skin and bones, isn't she?" The dowager glanced at Arabella, her face lined with undeniable concern. "It is all the walking she does. We could always tell when life was particularly difficult in her uncle's home. She would walk for hours every day, avoiding the necessity of returning there. She had grown almost gaunt the past months, and she walked for hours on end every day. She had to have been missing meals to have been away from home as long as she was. It is a miracle she hasn't been ill before now."

They turned down a corridor of bedchambers—the family wing, no doubt.

"I first considered the possibility of inviting her here almost a year ago," the dowager said. "Sorrel's younger sister and our Stanley were married, and the house was all but empty." The dowager's mouth turned down in lines of disappointed frustration. Though her volume did not increase, her words grew more vehement. "I should have acted upon that impulse sooner."

"Well, she is here now," Linus replied. "She will regain her strength; I've no doubt."

"But what of her spirit?" The dowager seemed to address the question toward herself.

Linus hadn't a ready answer to that. He didn't think Arabella's spirits as low as all that.

The dowager motioned to the last door in the family corridor. "This is hers."

Linus carried his coughing bundle inside. The room was nearly bare. The furniture was fine and well maintained. The linens were not worn. Yet everything else about the space reminded him of his own home during their very lean years.

The dowager must have noticed his reaction. "She was not permitted to bring very much with her from her uncle's home."

Linus crossed to the bed and gently laid Arabella on it. The dowager pulled another blanket over Arabella's shivering frame. Linus moved a chair over for her.

The dowager sat. "Thank you."

Linus watched Arabella. She appeared to be sleeping but was clearly not resting. He hoped whatever ailment had laid her low would prove short-lived. Only with effort did he keep himself from reaching out for her hand once more. With the dowager watching, he didn't dare. Calling her by her Christian name and being found alone with her despite her being rendered nearly insensible with illness had already pushed the acceptable boundaries. The dowager was watching the two of them rather closely as it was.

Dr. Scorseby arrived. Linus could think of no innocuous reason to remain, and he was not ready to admit to the reason he hated to leave. He watched Arabella for a drawn-out moment, wishing he could take her hand or sit beside her to offer some comfort.

He slipped quietly from the room. During the slow walk to his own bedchamber, he had time to think over the state of things. His sisters had gone to great lengths to find a lady to catch his eye. Without warning, a completely different lady had captured a bit of his heart.

Chapter Fifteen

ARABELLA COULD NOT REMEMBER EVER being so cheerful while simultaneously so ill. Linus had managed the impossible.

"Why do you not seem as interested in this as I am?" He held up his book on land management, eying her with an expression of disdain that she didn't believe for a moment. "Is it not absolutely riveting?"

Even the maid sitting near the door for propriety's sake didn't bother hiding her amusement at his jesting question.

"I will confess," Arabella said, "the bit about soil type influencing the frequency of changing one's crop did set my heart racing a bit."

"I believe I was asleep for that part."

She shook her head at his intentional nonsense. "I happen to know you were paying very close heed to what you were reading, focusing very intensely."

"Mostly because it felt like reading a foreign language." He set the book on the floor beside his chair. "That does not bode well for my future as a landowner, does it?"

She coughed, something she couldn't seem to stop doing. Linus's sister who lived in Lancashire had sent instructions for tisanes and tonics to aid the children's illness a week earlier as well as information on adjusting the dosages should adults be likewise afflicted. Arabella felt better than she would have without that help, but she did not feel truly well.

"This might be an unforgivably personal observation," she said once she'd regained control of her voice and breathing, "but you do not seem very enthusiastic about your responsibilities."

"And this might be an unforgivably sullen response, but . . . I'm not." He absentmindedly waved a hand as if dismissing the confession. "This was never meant to be *my* responsibility. I cannot seem to fully resign myself to it."

"You told me during our garden walk that you were the younger son."

"My brother and I both served in the navy during the war, but only I survived." He made the admission quickly, quietly.

"How long ago?"

"Almost eleven years. At times, it feels like only eleven days." The look he gave her clearly communicated his belief that she would find the continued rawness of his grief ridiculous.

"Someone I loved very deeply, someone infinitely dear to me, died eleven years ago. While I have more or less stopped expecting to see him in the places he once frequented, I do not miss him any less than I did then."

"Your father?"

That was not a question with a straightforward answer. And she knew that was not what he was truly asking. "I told you that both of my parents died when I was six. Do you truly believe I am only seventeen?"

He smiled broadly. "I *never* guess a lady's age."

"I have only the vaguest memories of my parents," she said. "This gentleman was . . ." She had never before attempted to explain the role he had played in her life. "He was a surrogate. He was family to me, the only family I have ever known."

"What of your aunt and uncle?"

She dropped her gaze. Her voice quieted as well. "They never considered me family."

"The Jonquils think of you that way, you know. Lord Lampton was fierce in his care for you. The dowager interrogated Dr. Scorseby for a full quarter of an hour the night you took ill. Charlie drove to Collingham to obtain a particular variety of herb my sister insists is most efficacious. Lady Lampton decreed that none of the guests are to disturb you without your express invitation."

Even Lady Lampton had come to her defense? "This illness has meant I haven't been very helpful to them."

"Arabella. You are far more to them than a helpful companion. You are far more than that to—" He cleared his throat and didn't finish the thought.

How tempting it was to create her own ending. She didn't dare. Life had disappointed her too many times to invite more heartache.

"More than that to the club?" Laughing was a far better option than tearing herself apart over Linus's possible feelings for her.

"Yes." He emphasized the word all out of proportion. "You are drafting our bylaws, after all. The club depends upon you."

"I will fulfill my duties to the best of my ability."

Still sitting casually in his seat, he snapped her a very smart salute. "I have every confidence in you."

"I thank you, Lieutenant Lancaster."

His mouth twisted. "I miss being called that." There was loneliness in the admission.

Her heart ached for him. "We could make it a club rule that you are always called Lieutenant Lancaster during meetings."

His smile was one of gratitude more than anything else. "What ought we to call you?"

"I've never been called anything but Miss Hampton or Arabella."

"You could be Captain Hampton." He laughed. "The tongue gets a bit caught on that."

"If I'm a captain, don't I outrank you?"

"Do you mean to start giving me orders?"

She nodded solemnly. "Of course. I will be insufferable."

"Excellent."

Seeing him lighthearted once more lifted her spirits.

"What is your first order, Captain?"

"I will require you to reread your text on switching out crops," she said. "I have heard a rumor that you were sleeping at that point."

His features settled in an expression of distaste. "Couldn't you just have me flogged instead?"

"Do you really dislike the topic of land management so much?"

He pushed out a heavy breath. "I probably wouldn't mind the reading if it weren't the predecessor to being a staid, boring landowner."

"If you will be miserable in that role . . ." She wasn't certain how to end the thought. She wouldn't suggest he walk away from his duties, yet she hated the thought of him being unhappy.

"The land was my father's," he said. "The home was my family's. I won't leave it to the care of yet another steward. I will do what is expected of me."

"But you will be unhappy."

"I am not a man of many talents," he said, "but I have a knack for finding satisfaction even in less-than-ideal circumstances. I'll manage it again somehow."

"Would you rather be at sea?"

He thought on it a moment. "At the risk of sounding terribly demanding—"

"It's far too late for that, Lieutenant."

He snorted. "You're troublesome, do you know that?" It was a good-natured remark, one filled with cheer.

"What is your 'terribly demanding' position on being a landowner versus returning to sea?"

"Only that I think I would be happier in a role I chose for myself. I've never been granted that. I went to sea all those years ago because my family was destitute. I'm returning to land now because I am the only son my family has left."

How well she understood his frustration. "Life is far more difficult when one is forced onto a path not of one's choosing."

He nodded slowly. "I'd feel a little less helpless if I had choices."

"You may not have an alternate path," she said, "but you can choose how you intend to walk the one you are on. Find a way to make life more your own, something more appealing and familiar to you, something you can feel excited about."

He made a show of pondering. "How difficult would it be to rebuild the family home as a ship of the line?"

"Easiest thing in the world," she said with a laugh.

"Do you know, I'm beginning to doubt the dowager's word. She told me you were terribly quiet, and she never once mentioned how funny you are."

She must have blushed all the way to her hairline. "Most people *would* say I am quiet. I don't know that I've ever been described as funny."

That seemed to surprise him. Why would it?

"Perhaps it is the result of your influence on me," she suggested.

He fought back a smile. "Are you saying I'm loud?"

"I'm certainly not saying you're funny."

He laughed. How she loved the sound, especially knowing she had inspired it. A closeness had developed between them during the days of her convalescence. He visited her regularly. They talked and laughed. Despite her illness, she smiled more than she had in recent memory. What would she do when he left for Shropshire?

"I can see your thoughts are wandering," he said, "no doubt back to the land treatise. I can begin reading it if you'd like." His humor faded a bit. "Or I could go, if you'd prefer to rest."

She shook her head no. In a voice just louder than a whisper, she said, "I'd like you to stay."

A sparkle entered his eyes. He leaned forward in his chair. His fingers brushed the very edge of hers. She tried to breathe, but her lungs fought the effort. His hand slid over hers, their fingers intertwining. Her pulse thrummed through her.

They sat thus—hands held—for long minutes, talking, smiling, enjoying each other's company. Only when the time came for her to take the prescribed tisane did he rise to leave. Watching him go, her heart sank. Her gaze remained on the door, hoping to see him step inside again. As the day wore on, she watched for him, longing for his company. She, who had been so alone for so long, had found someone with whom she felt she belonged.

Under normal circumstances, Linus would have more or less enjoyed an evening of impromptu dancing and interacting with guests. Though he was not the most social of gentlemen, he did appreciate conversation and friendly company.

But Mrs. Blackbourne had been on his scent for hours. Dodging her required more of his time and effort than he would have preferred to spend. The remainder of his energy he poured into helping Harry ease their brother-in-law's misery in order to lessen Persephone's worries. He would rather have spent the evening talking with Arabella. Holding her hand. Seeing her smile.

His visits with her the past few days had been the highlight of the house party for him. She enjoyed his stories of the sea, and though she had never left the immediate vicinity of Collingham, she was an observer of people and nature and had shared with him fascinating stories of her own. She helped him sort out his difficulties, and he hoped he had offered her support in return.

Now, four days after the onset of her fever, she was recovered enough to have joined the gathering, though she did not participate. Scorseby had spent nearly the entire evening glued to her side, occupying the only chair near Arabella's. Linus didn't fully trust himself to be civil to the interloping physician, so he'd kept something of a distance.

His attention, however, remained on Arabella. Her coloring had not entirely returned to a hale and hearty hue. She tucked her hands under her lap blanket as if to warm them. More worrying than the lingering hints of illness, she looked tired. Did Scorseby not see it? He was a man of medicine. How could he continue to tax her as he was? Did he not care at all for her well-being?

A couple approached Arabella and Scorseby, striking up a conversation Linus could not possibly overhear. Who were they? Arabella did not appear particularly pleased to see them.

Scorseby rose, offering a bow to the couple, then one to Arabella. Then he walked away, leaving her in the company of the as-yet-unidentified lady and gentleman. She did not look at all comfortable with the arrangement. Linus inched closer, attempting to sort out the situation.

Charlie happened past in that moment. Linus held him back. "Who is that talking with Miss Hampton?"

A quick look. "Her aunt and uncle."

Hence the displeasure on Arabella's face. She had mentioned before that her relatives were not always kind.

Something was said that left her paler than she was already. She shook her head vehemently. Her uncle pointed a finger. Her aunt leaned in and said something further. How could Linus intervene without drawing attention?

Perhaps the dowager might step in.

Arabella's uncle snatched her arm and pulled her to a stand, her lap blanket slipping to the floor. She attempted to bend to pick it up, but her aunt propelled her forward, away from the chair she had occupied. Her gaze darted about the room, searching, he would guess, for an escape. Her look of discomfort had changed to one of worry.

Linus sprang into action. He would make absolutely certain Arabella was safe and free of her aunt and uncle. No one would be permitted to cause her misery while he was in a position to intervene.

Linus spotted Adam not far distant and crossed to him immediately. A man of the navy, he understood the importance of assembling the right fleet. Something of the urgent nature of the situation must have shown in his face because Adam was on his feet by the time Linus reached him.

"Miss Hampton's been dragged from the room by her aunt and uncle," Linus said. "Multiple sources have told me they're not kind people."

"Say no more." Adam caught Harry's eye and, with a flick of his hand, motioned for their brother-in-law to join the rescue mission.

Linus took charge. "She passed through this door." He led them in that direction.

Lord Lampton crossed their path. "What's happened?" He eyed them all in turn.

"I saw Miss Hampton forcibly removed from the drawing room," Linus said. "She looked nearly panicked."

Lampton glanced over the room. "Where are her aunt and uncle?"

"They did the removing," Linus said through a tense jaw.

Lampton nodded firmly and joined their brigade.

A moment later, they were in the corridor outside the drawing room. A woman's voice echoed from not far away. Her words were not clear. A sharpness edged her tone.

Linus moved with determined steps toward the sound. So help him, if the Hamptons had mistreated Arabella in any way, he'd likely not be able to maintain his civility.

A hand grasped his arm, holding back the charge he meant to lead.

"For Miss Hampton's sake, I'd best take command on this," Lord Lampton said. "We have a family connection, and this is my home. There will be fewer eyebrows raised." He spoke without the ridiculousness one usually associated with the frivolous earl. "But"—Lord Lampton met Adam's eye—"your ability to intimidate would, I am certain, help tremendously."

"I have never abandoned a lady in distress." Adam growled the words. "I won't start now."

Linus and his brothers-in-law flanked their host as they turned a corner and came upon the very people they sought out. Arabella's aunt and uncle stood with their backs to the gentlemen. Arabella, however, was in full view.

Worry filled every inch of her face. Linus reminded himself that it was best for Lord Lampton to undertake the intervention. He would support the effort, but he needed to clamp down the urge to rush in. *Strategy over might.*

They'd moved close enough to overhear what Arabella's aunt was saying. "I knew you would be a failure. I knew it. You still wander the neighborhood like a vagabond, earning the ridicule of everyone. You've done nothing at all useful this entire evening. And to have incurred the expense of a doctor after only a fortnight here"—Arabella's expression crumbled as her aunt continued the tirade—"pushes the bounds of what little value you bring. They will send you back in disgrace."

"I am certain they won't." Arabella spoke with an edge of panic.

"All is not lost," her aunt said. "The duchess's brother has shown something of an interest in you. Why, soon, everyone will be speaking of it."

Adam shot Linus a curious look, but he wasn't entirely sure what to make of this either.

Mrs. Hampton pressed onward. "He simply must come up to scratch before you've pushed Lord Lampton beyond enduring."

Lampton had reached Arabella's uncle and slapped a hand on his shoulder with enough force for the sound to disrupt her aunt's remarks. "I thought we appeared short two guests." Though the words were innocuous, his tone was not. Beneath the jest was something far more threatening. Even Adam looked a little impressed.

"Lord Lampton," Arabella's uncle sputtered even as his gaze widened, sweeping over the group of gentlemen who had arrived. "Your Grace. Mr. Windover. Lieutenant Lancaster."

Linus let the title stand uncorrected. Given half a chance, he would gladly summon every ounce of lieutenant he had beneath his veneer of decorum.

Mrs. Hampton dropped a hurried curtsey. "A pleasure, sirs."

"Are these the guests you were looking for?" Adam's impatience colored his question.

"They couldn't possibly be," Lord Lampton said. "Well-mannered guests would never question their host's graciousness."

The Hamptons eyed each other with growing concern. Arabella's gaze fell on Linus and lingered there. He offered what silent reassurance he could.

"If we have given the impression of questioning your graciousness, Lord Lampton, it was unintentional," Mr. Hampton said.

The earl was unmoved. "You accused me of begrudging your niece the doctor's care she needed and further insisted that her only value in my household is as a laborer. You have called into question my adherence to the gentlemen's code and cast aspersions on my mother's ability as a hostess."

Lampton did not mention the heavy hints at Arabella's pursuit of an advantageous match.

Mrs. Hampton's solicitous expression grew almost desperate. "We were simply having a family discussion. We hadn't meant to insult you."

"Perhaps it was I whom you meant to 'insult,'" Adam said.

Mr. and Mrs. Hampton's faces blanched.

"You have implied that I would allow my family to remain the guests of a host and hostess whose humanity cannot be relied upon. No one questions with impunity my devotion to my family's well-being and happiness."

Harry jumped in. "Personally, I'm excited. I've not served as a second in one of the Dangerous Duke's duels in ages."

"Being the well-mannered host I am, I will offer you an escape," Lampton said. "Your carriage will be at the front portico in a few minutes."

"I'll see to it myself," Harry offered, "though I would far rather have met for pistols at dawn." He turned crisply and walked toward the front of the house with enough determination to erase any doubt that he meant to make certain the Hamptons' conveyance was not delayed by even a second.

Mr. Hampton's gaze slid slowly from his host to Adam. Linus heard him swallow.

"Take the escape Lampton has offered you," Adam said. "I am not so generous as he."

"Dear." Mr. Hampton offered his arm to his wife. "Perhaps we had best return home."

"Excellent," the earl answered before she could. "I will accompany you to the entryway."

He walked with the Hamptons, giving the impression of a guard overseeing the movement of prisoners rather than a host seeing off his guests. For his part, Adam appeared reluctantly impressed. Though Linus had no doubt Lampton and Adam would continue to grate on each other, he felt certain they'd gained a bit of mutual respect.

Adam turned his full attention to Arabella. "I am sorry we did not arrive sooner to spare you this ordeal, Miss Hampton. Linus rallied the troops as quickly as he could manage."

"Thank you," she whispered.

Linus met Adam's eye. He received a quick nod before Adam turned and walked back in the direction of the drawing room.

Arabella took a shaky breath.

He eyed her more closely. "You are crying."

She swiped at her cheek with her fingers. "These past weeks have spoiled me. I am no longer immune to their unkindness."

He set his hands gently on her arms. "This vitriol is not new, then?"

She shook her head. "I'm not usually so overset by it. I'm simply so tired. I don't feel well and—and I don't have the strength just now to—to—" Tears choked her voice.

Linus's heart broke at the sight of her suffering. He did not doubt that she had endured tirades worse than this one. But illness and worry and upheaval took a toll on a person. She was struggling under that weight.

There, in the quiet stillness of the corridor, he put his arms around Arabella and held her tenderly. She tucked herself into his embrace. A contentment he'd not felt in some time, perhaps ever, settled over him. She was a salve to his loneliness, to his aching uncertainty. Did she find solace in his embrace in particular? Or was she simply reaching out to the nearest person willing to offer her a respite? He wasn't certain he was ready to face the answer to that question. Not yet.

Neither could he ignore her aunt's words regarding him. Whispers had begun, rumors wondering about his connection to Arabella, about his intentions. Had Arabella heard them as well? Was she upset?

Linus did not wish to cause difficulties for either of them. He would offer her this embrace, this comfort, but then he needed to maintain a purely friendly degree of interaction. Both their reputations required it. Both their futures as well.

As Arabella had said, "Life is far more difficult when one is forced onto a path not of one's choosing." He would not bring her more difficulties; life had given her plenty already.

Chapter Sixteen

OLIVER WAS NOT YET HIS usual interactive self. Neither was Caroline. Both sat with Linus on the back terrace of Lampton Park, Oliver in his arms and Caroline resting against his side. The fever that had laid the children low had run its course. They were well enough, though still weary.

Linus had offered them a change of scenery and, in so doing, had given himself an excuse to leave the house. Persephone had taken to eying him with a little too much curiosity, and she was not the only one. Dr. Scorseby had come to check on Arabella and the children and had been pointedly cold toward Linus. When Linus had referenced Arabella in a conversation with the dowager, interested looks had been exchanged all around the room. He'd needed an escape.

"Lampton Park is very beautiful." He spoke as much to himself as either of the children.

"The Meadows is beautifuler," Caroline said. "We have a ceiling of trees. And there is a place on the river where all the leaves are. And the nursery is magic."

Though she was more sedate than Artemis had ever been, her colorful and eager imagination was forever putting him in mind of his sister as she'd been in those long-ago years before he'd left home.

"That sounds wonderful," he said.

"I like the Castle," Oliver weakly declared. He was hardly keeping his eyes open.

"Of course you do," Linus said. "The Castle has a gibbet, you know, and you and your father are very fond of gibbets."

"Don't tell Mama." Oliver rested his head more fully against Linus's shoulder.

"What is a gibbet?" Caroline asked.

Lud, he was not good at choosing appropriate topics for children. "A gibbet is something that very grumpy dukes keep on their grounds as a way of reminding people who visit that they are very grumpy dukes."

"I do not think the duke is grumpy."

Linus had only just recovered from hearing Lord Lampton disagree with the universally accepted assessment of Adam's character. Now here was another member of the Jonquil family who seemed to have seen through his exterior. "You don't?"

"I think he is sad." She adjusted her position, placing herself more comfortably against him, her little legs bent beside her. Linus shifted Oliver to one arm and rested his now free one around her shoulders. "When he was in the nursery holding Olive, he looked sad."

"He was probably sad because his son was ill. That makes fathers sad."

She seemed to think on that a moment. "My papa was sad that Henry and I were ill. Mama was more sad."

Linus leaned back a little, settling in more cozily on the wicker settee. "I would wager they were both equally sad; it was simply easier to see that your mother was. That is often the case with mothers and fathers."

"But the duchess didn't look as sad as the duke," Caroline said.

He laughed lightly. "The duke and duchess are the exception to a great many rules."

"Were you sad that we were ill, Minus?" She had begun calling him Minus, though whether it was because she did not actually know how to pronounce his name or that she had fashioned him a nickname, he could not say.

He squeezed her shoulders. "I was very sad that you and Henry and little Lord Falstone here were unwell. I missed making boats with you down by the river. I missed seeing you ride your pony, as I hear you are quite an accomplished equestrienne, and I missed your smile."

"Do you love me?" she asked quietly.

"Of course I do, dear." How could he not adore this sweet child?

She sat up straighter, forcing his arm to drop away. With an expression of such earnestness it melted his heart, she said, "You cannot marry me."

"I cannot?" He kept his smile hidden away, not wishing to make her think he was laughing at her.

"I am going to marry Edmund." Her brow pulled in worry even as her mouth turned down in a frown. "He says he won't marry me though.

That makes me hurt right here." She tapped her chest just above her heart.

The poor child.

Linus pulled her close once more. He didn't know who Edmund was, whether his objection came from being far too old to harbor any matrimonial potential for a six-year-old—though why a grown or nearly grown man would feel the need to crush hopes that would peter out on their own as it was, Linus couldn't say—or perhaps a very young boy who objected on the grounds that, being young and male, he found the very idea of love and matrimony a touch nauseating. Still, Linus could sense her heart was aching. He'd not been around when Artemis had experienced her first bouts of lovesickness, nor had he been able to soothe her broken hearts.

"If Edmund does not come up to scratch, my dear Caroline, you simply visit me in Shropshire, and I will marry you myself."

She giggled a little, and the sound did him good. "You cannot marry me."

"Because of Edmund?"

"No, because I know who you should marry. You cannot marry both of us."

He looked down into her upturned face. "Who is this mystery lady?"

She clamped her mouth shut, not preventing the smile beneath it, and shook her head.

"Shall I try to guess?"

A nod.

He had found during his brief interactions with Caroline that she enjoyed theatricality nearly as much as Artemis. He employed it in that moment as he made a show of pondering his first question.

"Is this lady kind?"

Another nod.

"Is she beautiful?"

"Yes." A spoken response added some weight to the answer.

"Have I met her?"

Caroline giggled. "Yes."

"Is she . . . Artemis?"

"You can't marry your sister, silly." This was the most life he'd seen in Caroline since before the fever.

"That's right. Hmm." He tucked her up against him as he tried to think of more questions. "Do I like this lady?"

"Janey says you *love* her," she said.

"That I love *Janey*?"

Caroline shook her head in amused exasperation. "That you love the lady you should marry. Everyone is saying you will."

Everyone is saying. Linus knew who "everyone" was talking about where his interest was concerned. He would do well to direct Caroline's thoughts elsewhere rather than feed the fire.

"Is it Mater?" He used the name her family used, unsure if Caroline would realize who he meant otherwise.

She laughed so hard her shoulders shook. He laughed right along until she began to cough, her lungs still struggling from the illness. He rubbed her back and tried to soothe her as she fought her way through the onslaught.

By the time the coughing fit settled, she was noticeably worn down. She leaned heavily against him once more. "I do not like being ill," she said.

"I do not like seeing you ill." He held her tenderly, wishing he knew how to better comfort her.

Oliver was sleeping soundly, which Linus thought was a good sign.

He drank in the moment: a beautiful vista, children in his arms, peace in the world, at last, and a feeling of home. How much more powerful and comforting would the experience have been if he'd been at his own home, with his own children? Even if he proved as ill-suited to estate management as he feared, moments like this one would make the undertaking well worth it. The possibility was almost enough to make him anxious to return home rather than dread the necessity of it. He'd have a home again. And a family.

Arabella came quite unexpectedly into view, walking up the pebbled path that led to the terrace from a side garden. She wore her walking shoes and very sensible bonnet. Had she executed another escape? Who was she running from now? Or what? A household whispering and conjecturing would send even the stoutest of hearts fleeing.

She came up the terrace steps and saw him there. Her eyes darted over his situation and she smiled. "You are very popular it seems."

Caroline lifted her head enough to look at the new arrival. "Minus is sad that I am ill."

Arabella leaned forward and touched her hand to the little girl's cheek. "You do not feel feverish. That is a good sign."

Standing as close as she was, Linus could make out the individual flecks of brown in her blue eyes, the slope of her nose, the charming width of her mouth. She was intriguing and mesmerizing. She was also worried about something; he could see it in the heaviness of her expression and the uncertainty lingering deep in her gaze. Her pallor and dark-circled eyes spoke of continued illness as well.

Caroline's little hand reached up, and a single finger hooked around the chain hanging from Arabella's neck "What is this?"

Linus was curious about it himself, though he had never asked.

"It is a necklace," she said.

"The bead is pretty," Caroline said, sliding it along the chain. Her curiosity held Arabella hostage.

"Yes. I have always thought so." She made a small effort to free herself but was not permitted.

"Where did you get it?"

Linus watched a swallow bob up and down in her throat. "It was gift," she said quietly.

Caroline pressed her hands together. "From a sweetheart?"

Arabella stood straight once more, finally able to do so. "Not a sweetheart," she said.

Linus's curiosity was piqued. "From your parents?"

She shook her head. "From Caroline's grandfather, actually."

Caroline sat up. "Papa's papa?"

Arabella pressed her open palm to the bead and smiled, the expression both fond and mournful. "I knew him when I was a little girl. He was always very kind to me."

Lord Lampton had said his late father had adored Arabella. The fondness appeared to have been mutual.

"Do you miss him?" Caroline asked.

"Ever so much." The pain in Arabella's expression pierced him. This connection she'd had to the late Earl of Lampton was, he felt certain, a crucial piece of her puzzle. Her gaze rose to the house behind them. Such sadness. Such grief. "He used to live here, you know."

"My papa used to live here."

Arabella managed a smile, though Linus could see that it took effort. "I know. I knew your papa when he was just a boy."

"And Uncle Flip?"

"I knew all of your uncles. They were my friends."

Caroline sighed, the sound one of contentment, as if knowing that Arabella was connected to them brought her solace. Linus could appreciate the desire. A gulf often opened between him and his family, he having been apart from them for so much of their lives. He too clung to every connecting thread he could find.

"And you live here now," Caroline said.

"I am very fortunate." Arabella met Linus's gaze for just a moment. There was discomfort in her posture that hadn't been present before. "I am trying very hard not to cause difficulties for anyone, including myself."

"Have you encountered a great deal of trouble?" he asked.

"Enough."

She'd heard the whispers, no doubt. She didn't seem to want to be ensnared by them any more than he did.

"I'm sure everything will be fine," he said.

"I hope so." She took a quick breath. "I will not disturb you further. I hope you are feeling better soon, Miss Caroline."

She slipped quickly into the house. She was worried. He was a bit worried himself. A little distance was likely best. The whispers would die down without evidence. Then they could both breathe easier.

"Will you tell me a story?" Caroline asked. "Mama always tells me stories."

He adjusted his hold on the children and made himself more comfortable, pushing back the question of Arabella Hampton to be answered at another time.

"There was once a little girl named Caroline, who lived under a ceiling of trees."

Chapter Seventeen

THE RIVER TRENT, ACCORDING TO longstanding folklore, was so thick with fish that no effort was needed to catch a bounty. Lord Lampton had invited the gentlemen of the house party to test that ancient tradition. He, however, was focusing far more attention on telling stories than dropping a line in the water.

"Imagine my horror when Carrington arrived, at a ball mind you, sporting a horse collar knot." Lampton tutted and shook his head. "I could not bear to look at him the entire remainder of the evening. Quite put me off. My dancing suffered for it, I will tell you that."

"Imbecile," Adam muttered under his breath.

Though his eyes were focused on his line bobbing in the water, the tension in Adam's posture belied the relaxed nature of their outing. The Dangerous Duke was displeased.

"In case there was any confusion," Linus said, "drowning does fall under the broader category of murder, and you did make a vow to your wife."

Adam eyed their host for only an instant. "Lampton is the one who brought us here. I can always argue he was begging for a swim."

"A forced swim?"

"If it will shut him up."

The duke and earl's interactions had been less antagonistic since their joint effort to toss out Arabella's aunt and uncle. What had worsened relations? "Is this because Harry has defected?"

As if to punctuate the question, Harry laughed as Lampton mimicked the very awkward way in which the Prince Regent moved about. The two had become surprisingly fast friends, both finding in the other a willing comrade in ridiculousness. Only the evening before they had exchanged a series of increasingly absurd remarks. Linus had managed to hold back his laughter only with great effort. Adam had looked thunderous, as he did now.

"Harry can spend time with anyone he wants."

Linus adjusted his footing and gently guided his fishing line a bit closer to a small eddy in the river. "You're jealous, then?"

"Not in the least." Beneath Adam's grumpy exterior was an undeniable sincerity, even a little amusement. "He distracts Harry. It is perhaps the only thing I actually like about the idiotic earl."

Linus eyed him sidelong. "I thought Harry was meant to distract Lampton, not the other way around."

"So long as they're both leaving me alone."

A cool breeze shook the trees nearby and sent added ripples over the water.

"You didn't have to come along today," Linus reminded him. "With Lampton and Harry both gone, the house would have been quiet."

Adam rolled his fishing pole in his hand. "I like fishing." A shockingly unterrifying declaration. "I am not often afforded the opportunity."

"Why not? You have an enormous lake at the Castle."

"I also have enormous responsibilities." Adam began slowly pulling in his line. "There is little time for leisure when I am at home."

There was a bit of irony in that. "For my part, I seem to have nothing but leisure since leaving the navy."

"Wait until you're back at your estate. That'll keep you busy enough." The duke recast his line. A peacefulness hung about him that one did not usually see there. It seemed he really did enjoy fishing. Did Persephone know as much? She would likely insist that her husband make time for something that brought him pleasure and a release of strain. Perhaps Linus ought to mention it.

Linus's line drifted on the current a bit past where he wanted it. He reeled it in and recast. Charlie seemed to have lost all interest. His pole sat abandoned on the shoreline, and he walked along a rocky outcropping a bit apart from the other gentlemen. He was alone but didn't seem overly bothered by it. He likely felt out of place amongst this gathering of people so much his senior. He was not a child, but neither was he truly grown yet. It was a difficult place to be.

Harry sat on a rock not far distant, his line bobbing about without receiving the least attention. "If I don't catch anything, I plan to blame you, Lampton. I suspect you've cast a spell of some kind."

"I, for one, intend to blame the weather," Lampton replied, swinging his quizzing glass on its chain. Who wore a quizzing glass on a fishing expedition? It was beyond odd. "The summer has been unseasonably cool."

"I suspect your lack of fish will be the result of your pole leaning against that tree instead of being in the water," Harry said, "though I'm no expert."

Lord Lampton tugged at his cuffs, then fluffed his cravat. "The fish are, no doubt, so impressed with this knot my valet created that I hardly need to entice them with a hook and bait."

"They'll land on the bank out of sheer joy, is that it?" Harry grinned.

Oh yes. Harry had most certainly defected.

"Indeed." The earl set a foot on a slightly higher rock, striking a pose worthy of the most dramatic of portraits. "And if this weather continues as it has, we'll have another frost fair this winter. I will commission an ice sculpture of my success here today. I am certain Mother Nature sent this spell of weather specifically so I could do so, which I think was very sporting of her."

"This weather is nothing to celebrate," Adam tossed back. "We've had crop failures throughout the kingdom. People are suffering. You should be praying for this cold spell to pass, not continue."

"But think of the ice sculpture," Lord Lampton implored.

Adam turned to face him more fully. "You've been present when this has been discussed in Lords. Were you not listening when we were told of those pouring out of Wales, hungry and broken by their losses, or when we discussed the famine plaguing Ireland because of this weather? Do not make light of this."

"My good man," Lampton sauntered a bit closer, "I am happy to share my ice sculpture with anyone who wishes to enjoy it."

Adam tossed his pole onto the bank and moved toward Lampton. His stride was not one of friendly camaraderie. Linus eyed Harry, unsure how quickly they ought to intervene.

"I first took up my seat in Lords when I was twenty-one years old." Adam's voice tightened with each word. "For six years, I served there with your father. For six years, I watched him as an example of how a gentleman fulfills his duties. I admired him. Deeply."

Some of the earl's bravado died, replaced by a tension of his own.

"For his sake," Adam continued, "I have held my tongue while you have pranced and preened about that chamber. I have held out hope that eventually you would decide to live up to his legacy. But you never do. He was a gentleman worthy of that title. You, sir, are a disgrace to his memory."

"How dare you." The earl didn't sound the least superficial now. "How dare you stand on my father's land and question his legacy."

"So long as that legacy is borne by the likes of you, I will question it at every turn."

The two men stood within throttling distance now. Linus tucked his fishing pole into the space between two rocks and stepped closer to the combatants, ready to jump in should it prove necessary. Harry made his way over to him.

"I know what it is to be a too-young member of Lords," Adam said, "without a father to guide me, without the first idea of how to be a gentleman of worth. There are others in that chamber in that same position, and they look to you, Lampton. You draw attention, no doubt on purpose, and they see you. They see the example you set, and you are teaching them to be frippery wastes."

For the first time in the course of Linus's entire acquaintance with the earl, Lampton looked almost threatening. A harshness settled in his eyes and in the tenseness of his features. There was something in the set of his shoulders that, to Linus's experienced gaze, spoke of one familiar with battle. "You, Your Grace, are teaching them to cast judgment and aspersion without bothering to know the entirety of a situation. For why bother discovering what one does not know when one can simply assume the worst and judge accordingly."

Adam pointed an accusatory finger at Lampton's face. "You think I do not see what you are? I watched you toss those weaselly Hamptons from your home with all the precise determination your father possessed. I know when Miss Hampton grew ill, you saw to her care without hesitation. I have seen your attentiveness to your mother. You know how to be worthy; you know how to be strong and capable. You choose not to be."

Lampton, to his credit, didn't flinch or squirm as most men would have. He raised an eyebrow, not unlike Adam's signature look. "You wish to speak of masks? To all the world you appear hard and cold through and through. You are known as the Dangerous Duke. You are feared and fearsome and, if rumors are to be believed, are more heartless than the devil himself. Yet I have watched you. You are tender with your son. You look at your wife with an affection that belies the moniker you have encouraged over the years. I remember well enough the gentleness you showed your quiet and tenderhearted sister-in-law during her debut in Society. You may feel justified in decrying my frivolous behavior, but you, sir, are more of a counterfeit than I will ever be."

Linus inched closer to them. Mentioning Adam's family was perilous, whether or not Lampton knew as much. Harry watched the gentlemen but looked more curious than concerned.

"Do what you will with your father's legacy," Adam said. "That is yours to dispose of, but I will not stand silently by while you cause innocent people to suffer."

"I certainly hope you mean to explain that remark," Lampton said tightly.

"Life has dealt your wife a difficult enough hand without you adding to her misery."

Lampton's nostrils flared. "You would dare speak of my wife."

"I would dare defend her," Adam growled back. "She is unhappy, and you, sir, with your ridiculous and exasperating behavior contribute to that daily." They stood nearly nose to nose.

"This is how you live worthy of your father's title?" Lampton snarled.

"Better than the way you live worthy of your wife's devotion."

At that, a brawl worthy of the seediest den of villainy broke loose. Gentleman Jackson himself would have been impressed with the immediate and vicious round of fisticuffs that ensued.

Linus took a single step before Harry grabbed his arm and held him back.

"Let them work out some frustration," Harry said. "This has been building for days."

"But Persephone—"

"Is going to kill us either way."

He had a point.

Charlie arrived at Linus's side a moment later, his eye on the men circling each other nearby, fists at the ready, taking regular jabs, more than half of them landing with force. "Your brother-in-law doesn't fight dirty, does he?"

"Of course he does."

That brought a little worry to the young man's face. "I don't think Philip has scuffled with anyone since we were kids. He's going to get killed."

"Adam, I think you have a fish on your line," Harry called out.

"Shut up, Harry," came the response.

Harry nodded sagely. "I believe you can rest easy, Mr. Jonquil. If Adam were determined to actually kill your brother, he wouldn't have taken the time to put me in my place."

Charlie looked to Linus for confirmation.

"He does fight dirty," Linus said, "but only when he has to. This fight seems fair enough. Besides, I think your brother is making a good showing for himself."

It was nothing short of the truth. Both men looked equally worse for the wear. Not many gentlemen could have scuffed up the Duke of Kielder without finding themselves inching toward their own deathbed. The lanky, dandified earl was proving fierce.

"Well, how about that," Charlie said quietly. "Philip is good for something after all." He watched only a moment before venturing back toward the river and the rocks he'd been wandering on before.

"There's a chasm between those two brothers," Harry said.

Linus nodded. "A bigger one than I think the earl realizes. And one the poor boy doesn't know how to cross."

They turned their attention back to the combatants. The fight hadn't progressed, but neither had it really ebbed. Obviously neither participant was bent on the other's destruction. Harry had been right, it seemed. They were merely boiling over a bit. It'd do them both good.

Lud, maybe the earl and his brother ought to go a few rounds. At least it would be some interaction, which Charlie needed rather desperately.

"How long do we let this continue before sending them both to the nursery, where they belong?" Harry asked with a smile.

Just as Linus opened his mouth to answer, a splash interrupted. He turned immediately to look where Charlie had been standing and saw an empty outcropping of rocks. He'd fallen in.

Linus rushed in that direction, pulling off his jacket.

The fight ended abruptly.

Lampton called after him, though a bit breathless. "Charlie swims very well. No need sacrificing yourself."

Sure enough, the young man was expertly making his way back to shore a bit downstream. Lampton and Adam moved to where Linus stood watching, one on either side of him.

"I ought to have known Charlie would fall in if we brought him," Lampton said. "He is forever getting himself into scrapes. I can't take him anywhere."

"How many places do you take him?" Linus asked a bit under his breath.

Lampton didn't answer but called out to his brother instead. "You'd best head back to the house and change. Try not to fall into a ditch or something on the way there."

Charlie tossed his brother what was likely supposed to be a glare, but a painful degree of embarrassment filled his expression. The young man dragged himself away, head hung a little, steps slow and heavy. Poor Charlie.

Harry joined them on the bank of the river and eyed Adam and Lampton. "You two look like a couple of tomcats after an alley brawl."

Adam's mouth pulled into a tight line. "No one tells Persephone."

"Or Sorrel," Philip added. "If my wife finds out, she'll make this bout of fisticuffs look like a ballroom waltz."

"Mine as well." Adam turned to Philip and held out his hand. "A vow of secrecy?"

Philip shook it firmly.

Harry grinned and turned to Linus. "Shall we vow to keep mum as well? I, for one, am not nearly as afraid of their wives as they clearly are."

"I am," Linus said. "One of those wives is my oldest sister; I know how fearsome she is. And Lady Lampton wields her walking stick like one who knows precisely how to put it to good use."

A corner of Lampton's mouth, the corner not trickling blood, twitched upward. "She most certainly does."

"That settles it," Harry said. "If anyone asks, these two were attacked by a bloodthirsty trout."

"Make it a lamprey, and I'll go along with the tale," Lampton said. "To be attacked by an eel would make a far better story."

"What of you, Adam?" Harry asked. "What type of fish shall we say you scuffled with?"

Adam eyed Lampton for a drawn-out moment. "A minnow."

They all laughed at that. Adam even smiled ever so slightly. Lampton sketched a brief bow of acknowledgment. It seemed they'd brokered a peace. Had they done so a few days earlier, Linus might have taken advantage of some additional free time to spend with Arabella. That, however, would only have further fueled the gossip now hovering about them.

He would not cause her more distress. He would keep his distance and both their reputations intact. No matter the misery of denying himself her company, he would do what he must for her.

"Lieutenant Lancaster, thank you for coming."

Linus stopped in the doorway of a small sitting room. He offered a brief bow, his attention a little pulled. Lady Lampton had sent a note requesting a brief audience with him. Seeing Persephone in the room as well was unexpected.

"Please have a seat." Lady Lampton motioned to a straight-backed chair placed on its own, facing the two wingback armchairs the ladies occupied.

He offered no objections, though he harbored plenty of suspicions. "What can I do for you?"

"You were at the river today, I believe." The countess, with her stiff posture, unyielding gaze, and firm, frilless tone, was surprisingly intimidating.

"I was," he said.

The ladies exchanged the briefest of glances before turning their attention to him once more.

Persephone spoke next. "Tell us about the eels, if you would. We have heard some very strange rumors."

Ah, lud. They knew about the fight, at least some of it. And, it seemed, the ridiculous plan to blame the fish had been carried out.

"All I will say is that fish are not very bright."

Lady Lampton was undeterred. "Which one swore you to secrecy, the eel or the minnow?"

"I have fought plenty of battles," Linus said. "I stay out of them whenever possible."

"Both," Persephone said with a crisp nod.

There was no keeping secrets from his sister. There never had been.

"He promised me he would behave." Persephone's lips tensed in frustration. "I simply wanted one gathering where he didn't send everyone fleeing in fear."

"Believe me, Lampton was not fleeing."

That brought curiosity to both ladies' faces, though only Persephone seemed surprised.

"Philip is more than capable of defending himself," Lady Lampton said. "I imagine he held his own against the attack."

Though he was likely being a little disloyal to the gentlemen, Linus felt compelled to explain things a bit better to the ladies. "At the risk of interjecting where I'm not welcome, Lady Lampton, your husband was not the one attacked. "

Now they both looked shocked.

In for a penny, as the old saying went. "They have been at each other's throats since before this house party. Things boiled over at the river. There was an argument. Adam expressed concern that Lampton is at times neglectful and causes misery." Linus looked fully at Persephone. "You know Adam's feelings on that."

She nodded, both weariness and pride in the gesture. "He never could bear for anyone to be hurting without rising to their defense. He does not always pause to think before rushing in."

"Well, he didn't this time either. Lampton took umbrage at the insinuation and belted him. Adam, being Adam, slugged back and . . ." Linus shrugged.

"Why did you not stop them?" Persephone asked.

"For one thing, they would have torn me to pieces. For another, they are grown men; they don't need me to play nursemaid."

"The current state of their faces says otherwise," Persephone answered drily.

Lady Lampton, who hadn't spoken in a while, eyed him closely. "Who was it your brother-in-law accused my Philip of mistreating?"

For a man who'd bemoaned being an overlooked outsider in this gathering, he'd certainly been pulled into the thick of it.

"I would rather not say, Lady Lampton."

"Come out with it, Lieutenant," she said. "If something upset my husband enough to result in today's fiasco, I have a right to know what it was."

From now on, Linus intended to fully embrace his membership in the club of misfits and leave everyone outside of it to sort their own difficulties. He and Arabella would be perfectly happy not navigating these treacherous waters.

"I should warn you," the countess pressed, "I am both determined and impatient, and I'm not afraid to use your sister to get the truth out of you."

"I will happily help," Persephone said. "I want to know what accusation Adam flung at him. Whom did he say Lord Lampton was mistreating?"

Linus slumped in his chair. How had he found himself in this situation? "Lady Lampton," he said. "Adam said he believed that Lampton was making his own wife miserable."

Persephone turned to Lady Lampton, who had paled even as her brow had drawn down in confusion. The countess's eyes held worry, pain.

"He ought not to have said that." Persephone set her hand on Lady Lampton's. "He means well, but he doesn't always know how to help."

Linus slipped quietly from his chair. He met Persephone's eye and motioned silently to the door. She nodded.

Stepping into the corridor, he sighed his relief even as he cursed his own recklessness in placing himself in such an awkward situation. Perhaps home, with its emptiness and loneliness, would not be such a bad thing after all.

Chapter Eighteen

No specific entertainment was planned for that evening. Though the dowager explained it as a desire to allow her guests and that evening's additions to interact more freely, Linus thought she looked a little weary, the weight of hosting a two-week-long party apparently taking a toll. Arabella, sitting beside her, looked more tired still. And yet Linus kept to the other side of the room. He'd found himself in enough entanglements without adding "fueling gossip" to the list.

Lampton was in rare form that night, making any number of inane observations, all of which were roaringly funny if one assumed that was his aim. After that afternoon's scuffle, Linus felt certain the earl's frivolity was, in large part, an act.

"I was justified in pounding him," Adam muttered a full half hour after dinner, having been subjected to the commentary during the meal and the "performance" afterward. Both he and Lampton were sporting poorly concealed cuts and bruises. "There are few things as wasteful as a gentleman who chooses to be frivolous when he is fully capable of being an asset in the world."

Linus eyed him sidelong. "What about one who chooses to be dastardly when he is fully capable of being at least a little bit personable?"

"Lampton already sermonized on that score. If you start preaching to me, I will drag you back to the river and grant you a renewed acquaintance with water."

Linus always had enjoyed Adam's flare for creative threats. "You mean to drown me?"

"You and then Harry. Then Lampton. And then your overly dramatic sister. That would simplify my life tremendously." The return of Adam's irritability put Linus firmly in mind of Caroline's declaration that the duke was not grumpy but sad.

He watched his brother-in-law as the evening wore on. There was, in fact, a degree of sadness in his expression but a vague and old one. Persephone said Adam still deeply mourned his father's passing. She'd also said he'd experienced true sadness when Daphne had married and left home, and she expected the same to be true of Artemis's departure. How much of Adam's fearsomeness was grief, sorrow he did not know how to work through?

Linus felt much of that same irremovable heartache. His mother had died so long ago, yet he missed her every day. His father's loss had been slower and, in some ways, more tragic. He had felt a sense of relief when the pain of such a slow decline had finally ended, but his heart had broken anew at losing his last remaining parent.

In a rush of unexpected emotion, his heart told his head what it had tried so hard to ignore. Those losses were difficult and heavy, but none was so raw as Evander's death. They had been as close as two brothers could be, even before their time at sea had forged an even deeper bond. Evander had been his closest friend, his only confidante, the one piece of his family he hadn't lost. He had clung to that, to the fragile strand that held him to the life he'd known.

That strand had snapped on a cruel November day eleven years earlier. War did that. It stole things that could never be given back.

The reminder lay heavy on his heart. He could not sit with Arabella as he would prefer and allow her influence to lift his spirits.

He drifted toward the dowager, intending to make his excuses. The evening's gathering had lost its appeal.

The "good evening" he'd meant to offer his hostess died unspoken at the look of concern in Arabella's eyes. That set him to studying the dowager countess a bit more closely. What had appeared to be fatigue looked, on closer inspection, more like true illness.

Arabella moved to his side, her own appearance less than hardy, and whispered, "Will you sit with her? I need to alert Lord Lampton."

"Of course."

He took the seat she had occupied, watching as she slowly, wearily made her way toward the earl.

The dowager sat with her shoulders a bit slumped. She slowly shook her head, her mouth pulled into a tight line. She seemed to know that her illness had not been kept hidden and disliked the fuss she anticipated.

He kept his first remark light. "It appears grandmother could not resist the urge to rock her ailing grandchildren."

She sighed, the sound one of annoyance. "That physician warned me not to, but he is something of a fusspot."

"And, therefore, you didn't listen."

One corner of her creased mouth tipped upward. "I have never been good at obeying orders."

"There are few things as formidable as a tenacious woman," he said. "Of course, one need only look at my sisters to know where I learned that truth."

Her smile was still genuine but weaker than usual. "Perhaps, Mr. Lancaster, you would be so good as to solve a mystery for me."

"I will promise to be of any assistance I can."

"You have been very sweetly attentive to our Arabella in the time you've been here. Why do you seem to be avoiding her now?"

That was certainly a direct question. "It was brought to my attention that whispers have begun, speculating on our connection and my intentions. Though I miss her company, I am attempting to quiet the gossip."

"A difficult thing once it has begun."

He nodded. "I know."

"And you are an exemplary gentleman; I hope you also know that."

Lord Lampton arrived. Though his dandification was not entirely absent, Linus saw precisely what he had seen on a few occasions: his unwavering gaze, the firm set of his jaw. In that moment, he was not ridiculous in the least.

There are few things as wasteful as a gentleman who chooses to be frivolous when he is fully capable of being an asset in the world.

"You have come to send me to bed, have you?" The dowager was clearly frustrated at the necessity, though she did not argue it.

"I have come to assure you that Sorrel means to oversee the remainder of the evening, which is something of a miracle unto itself." He added the last in a low aside.

"I should have grown ill months ago," the dowager said.

Lord Lampton helped her stand. Linus rose as well. Arabella looked on.

"Come now, Mater," Lampton said. "You have earned an extra bit of rest tonight."

"Have I also earned an extra cup of chocolate in the morning? I think I have."

Lord Lampton chuckled as he led her away.

Arabella remained, watching them go. "I am afraid I will not be much help, being ill yet myself."

"She will understand," he assured her. "Indeed, you can offer something none of the rest of us can."

She looked at him once more, curiosity in her expression.

"Empathy," he said. "You know how she feels."

Arabella's gaze dropped for a moment before returning to his face. "I know there have been whispers. I'm sorry to have caused you trouble."

"Those whispers are problematic for you as well," he pointed out.

"I am a poor relation turned lady's companion. I have far less to lose."

Did she truly think *he* was the one who would suffer most should the whispers grow too loud?

"You've been so kind." Regret filled her face. "Now that kindness has caused you grief."

"We'll both emerge from this fine; I'm certain of it," he said. "I have my home to return to, and you have this one."

Her hand moved to the bead on her necklace, though Linus doubted she made the gesture consciously. "I had best go see if the dowager needs anything. Thank you again for your goodness while I've been ill."

"And thank you for your patience the many times I've told you of my problems."

She nodded. "That is what friends are for, Linus Lancaster."

Friends. That was not the word he wanted to hear, but it was the only one permitted between them.

Chapter Nineteen

MATER WAS, QUITE POSSIBLY, THE world's most cooperative invalid. Arabella took on the task of seeing to her comforts and found it quite an easy thing. She was thanked regularly, and Mater had no qualms about simply requesting the things she wished for. If these were the circumstances under which Arabella would pass her years as a companion, the experience would not be an unpleasant one. She would be needed and appreciated.

The future she now anticipated was far better than the one she'd faced at her aunt and uncle's house. Indeed, when they had berated her only two evenings before, a veritable army had come to her defense. She would be watched over in this house, even after the guests were gone.

Even after *Linus* was gone. She pushed aside the disappointment that realization caused.

She knew perfectly well her aunt had been behind the rumors that had driven a wedge between them. No gentleman wished to have his hand forced. If not for that, would he have continued sitting with her, his hand wrapped around hers, bringing a smile to her face and a sense of belonging to her heart. The house party was not yet over. Perhaps in the time remaining, they could regain some of the connection they'd had. She hoped so.

Lady Lampton arrived in Mater's rooms midmorning and, with a comfort that spoke of familiarity, took a seat near her mother-in-law. There was a closeness between the two ladies despite their disparate personalities.

"You have Philip in an absolute panic, you know," Lady Lampton said. "So I thank you for that."

Mater smiled. "I will assume, then, he is no longer making a drawn-out spectacle of himself for the 'benefit' of our guests."

"Less of one, at least." Lady Lampton did not seem particularly annoyed. Indeed, the same fondness Arabella had seen in her face as she'd spoken of the blessing of having a kindhearted husband returned. "One would think that after bloodying himself brawling at the river, he would tiptoe more carefully around His Grace's temper. Yet he seems determined to continue provoking him."

Mater and Arabella exchanged looks. They both knew full well Philip's reasons for testing the duke's endurance, but as they involved Lady Lampton, revealing those motivations did not seem at all the right thing to do.

She eyed them both with growing suspicion. "I have stumbled upon something, it seems."

"My lips are sealed," Mater said.

Lady Lampton turned fully to Arabella. "And what about you? Do you know all our secrets as well?"

She offered her ladyship a dry look. Lady Lampton was perfectly aware of the fact that she was privy to a great many secrets.

Mater pieced things together on the instant. "How many of us have told you things in confidence?"

"All of you," she admitted.

Lady Lampton seemed surprised. "Even Charlie?"

Arabella nodded.

Despite the lingering effects of illness, Mater's gaze sharpened on her. "What is weighing on that boy's mind? I see it in his face and in his posture. It has been there for some time, truth be told, but has grown more pointed of late. He won't talk to any of us."

Arabella would not divulge what he had confided in her but wished to ease some of his mother's worries. "He and I have shared a special kinship ever since the day he ruined my best morning dress by splattering it from top to bottom with thick, putrid mud."

Mater laughed at the memory. "I was so put out with him. The mischief he has caused over the years. You'll remember, I packed him up, along with Caroline, who was staying with us at the time, and hied him off to Havenworth."

"My other gowns were most grateful to you," Arabella said.

But Mater's amusement turned to regret. "I was especially frustrated with him because I knew your uncle did not allow you sufficient pin money to replace what Charlie had ruined."

"He did on that occasion," she said, "which, I assure you, came as an utter shock, both to me and my aunt. She, in fact, was rather livid. She never could countenance any of his finances being used for my benefit."

"I didn't realize your uncle kept the truth of it a secret." Mater's remark made little sense.

"Kept what truth a secret?"

She smiled gently. "I replaced your gown. I could not bear the thought of you suffering because my nearly grown baby could not seem to keep himself out of trouble."

"*You* replaced it?" Had Mater truly been so aware of and concerned about her situation long before inviting her to the Park? "That was very kind of you."

"I ought to have done far more than that." Sadness touched her words, even a bit of guilt.

Arabella could endure receiving her position out of kindness, even charity, but guilt and pity were not to be borne. "You have done a great deal for me," she reassured Mater. "I am happier here than I have been in some time." In eleven years, in fact.

"I can honestly say the same." Lady Lampton spoke with more emotion than Arabella had ever heard from her. "My home life was one of constant rejection and sorrow. Being an"—she swallowed back a word before finally allowing it free—"an invalid meant enduring endless disdain and dismissal, even from my own parents. Yet this past year and more, I have been met with acceptance and loving kindness." She took hold of her mother-in-law's hand. "I have not been left to walk alone."

"My husband always wished for a family of daughters," Mater said. "He, of course, would not have traded his sons for the world, but he longed for girls of his own." A mixture of nostalgia and grief filled her voice. "He often imagined this house filled with a family of strong, caring, fierce women. I see that dream of his coming true all around me."

Quite to Arabella's surprise, Mater took her hand with the one Lady Lampton was not holding. Oh, how she hoped that meant Mater felt her late husband would have approved of Arabella's presence and of the woman she had become, that he had, in some degree, imagined her a part of his home.

"And for my boys' sakes, I am grateful that they share their father's appreciation of intelligent and resolute women. They are so very like him."

"I think you would be wise to tell Charlie that." Arabella hoped she was not betraying a confidence. "And in the most specific terms you can."

Mater's pained gaze turned fully on her. "Charlie doesn't remember him, does he?"

"Not well." She disliked speaking a truth she knew would cause Mater further sorrow. "I think knowing him better and knowing that his father lives on in him would mean a great deal."

Mater squeezed her hand. "I will do that."

"And will you also start taking the powders Dr. Scorseby prescribed you?"

Mater's eyes opened wide, as did Lady Lampton's.

"I told you everyone has been telling me things," Arabella said.

Mater, in tones of mock outrage made all the more entertaining by the twinkle in her eyes, said, "Then you can just tell that nosey physician that I have, indeed, been taking his nasty powders and they are working every bit as well as he said they would."

"You have been ill?" Lady Lampton pressed. "Beyond this current bout, that is?"

"Nothing at all serious," Mater insisted. "A touch of dyspepsia is all. Dr. Scorseby makes everything out to be a crisis. I think he enjoys the feeling of panic."

Lady Lampton smiled knowingly. "He does have a flair for drama, does he not?"

Drama? Panic? Arabella hadn't noticed either. It seemed, despite being in company with him evening after evening, she didn't know him very well.

"What dramatic pronouncements has he made about *your* health of late?" Mater asked her daughter-in-law.

"Only that I am in no more pain than can be expected for one with an utterly broken body," Lady Lampton said. "And that he does not expect my situation to improve, though he has instructed me not to give up hope."

"Hope is a powerful thing," Arabella observed. It had sustained her through her darkest days.

"As is a friend and a reliable confidante," Lady Lampton said to her. "And we have been fortunate enough to find that in you, Arabella."

Hearing herself called by her Christian name proved more moving than she could have predicted. For the first time in a very long time, she felt as though she belonged.

A knock sounded on the door of Mater's sitting room, though it was slightly ajar. They all looked in that direction as Linus peeked his head inside.

Linus. Arabella held her breath.

"Forgive the interruption," he said.

"Nonsense, Mr. Lancaster." Mater waved him inside. "The infirm are always in need of diverting company."

"I take leave to doubt you are so very near death's door." He stepped inside, offering quick dips of his head to Lady Lampton and Arabella before taking Mater's outstretched hands in his own. "You appear in better health than you did last evening."

"Whether or not that is true, I will thank you for saying it." She indicated he should take the only vacant seat in the sitting area, the one directly beside Arabella.

He did so and then, without looking at her, said, "I am surprised your Dr. Scorseby is not here looking after . . . everyone. He asked about you at least a dozen times last evening after you had retired."

She returned his teasing in kind. "I am surprised your Mrs. Blackbourne is not here looking after . . . you. She ran you to ground at least a dozen times in the first quarter of an hour she was here last evening."

Mater grinned unrepentantly. Lady Lampton's amusement showed as well, though in an expression more subdued than her mother-in-law's.

"Ah." Linus looked around at the lot of them. "I see I have stumbled into a gossip circle."

"It was not a gossip circle until you arrived," Mater said. "I fear you may be a bad influence."

"Well, I have come with news, so perk up your ears, ladies."

Arabella could not hold back her amusement. He lightened her spirits like no one else. He even managed to pull a fully bloomed smile from Lady Lampton, something she had not often seen.

"Unfortunately," he added, "the first part is sad news. I have received word from my estate of a difficulty that must be seen to immediately." He turned his full attention to Mater. "I have to leave within the hour."

He was leaving. Within the hour. Arabella tried to swallow, but her throat felt too tight. A stinging started at the back of her eyes.

"Oh, that is sad news." Mater's mouth turned down in disappointment. "It cannot possibly be put off?"

"I spoke with my brothers-in-law as well as your two oldest sons, they having more estate experience than I do, and all four agreed that I must go personally and that time is rather of the essence."

Mater and Lady Lampton both expressed their disappointment. Arabella could not quite find words.

He was leaving.

There would be no returning to their earlier friendship, no chance of pursuing something beyond. She'd not admitted to it before, but she had hoped for that. She still did.

"What is the second part of your gossip?" Mater asked. "Is it sad as well?"

"It might be a little for you," he said. "But on the whole, I believe it is good."

"You certainly have me intrigued," Lady Lampton said.

"I have presented an idea to your eldest son," he said, "one he finds acceptable enough for me to bring here to you." He paused only a moment. "I wish to take Charlie to Shropshire with me."

"Charlie?" Mater clearly found that as surprising as Arabella did.

"I have enjoyed his company during this house party. He is a good and sensible young man, but he is also a little lost." Linus's tone softened ever further. "I believe he could benefit from some time spent out of the shadows cast by his brothers, and I suspect he needs a little guidance, something he seems very reluctant to seek from any of those brothers."

"He would likely land himself in one pickle after another," Mater warned. "That can be a lot to deal with."

Linus looked unconcerned. "I firmly believe a lot of his mischief arises from boredom. There is work aplenty to be done on my estate. He will be very busy, but he will also be the only other one there, and I think that is what he needs just now."

Mater wove her hands together, then lifted her intertwined fingers to her lips, thinking. Arabella watched her, ready to provide support if this discussion proved too much for her weakened constitution. She ought to have known that this formidable lady was made of sterner stuff.

"Being the youngest has always been difficult for him," Mater said. "I think more so now that they are all grown and he is very nearly as well. They are successful, respected, and, in many ways, very important in their various spheres. That is, as you said, a large shadow to try to escape." Mater lowered her hands to her lap. "I have struggled to know how I might help him. Philip has tried, but his efforts are hampered by the fact that he is unwittingly part of the problem."

"I know Charlie needs to return to Cambridge when the new term begins," Linus said. "I will see to it that he does. But I believe he will benefit greatly from time away from both his studies and his, for lack of a better word, insecurities."

"You would do that for our Charlie?" Mater's voice broke a little.

"Do not ascribe to me too many selfless motivations," he said, his voice lightening, no doubt in response to her tone of concern. "His company will do me good as well. My estate is very empty and a little lonely. Charlie feels he has too much family nearby, while I very much wonder why I have none at all."

Mater reached over and patted his hand. "We will miss both of you as our party winds to its conclusion, but I believe this is for the best."

"I agree," he said.

"Have a safe journey," Lady Lampton said. "Don't let Charlie drive the coach."

Linus laughed and dipped his head, then turned slowly to face Arabella. "Might I beg a moment, Miss Hampton?"

She had not been expecting that. A little perplexed, she walked with him to the door and a single step into the corridor.

"You seem to be relinquishing your membership in our club, Captain Hampton."

"Whatever do you mean, Lieutenant Lancaster?"

He motioned back through the open doorway. "This is not a gathering in which you appear to be an outsider. It seems to me you are finding your place amongst this family."

"I believe I am." The realization struck her in that moment. "I truly am."

Unmistakable relief entered his eyes. "I am beyond pleased. You deserve all of the happiness in the world, Miss Hampton."

"What about you? You will be alone at your estate."

He smiled. "I will have Charlie. According to his family, that will keep me very busy."

"He will return to school soon," she reminded him.

"By then, I fully intend to have implemented your excellent advice and have found a means of making the life of an estate owner and man of the land suit me better."

"You will be happy?" she pressed.

"I will be happy."

There was some consolation in that. He was leaving, but he was leaving more hopeful than he had arrived.

He took her hand. She willed her heart to calm as he raised it to his lips. He pressed a kiss to the back of her hand. She held her breath.

Linus stepped back, relinquishing her hand. "Goodbye, Miss Hampton," he said and walked away.

With those three words, he broke her heart.

Chapter Twenty

LINUS RECALLED WITH PERFECT CLARITY the moment he first saw the ship that would take him away from England, away from the only home he'd ever known. He'd been little more than a child, and he'd been afraid. Yet there'd been an undeniable surge of anticipation beneath his trepidation.

He felt that same contradiction all over again as the traveling coach pulled up the drive leading to the Lancaster family home. He was anxious to see the old place, to make certain that his brother's inheritance was properly cared for, yet a growing part of him wanted to demand the carriage be turned around and pointed in any direction other than home. His memories always grew louder in Shropshire. He couldn't outrun them here.

"Your house is Tudor." Charlie watched their approach.

"It is also much smaller than Lampton Park's manor house," Linus acknowledged. "You will likely find it absurdly 'quaint.'"

"A thing doesn't have to be impressive to be valued." Charlie sat with his face all but pressed to the glass of the carriage window, looking closer to nine than nineteen.

If Linus had years' worth of only pleasant memories of home and family, would he be as eager at their arrival? Would he ever be?

Charlie looked back at him. "Your father's scholarly income was enough to sustain a home and estate this size?"

Rather than rehash the details of Father's decline and the necessity of scraping together money for their subsistence, Linus simply nodded. Had Father remained healthy, his income would have been sufficient, though only just.

Charlie returned to his inspection of the house they'd pulled to a stop in front of. "A family could live here."

"A family *did* live here," Linus whispered.

The footman opened the carriage door. Charlie descended without hesitation. Linus sat a moment, rallying his courage. How was it a naval man who'd fought in countless battles, who'd traveled the seas for years on end, quaked at something so harmless as stepping inside his childhood home?

He could not remain in the carriage forever. This was not the first time he'd been home since Evander's death. He'd survived the other visits; he'd certainly survive now. Except, this wasn't merely a stop-in before returning to duty, as it had always been in the past. This *was* his duty now.

Linus took a breath. Then another. He set his sights on the narrow strip of light spilling in from the open carriage door and moved toward it. Then through it. He stepped onto the pebbled path, slowly lifting his gaze to take in the house. For the briefest of moments, his mind saw it as it had once been: broken windows, the exposed wood in desperate need of tarring, the white paint cracked and peeling off the wattle and daub. The land had not fared much better. The lawns had been overgrown and untended. The ornamental gardens had been left to grow wild. They'd had means and time enough only for the gardens that produced food.

It looked so different now. First Adam and then Daphne's husband, James, had taken on the restoration of the Lancaster family home. They'd managed it. Evander would have been elated. He'd talked often of wishing to put the house and estate to rights. Linus only hoped he didn't undo all the good done here. He owed that much to his brother.

Mr. and Mrs. Tuttle, butler and housekeeper, stood on either side of the door, waiting for him. Charlie hadn't stepped inside yet. He watched Linus. The servants lined up beside Mrs. Tuttle hadn't looked away from him either.

He was the master of the estate now. Lud, he wasn't at all used to that. He was expected to arrive in grandeur and lead the return to the estate. They all awaited his nod of acknowledgment, his words of approval, his instructions. Why did it have to be this way? The staff knew their roles better than he ever would. He would far rather arrive, ask them how they were getting on, and allow everyone to go about his or her own business.

"Find a way to make the role your own," Arabella had said.

Significantly altering the expected routines and tasks everyone undertook would impact the servants. After all they had done the past years to help restore his family home, he would not repay them with upheaval. He could make adjustments elsewhere, but not in this.

He stepped past Charlie and to the doorway. The Tuttles offered a bow and curtsey respectively. He acknowledged that in the expected manner.

"Welcome home, Mr. Lancaster," Tuttle said.

The customary response would be to declare himself pleased to be home, but he'd rather not lie. "I hope you received my note warning you that we would be having a visitor."

"We did, sir," Mrs. Tuttle said. "But you did not specify which bed-chamber you wished Mr. Jonquil to be placed in. We've tried sorting it on our own but would like your advice. You'd not wish him in the nursery."

He shot a grin at Charlie, who made a dramatic show of being relieved.

"And Miss Daphne's bedchamber'd be too feminine for a gentleman to feel comfortable staying in." Mrs. Tuttle spoke with utmost conviction.

That was certainly true.

"The master's chamber is yours," Mrs. Tuttle continued. "You'd not intended to place him in the mistress's bedchamber, I'd not think."

"Certainly not." He laughed at the picture that inspired.

Mrs. Tuttle nodded. "Then, your only remaining options are either Miss Persephone and Miss Athena's bedchamber or the one you shared with—"

"The girls' room." He turned back to Charlie and motioned him for-ward. "Let us settle you in."

"Mr. Lancaster." Mrs. Tuttle spoke before Linus could take a single step inside. "The girls' bedchamber is—"

"More than sufficient." He stepped inside the house.

With the same determined stride he'd learned to strike during tense moments on ship, he crossed the entryway and around the turn that led to the main staircase. Ghosts of his past followed him all the way there, whispering in his ears and echoing in his thoughts. Daphne, tucked into corners reading a book. Artemis, running down the corridors, giggling. Persephone's perseverance. Athena's hopefulness. Father's struggles. Mother's . . . absence.

He shook his head, trying to clear it before the final member of the Lancaster family forced his way into his mind.

"Up this way," he told Charlie, who'd kept up with his quick pace. "Your room overlooks the side meadow. You'll like it."

They took the stairs without pausing. He was likely being a poor host, not allowing Charlie the opportunity to look around and become acquainted with the house. But Linus hadn't the endurance for it just then.

The corridor was quiet, as it always was during his brief sojourns in Shropshire. Having Charlie there would help. There'd be someone to talk with, someone to fill the gaps. And not just any someone but Charlie, whose company he thoroughly enjoyed. It would help ease the sting.

"This room here will be yours," Linus said. He pushed open the door to the room his older sisters had shared. It was empty. No bed. No bureau. Only a single chair near the window.

Charlie stepped inside and took a look around. "I'll admit, this is more rustic than I'd expected." He eyed Linus with amusement. "Are you hoping to accustom me to the sparse existence of a poor academic?"

"Perhaps I'm trying to convince you to think highly of your family's graciousness as hosts by demonstrating the opposite."

With a laugh, Charlie nodded. "Consider me convinced."

Mrs. Tuttle stood in the doorway. "I did try to remind you, Mr. Lancaster. You allowed Lord and Lady Techney to give the furniture in this room to the vicarage, as it was in terrible need of it. None of it was ever replaced."

She *had* tried to warn him; he hadn't listened.

"My apologies, Mrs. Tuttle, for not heeding you. I'm afraid I am not very well suited to this role."

Mrs. Tuttle smiled but not in agreement. In the next moment, a passing maid pulled her attention into the corridor once more and she stepped away.

Linus turned back to his young guest. "That leaves you but one option, really. Unless you're willing to sleep on the floor."

"Willing, yes. But not eager."

He slapped a hand on Charlie's shoulder and led him from the room. The journey was a short one, a matter of mere steps, yet it felt like thousands of miles.

Linus grasped the handle of the bedchamber he'd not entered in so long. For a moment, he couldn't turn it, couldn't commit to opening the door. Even when Father had still been alive and Linus had come to visit, he'd not occupied this room. He'd even stayed in the nursery more than once. He couldn't ask that of Charlie, no matter how painful the alternative.

This is my home now. I cannot live here with this room permanently closed off. He turned the handle and pushed open the door, its hinges protesting.

His heart thudded against his paralyzed lungs as he braced himself against the familiarity of the space. The furniture had been replaced some years earlier. The layout was different. None of that stopped the flood of grief he felt.

This had been their room. In these walls, he and Evander had been together, happy, hopeful. They had spoken of returning here on shore leaves for years, carefree for a time, enjoying the freedom that would come from having incomes to contribute to the family estate. None of that had happened. None of it.

"I'll leave you to settle in." He left, moving hastily toward the master's bedchamber, the one that now belonged to him. Even with the memories that room held of his father, it was not as painful as the one he'd just left.

He shut the door behind him, as if doing so could prevent these specters from finding him there. This was meant to have been Evander's home; its rooms would never be free of him.

"Look after them." Evander's voice echoed across eleven years. The pounding of cannons and the cacophony of voices that had filled that long-ago moment returned as well. Linus knew if he closed his eyes, he'd see the deck of the *Triumphant*, the thick smoke all around them, and Evander's face growing paler by the moment, grayer. Linus could taste the ash in the air. Smell the blood.

"The girls need you, Linus. And Father. He can't tend the estate on his own. Persephone's husband might not care what happens to it. You have to see to it, Linus. And the girls. Don't let Daphne disappear. She'll fade away, Linus. She'll fade away, and we'll lose her. We'll lose it all."

Linus coughed against the clog of tears in this throat. He'd tried so hard to be everything his brother had begged him with his last breaths to be. But he'd failed in so many ways. The girls had been looked after by Adam and Persephone. Daphne had struggled against the very fading Evander had feared. The estate had been tended to by other people. Linus had no experience with estates or land management.

"I don't know what to do, Evander. This was never meant to be mine."

Guilt ate away at him. Guilt that, for the most part, he didn't want the inheritance entrusted to him. Guilt that, having sat on the back terrace of Lampton Park with two children cuddled beside him, the expanse of a peaceful estate spreading out in all directions, watching the approach of a kindhearted, intelligent, caring lady who'd captured a bit of his heart, he was beginning to change his mind.

Of course, those vistas belonged to the Park, the children were not his, and Arabella was not here. He rolled his shoulders against the tension in his neck. What would Arabella think of his family home?

He wandered to the window. The grounds were not as extensive as those found at Lampton Park, nor were they as well manicured. But a great many walking paths traversed the lawns and gardens and stands of trees. The neighborhood itself boasted many more. She would have appreciated that. And she would have encouraged him, as she had before, to find ways to make the undertaking his own.

But what if his way of doing things only made the situation worse? What if he ran the estate into the ground? Linus couldn't bear the thought of breaking yet another promise to his brother. Yet doing nothing was not an option either.

One way or another, he needed to sort things out. He could not get on with his life until he did.

Chapter Twenty-One

MATER'S HEALTH RECOVERED FULLY BY the final evening of the house party. Her sons who lived near enough to attend the closing ball did so, even Harold, whose devotion to his clerical duties had, thus far, kept him from participating in all but one of the fortnight's activities.

The ballroom was exquisitely decorated. The planned supper would meet the expectations of even the most finicky of guests. The sparkle of candlelight on gemstones and the swirl of colorful gowns gave the space a dream-like quality. Though more guests could have been included on the list, the Lampton Park ballroom being quite extensive and the neighborhood boasting a significant number of fine families, Mater possessed that crucial ability in any hostess to compile a guest list based on considerations beyond mere size and space. She had honed her list to those who would, in one another's company, be most pleased and pleasant, and to a number which was at once impressive and somewhat exclusive. She had, in short, planned the perfect final event to mark the end of her time as mistress of Lampton Park.

Arabella watched Mater move about the room. Her expression showed nothing but pleasure and enjoyment, though there had been more than a hint of sadness in her eyes as she had prepared to greet her guests. Endings were always difficult.

His Grace sat near Arabella, apparently not caring to dance. Her Grace had accompanied Miss Artemis from the ballroom some minutes earlier, and the errand had not appeared to be a fully pleasant one. Arabella was not privy to the particulars of that family relationship, but she sensed a growing strain between them all.

Lady Lampton arrived in the seconds before Philip sauntered over, chest a bit puffed out, shirt points so high he could not turn his head independent of his shoulders. "Quite the crush, isn't it?"

"Your mother invited the perfect number of people," Lady Lampton replied. "Not a crush but a pleasant gathering."

"Do you not know, my dear, that if one is to have a successful party, it simply must be described as a crush." Philip cast wide eyes on them all. "Any other word would indicate failure."

"Your wardrobe indicates failure," His Grace drawled.

"Nonsense, my man." Philip motioned at his very colorful attire. He was the only one of the gentlemen not dressed in somber blacks and very dark colors. Philip wore brighter colors than many of the women. "My valet is a man of many talents. He gave his approval."

"Your valet needs spectacles," the duke countered.

"On the contrary." Philip smoothed his impeccable jacket sleeves. "The man deserves a knighthood."

"For enduring you?" His Grace tossed back. "That, Lampton, ought to earn him *saint*hood. Everyone in this household ought to."

"Your Grace, that brings us to my reason for coming to this corner of the room," Lady Lampton said, her dignity palpable.

Arabella glanced at Philip, knowing his goal was to rally his wife from her recent doldrums by earning the duke's ire. Philip did not let his mask slip even a moment.

The duke clearly expected a complaint of some kind and felt himself equal to enduring it. He was the Dangerous Duke, after all.

"While I applaud your willingness to defend those you feel are being mistreated," Lady Lampton said, "I want it made perfectly clear that no one is permitted to question my happiness in my marriage. Not you." She pointed a finger directly at the duke, then turned and pointed at Philip. "And not you. And if I ever hear that either of you have cast yourselves once more in the role of 'declarer of my happiness,' I swear, I will make the thrashing you gave one another at the river look like a child's quarrel."

A look of such deep relief crossed Philip's features that it nearly broke Arabella's heart. He kept his worries so carefully hidden, but his current expression spoke of a deeper pain than she had realized lingered there.

Philip held his hand out to her. "Will you join me for the next set?"

"I may walk better than I once did, but you know perfectly well that I cannot dance." Her feelings had been injured, that much was obvious.

His expression softened. "I hadn't meant for you to *dance* with me, dearest, only to *be* with me."

Some of her fight fled. She wove one arm through his, the other utilizing her ever-present walking stick. They walked slowly away from the small gathering of chairs.

"I like her," the duke said.

"She is a little frightening," Arabella admitted.

The duke nodded crisply. "That's *why* I like her."

And Arabella was finding she very nearly liked the duke.

"Have you been enjoying yourself, Miss Hampton?" Dr. Scorseby asked upon reaching the gathering of chairs where she had sat all evening.

"I have, actually."

He sat beside her. "Why 'actually'? Were you not expecting to be pleased this evening?"

"I wasn't certain if I had recovered enough of my energy to enjoy myself this evening," she said. "I am simply grateful to be feeling equal to the undertaking."

"Are you recovered enough to stand up with me for the next set?"

She was at a ball being asked to dance. Such a thing would have seemed impossible a few short weeks earlier. She had imagined it the evening of her aunt and uncle's attendance, when the other guests had undertaken a few impromptu sets. Her hopes had soared every time Linus had passed anywhere near her. He, however, had never asked. And when whispers had begun linking their names together, he'd grown distant. She understood the necessity, but it had still hurt.

Did he miss her, as a friend at least? Had he regretted his departure as much as she had?

"I can see that you are still fatigued," Dr. Scorseby said. "I will sit beside you instead and allow you to continue to rest."

He didn't have Linus's sense of humor nor his ability to lighten her worries with his presence, and he did not make her heart flip about whenever he was nearby, but Dr. Scorseby was an amiable gentleman. She appreciated that about him.

"Have you been terribly busy?" she asked. "I know the fever we've had here has been running the gamut of the neighborhood."

"I have hardly slept the past five days. While the illness is not a dangerous one, it is tenacious. I think the only person busier than I of late is the apothecary."

He did look tired.

"I hope you are taking care of yourself as well," she said.

"That is a difficult thing for a man alone. But I am making every effort."

"You will be pleased to know the dowager is taking her powders," she said.

"Excellent."

"And though Lady Lampton has not shared with me the particulars of her visit to your home, she does seem in better spirits."

He nodded firmly. "I hope she will choose to speak to her husband about the things that concern her. There can be such strength in a marriage." He looked at her then, his gaze warm and intent.

He was not making a general observation, not with such a pointed expression as he wore just then. With all the attention he showed her, it was only a matter of time before the whispers Linus had worked so hard to silence began to speculate about Dr. Scorseby. He, however, would likely not object.

A woman of her status, of her situation, had few options. She ought to have been elated, encouraged. Her hopes ought to have been soaring. In reality, she simply felt . . . disappointed.

Chapter Twenty-Two

CHARLIE PROVED TO BE ONE of the hardest-working people Linus had ever known, which was a feat considering he'd spent more than half his life in the navy. There was no task too menial or too exhausting for Charlie to willingly undertake. He'd helped clear out a ditch, repair a wall, even rebuild a tenant cottage destroyed by fire. It was an aspect of his character that had never had a chance to shine at his brother's precisely run estate. Charlie was not needed there, so he'd learned to not do anything.

Perhaps Lampton had a minor estate that needed looking after that he might place in Charlie's keeping. The young gentleman would flourish if given responsibilities and a bit of independence.

Linus had originally concocted the idea of setting them both to the exhausting manual labor usually reserved for groundskeepers and tenants as a means of giving Charlie an opportunity to work out a bit of his frustration and boredom. He had found, however, that the unusual approach to managing the estate suited him quite well. He, after all, was accustomed to the grueling work of a ship.

They'd been in Shropshire a full week, and both were exhausted but pleased. They sat down to their evening meal after having spent the day checking the drainage on the back acres. Theirs was a satisfied sort of tired.

"If I had realized you were bringing me here to serve as brute labor, I might not have come," Charlie said, tucking into the hearty stew Cook had prepared. "You are quite the demanding host, you know."

"I've got to get the work around here done one way or another, and I'm not going to do it by myself."

"Because you're so old, right?" Charlie smirked.

"I'm only barely your senior. Show a little respect."

"Yes, the old and infirm do demand some degree of reverence, like ancient stands of trees or those giant pyramids in Giza."

Here was another part of his personality that had blossomed away from the pressures of home. Charlie Jonquil was funny.

"I've half a mind to follow you back to Cambridge to see to it you're a little miserable." Linus's jest missed its mark.

Charlie grew more solemn, picking at his stew rather than devouring it as he had been. That had happened more than once over the past days. When Linus brought up the topic of university, Charlie pulled into himself once more.

"Do you want to return to Cambridge?" Linus finally asked the question he'd been holding back.

"Yes," Charlie answered, then quickly said, "No." He pushed out a breath. "Both."

"Are you unhappy there?"

He shook his head. "Not really."

"Charlie."

He shrugged and pushed his bowl away. "A little, I suppose."

Linus suspected it was more than "a little." When no further explanation was forthcoming, he pressed on. "I do not know much about a university education. I didn't even go to Harrow or Eton. I was at sea far too young. I can't begin to guess what might be amiss there for you."

"The dons have known nearly all of my brothers," Charlie said. "They are forever telling me what good students they were and how well they did in all their courses and how wise they were in what they chose to devote themselves to, that they understood how to prepare themselves for their futures."

"They do not say the same about you?" Linus asked.

"No, and it's not fair." Charlie leaned back, folding his arms across his chest, not in a petulant display but one far closer to self-protection. "My brothers all knew precisely what their futures were. It's easy to choose your studies when you know what your aim is."

"And you don't have an aim."

A tense breath whooshed from the younger man. "All the targets are taken."

One of the difficulties of having a great many older brothers. "You told me you have enjoyed your study of mathematics."

"It is fascinating." Charlie launched into a dizzying explanation involving a great many Greek names and a long list of various mathematical theories.

"The deeper we delve into the properties and relationships of numbers, the more we can learn about the world around us," Charlie said, growing ever more animated. "With mathematics, we can expand our scientific discoveries and our intellectual foundations. It is important and exciting and—"

"Exactly what you ought to be studying," Linus said. "Clearly, it captures your interest more than anything else."

Again, Charlie's enthusiasm waned. "But what would I do after my time at Cambridge? There are no pursuits in the field of mathematics beyond the academic."

Linus pushed his own bowl aside, knowing his young friend needed his full attention.

"Why do you dismiss the possibility of an academic career so wholly?"

Charlie shook his head, his gaze downcast. "Were I to become a don, I could not marry or have a family of my own. It would not be a matter of not being able to afford it, which is hindrance enough. A don is not permitted to marry."

"I know," Linus said. "My father was a don before he met my mother. He gave that up because he fell in love with her."

"She married him still? Even knowing he would have no income?"

"She loved him as well," Linus explained. "They both knew they would not live a lavish life, but they trusted their ability to make do. He had a bit of income from his father's estate, and his grandfather gave him this unentailed property."

Charlie appeared to be pondering that but not in a way that brought him reassurance. "I have some income from the Lampton estate but no property I might live on and no prospect of one suddenly materializing."

That was unfortunate for many reasons.

"Could you be happy in rented rooms or a small house near university? You could continue your study of mathematics. You could fully embrace the academics you enjoy. You would likely be given ample opportunity for presenting lectures and papers and such."

A little smile lit his face. "I would like that part of it."

"Perhaps it is not your long-term answer," Linus said, "but it does give you a target, one no one else in your vast family has claimed."

"That borders on the miraculous."

Linus could only imagine the struggle that constituted. His difficulty was quite the opposite. He had been given a target he had never intended to shoot for, one he was trying to find a way of appreciating.

"When you return to Cambridge, let that be your focus. Prepare yourself for the possibility of choosing a career down that path. You might change your mind. But I think you will be less miserable if you have a goal."

"I think you are probably right."

Linus tugged at his cuffs in a show of self-importance. "I usually am."

Charlie laughed once more. Linus had quickly come to appreciate that. This house had, even in the Lancaster family's leanest years, been a happy one. They'd found reason to laugh through their poverty, through their want. And when he and Evander had gone to sea, Linus had taken it upon himself to make certain his brother continued to be joyful when life aboard ship grew painful and difficult and, at times, soul crushing.

"Your father still pursued his academics even after leaving Cambridge and his donship, did he not?" Charlie asked, returning to his meal once more.

"He did. He published papers and returned to the university on several occasions to present them." At least while his mind had been whole. "He had a room here that he devoted to his studies. I imagine it resembled very closely the work spaces of the dons he'd left behind."

"He had the best of both worlds, then." Charlie seemed encouraged by the possibility.

Not wanting to lose that precious thread of hope, Linus rose. "I'll show it to you," he said. "It's not been changed or touched in many years."

"You do not mind?" Charlie asked. "I imagine it is important to you, having belonged to your father."

"I know how much you will appreciate it. And as you are here to be my brute-labor force, I suppose I can offer you a moment's happiness before sending you to work again."

Charlie laughed and rose as well. "You are a very magnanimous task master."

"Indeed."

They climbed the stairs. Father's study had been placed on the same floor as the family bedchambers. Persephone had once said Father chose the unusual arrangement because he had not wanted the conflicting pull of his family and his work to create a rift. If only he had recovered from his grief before senility had begun taking him away from them. The rift he'd tried so hard to prevent had torn open despite his efforts.

Reaching the study required passing his and Evander's bedchamber. Linus kept his gaze forward, not so much as glancing at the door. Though he was finding some degree of contentment and even pleasure in his role as master of the estate, he pushed thoughts of Evander from his mind, focusing instead on the study at the end of the corridor. Upon reaching it, he took hold of the handle and looked back at Charlie.

"Prepare yourself. This is very impressive." He rolled his eyes a little, knowing full well that to the casual observer, the space beyond looked like nothing but chaos.

"I will do my best to endure the splendor."

Linus pushed the door open. He had not adequately prepared himself for the rush of emotions that slid over him. Father had been gone for two years, longer if one considered how long ago his mind had rendered them strangers. Yet the pain was so fresh and new.

He hung back by the door as Charlie stepped inside, apparently mesmerized.

"He had so many books."

That was most certainly true. "He read them often. Studied them. Pored over them." Father was forever reading and digging for more ideas and insights.

"He specialized in myths, if I remember."

"Greek, in particular."

Charlie peered at the shelves, reading the spines, running his fingers along them. "What aspects of them did he focus on?"

"He attempted to reconcile the many different versions of the myths. And he was never more excited about his work than when he discovered a new insight, a way of viewing and interpreting them that no one else had thought of or seen." Linus had always found his father's interpretations fascinating, though he'd not always agreed with them. "It was the pursuit of new ideas that drove him."

Charlie nodded emphatically. "Mathematics is like that as well. There are so many possibilities, so many things to be discovered if only people would work at it and pursue it with passion."

Passion. That was the best word Linus could think of to describe his father's approach to his studies. It drove him and pushed him. In the end, though, it had consumed him.

"One must also find a balance," Linus warned. "To lose oneself in the theoretical and miss what is real is a tragedy indeed."

Charlie did not comment. Linus didn't know if he'd even heard. The young man was studying the space, perhaps imagining a similar one of his own but filled with numbers instead of Greek names, books on mathematics instead of mythology.

Father would have appreciated meeting another person pursuing an academic field of endeavor. When Evander had told Father that he and Linus were bound for the navy, that was the regret he expressed most vehemently: that they would be denied the opportunity to pursue knowledge. He felt certain his father had also mourned the loss of their company and had worried over their safety, but he hadn't expressed it in the same way.

For Evander, loss of *education* had not proven the ultimate tragedy.

For Linus, it was still a part of what he mourned about going away. He shared his father's love of the myths and the myriad things they taught about human nature and experiences. He would have liked to have studied it further, to have searched for his own interpretations and meanings.

He stepped farther inside and ran a hand along the top of the desk chair. The room had no permanent occupant now. Perhaps when Charlie left to continue his education, Linus might devote himself to pursuing his own.

Chapter Twenty-Three

ARABELLA TOOK TWO DAILY WALKS now: one long one traversing the neighborhood to clear her thoughts and one with Mater around the walled lawn surrounding the dower house. She was not overly familiar with this part of the estate. Her childhood romps with the Jonquil brothers had not included the area surrounding the dower house.

"It is very quiet here," Arabella observed.

"It's ghastly."

Arabella turned shocked eyes on Mater and received something of a smile in return.

"I confess I'm being a touch dramatic," Mater said. "I simply feel a little too much like an old workhorse sent to the back acres to live out its life in peace because no one has any use for it any longer."

Arabella nodded sagely. "That would explain the delivery of oats we received this morning."

Mater laughed lightly. "My husband often said that if you were free of your aunt and uncle's home, your personality would blossom. I am discovering that he was correct in that."

Arabella had often thought of the earl when they were apart, but she had not, until that moment, known if he had ever thought or spoken of her when she was not nearby. To know that he had, at least in a small measure, brought tremendous comfort.

"Mr. Lancaster told me he was surprised I didn't think you were talkative," Mater said as they turned a corner near the back wall.

"He told me he was surprised people didn't generally think I was funny."

Mater eyed her a moment. "You were different in his company. I don't know if you realized that. You were more sure of yourself, more at ease. You seemed happier."

"I was." Arabella plucked a leaf from a shrub as she passed. "But it amounted to nothing in the end."

Mater's expression was utterly empathetic. "Things do not always turn out the way we expect them to."

"Says the old, abandoned workhorse."

Mater slipped her arm through Arabella's. "Do not worry for me. I have plans."

"Do you?"

Mater nodded eagerly. "I am going to travel."

That was unexpected.

"I don't know where yet but someplace new and interesting. Of course, I would have to convince my companion to come with me, and we would have to keep it a secret from my sons, or else they'll worry themselves into a decline, and then where would we be?"

"I believe we would be someplace new and interesting."

Mater squeezed her arm. "Oh, I do like you, Arabella."

Just as she was beginning to think everything was wonderfully right in the world, her aunt appeared on the garden path and ruined the illusion.

"We appear to have a visitor." Arabella sighed.

"We can be gracious," Mater said. "For a while, anyway."

That was one advantage to being Mater's companion: the Dowager Countess of Lampton had no difficulty ridding herself of visitors who overstayed their welcome.

Curtsies and words of greeting were exchanged, then Aunt Hampton joined them on their stroll about the lawn.

"Has Arabella imposed her walking habit upon you?" Aunt Hampton asked. "Such an odd occupation."

"Is it?" Mater posed the question innocently enough, yet Arabella sensed something more strategic in the question. "I'll make certain to inform the Almack's patronesses, as they will likely wish to never walk again."

Though Arabella recognized the subtle jab for what it was, Aunt Hampton didn't seem to. "The patronesses? You speak with them often?" her aunt asked.

"Often enough," Mater said.

"Perhaps you might introduce me when we are in Town for the Season." Her aunt eyed Mater hopefully. "We are neighbors, and my niece is a member of your household. That was our arrangement, after all."

"I understand you left early the night you joined us for the house party." Mater's conversational tone didn't slip, but her posture had grown more rigid. "My son, in fact, spoke to me of it at length."

Arabella hadn't realized her misery had been discussed. She shouldn't have been surprised. Plenty of other people had been spreading word of her. Those "discussions" had sent Linus running for the hills. If only they'd had the same impact on Aunt Hampton.

"Our departure that evening stemmed from a mere misunderstanding, I assure you." Aunt Hampton was almost desperately insistent.

Mater held her chin at an authoritative angle. "I am not certain I can introduce to the patronesses someone with whom I have that kind of 'misunderstanding.'"

Aunt Hampton urged Mater aside. "We were simply concerned. Arabella had been ill. We were hearing rumors that a duchess's brother was showing her attention. We simply wanted to know that she was well and that she wasn't being taken advantage of. A gentleman of Mr. Lancaster's standing is less likely to have honorable interest in a mere lady's companion than he would in one of your more exalted guests."

"That 'mere lady's companion' will have vouchers to Almack's next Season." Mater appeared genuinely offended on Arabella's behalf. It was little wonder Arabella felt so safe amongst this family. "Furthermore, I certainly hope I would not be one to extend an invitation to a gentleman who would behave in such a caddish manner as you are implying."

"Forgive me." Panic edged Aunt Hampton's words. "Our concern that evening temporarily overcame our reason."

The desperation in the apology was not difficult to interpret: her aunt and uncle were depending upon Arabella's position in the Lampton Park household to further their own standing. Any threat to their connection to her was reason, in their minds, for great concern.

"In the end, we were right to be concerned." Her aunt, not one to be cowed long, pressed onward. "The young lieutenant left without a backward glance."

That was a truth Arabella couldn't deny.

Mater managed it though. "On the contrary. Mr. Lancaster's uneventful departure is evidence you made a spectacle for no reason." She urged Arabella on toward the dower house. "I will bid you farewell, Mrs. Hampton. I wish to lie down."

They moved with determined step, leaving Aunt Hampton little choice but to accept her dismissal.

"I may have to instruct the housekeeper to always tell your aunt that we are not at home to visitors; otherwise, all the powders Dr. Scorseby can procure will likely not be enough to prevent that woman from giving me indigestion."

"I don't know about the wisdom of that," Arabella said drily. "If she does not come by, how will I know if I am pinning my hopes on a gentleman who isn't likely to come up to scratch?"

It was more than Arabella had intended to confess, she having thus far not admitted that she'd actually had hopes of a future with Linus Lancaster. Mater didn't press the matter.

"We will simply have to travel somewhere where your aunt won't find us," Mater said, her tone light and laughing.

Arabella latched on to the humor, grateful for it. "And somewhere without gentlemen," she added.

Mater tossed her a mischievous look. "Where would be the fun in that?"

There was no doubt in Arabella's mind: life with Mater, though perhaps not the one she had always dreamed of, was going to be an absolute joy.

Chapter Twenty-Four

"Do the Nappers know I'm only nineteen?" Though Charlie's confidence had grown over the past fortnight, he still had many moments when his self-doubts resurfaced, always in regard to his being too young for something or simply unwanted.

Was this a common struggle for younger siblings? Linus didn't think Artemis had this particular worry.

"I would imagine they do," Linus said. "Yours is a well-known family. Your name and age and quite possibly your favorite color are likely public knowledge."

"My favorite color?" Charlie laughed a little. "How is it they know something I don't?"

"I will let you in on a secret." Linus leaned forward, closing the gap between them in the carriage. "The matrons' gossip circle possesses the second sight."

"Do they?"

Linus nodded solemnly. "They can see your future, provided that future involves one of their daughters."

"Or nieces?" Charlie asked a little too innocently.

Charlie hadn't been present when the Hamptons had pressed the idea of a match between himself and Arabella. Still, he'd apparently heard about it.

"I didn't imagine the rumors, it would seem."

"Unless I was imagining them too," Charlie said. "And Arabella as well."

"She started doing a lot more walking." That told a story unto itself.

"She was escaping the whispers."

"Either that or she found a treasure map and was seeking out her fortune."

Charlie shot him a look of commiseration. "And you won't see a single gold coin from the hull of any galleon we discover. Pity."

"Sunken treasure, you say? Lud, I should have encouraged the rumors."

"You should have *started* them."

Linus couldn't help laughing, something he did often in Charlie's company. The young gentleman had lightened considerably these past two weeks. His personality had emerged more. Though Linus knew better than to say as much out loud, the lad reminded him of Lord Lampton: quick with a smile, always up for a lark, and endlessly entertaining.

The carriage slowed. A moment later, both he and Charlie emerged in good spirits.

Their host and hostess welcomed them warmly. The Misses Napper, of whom there were three, seemed even more delighted than their parents. The vicar had been invited as well, no doubt to even up the numbers. He, however, was not a young man by any means. None of the sisters appeared terribly interested in their oldest guest. Charlie would quickly realize that being a little young was preferable in these situations.

They were soon situated at the dining table, Charlie on one side, sandwiched between the second and third daughters of the household. Though he at first seemed at a loss to know what he was meant to do, he quickly found his footing. He conversed easily, flirting harmlessly. He would be a favorite in Society in another few years.

Arabella would have been pleased to see Charlie doing so well. She spoke of all the Jonquils with such tenderness. Their happiness mattered to her, no doubt because their father had shown her kindness.

Arabella. How often his thoughts returned to her. Had Lampton adequately shielded her from her aunt and uncle? Was she finding her place in the dowager's household? Was she happy? Did she miss him? If Dr. Scorseby were even half as attentive as he'd been during the house party, Arabella had likely not even noticed Linus's absence.

He reminded himself of that firmly before focusing once more on the current evening's engagement. His companion was the oldest of the Napper sisters. She spoke very little, and he was not entirely certain why. She did not seem overly bashful, but neither did she give the impression of feeling herself above her company.

"Your family was kind to invite us this evening," he said.

"We have been anxious to make yours and Mr. Jonquil's better acquaintance." Miss Napper then returned all her attention to her plate.

This was different from Daphne's bashfulness. Even when she was at her most timid, she made a concerted effort to try to converse and interact. How ought he to respond? He didn't wish to make the lady uncomfortable, yet neither did he want to leave her feeling neglected. Around him, the others' conversations swirled unhindered.

Mr. Napper spoke, pulling Linus's attention to him. "I understand you and young Mr. Jonquil here have been quite busy laboring about your estate." His feelings about that laboring were not apparent in his tone.

Still, Linus was not ashamed of the work they were doing. Indeed, it brought him his first glimmer of excitement about the life he had returned to England to live. "I am a naval man, accustomed to the arduous labor necessary for survival at sea. Were I forced to adopt a life of unending leisure, I am certain I would run mad."

While Mr. Napper did not appear to truly agree, his nod indicated that he at least understood.

Not wishing Charlie to be questioned for his assistance, Linus continued. "Mr. Jonquil has been a tremendous help, enduring my odd propensity for working at the tasks most gentlemen consider beneath them. Perhaps I will convince him to seek a career in the navy as well."

The suggestion sent the younger Misses Napper into a running dialogue, at once insisting that Charlie would be the very best of sailors, dashing in his uniform, and, at the same time, in such danger at sea that they could not countenance the idea. Linus could not have planned this evening better if he had tried.

The physical work had helped give Charlie a sense of purpose. Their growing friendship and camaraderie had given him a feeling of belonging and importance. But few things did as much good for a young man's too-often fragile sense of worth than the notice of a young lady. Being the last in a large family of brothers who were not exactly hideous had likely meant he'd been many times overlooked.

"If the two of you are not opposed to arduous tasks," the vicar said, "there is a patch of loose slate on my roof. You would save me the trouble of climbing up there myself."

Though the vicar obviously spoke in jest, Charlie, without hesitation, said, "I can be there in the morning."

He met Linus's eye, confidence in his expression. Linus felt a surge of pride. Here was the person Charlie ought to have been all along: one who didn't question whether he could make a difference or wonder if he was needed. Now if only Linus could find an equal measure of that for himself.

Chapter Twenty-Five

ARABELLA AND MATER WERE ELBOW deep in plans to improve the dower house's back garden. They walked its environs every day and had quickly discovered an unfortunate lack of shade trees and fragrant flowers. Philip had happily granted his mother full reign over her new dominion.

Mrs. Hill, the housekeeper, maid, and general servant at the dower house hurried into the sitting room and announced, "Dr. Scorseby to visit the both of you."

"The both of us?" Mater asked with a laugh.

Heat warmed Arabella's face. She knew perfectly well the local physician came to visit *her*, Mater having been faithfully following his advice of a few weeks earlier and, as a result, not at all in need of his attention.

Arabella had no real experience with suitors and could not say with any certainty quite how she felt toward him. She enjoyed his company and, generally speaking, looked forward to their conversations. But she experienced none of the contentment and ease she'd known with Linus. She also felt no flutterings inside or surges of anticipation at seeing him again.

She didn't miss the doctor between his visits, but she'd missed Linus every day since he'd left for Shropshire. Her attachment to him was hopeless and one-sided, but it was real just the same.

Arabella firmly told herself to keep her mind on the present rather than losing herself in the past.

Dr. Scorseby offered a very proper bow upon arriving. Mater invited him to sit.

"How kind of you to visit us," Mater said. "What brings you around?" Mischief filled her eyes and tone.

Dr. Scorseby answered seriously. "I came to the Park to look in on Lady Lampton."

"How is she?" Mater's expression transformed to one of concern.

"All appears to be well," Dr. Scorseby said. "She is in good spirits, which is always beneficial." He turned to Arabella. "I had a very pleasant visit with your aunt and uncle yesterday. They seem quite pleased about your situation here."

She knew she was meant to say something in response. They were her family, after all. Yet she knew precisely why they were happy about her position. Theirs was not happiness *for her* at all but rather for themselves.

He nodded. "I found them to be in generally good health."

"And I find myself generally pleased," she said drily.

Only when Mater choked on a held-back laugh did Arabella realize how impolite her remark had been. Thoughts of her relatives' selfishness had pricked at her, and she had allowed the resultant annoyance to loosen her tongue inadvisably.

"Forgive me," she said. "I'm not certain what has come over me."

His features assumed the expression she had come to think of as his physician's face. "Are you feeling feverish? Faint? How have you been sleeping?"

Ever the man of medicine. Still, his questions offered her a way out of the increasingly embarrassing situation.

"I have not slept as well as I would have liked the past week or so. I have a lingering cough." It was true, no matter that she didn't believe exhaustion was the reason for her momentary lack of manners.

"Coughs can be very persistent." Dr. Scorseby said.

A knock at the front door reverberated throughout the dower house.

"Good heavens," Mater said. "Whoever that is knocking sounds likely to pound the door down." She rose and crossed to the window, eyeing the front door. "It is Bill from the stables."

They all turned to watch the sitting room door. A moment later, it opened, Mrs. Hill letting Bill in. His face was splotched with frantic color. His widened eyes searched, then found Mater. What had happened? The room held its collective breath.

"Ma'am," Bill said, a touch out of breath. "Word's come from Shropshire. Young Charlie's had an accident."

Chapter Twenty-Six

"He'll not sleep if he's in this much pain." The surgeon Linus had brought in to evaluate Charlie's condition did not sound overly encouraged. He had more experience than the local physician and was highly respected.

"What can we do to ease his suffering?" Linus hadn't heard yet from Daphne. He'd sent a missive, but messages took time to travel across counties. She would know an efficacious tisane or tea, but he might not receive word from her for days yet.

"I'll write up instructions for the apothecary," the surgeon said. "We've a few things that'll help."

That was a relief. Charlie was by now as much family to him as his own siblings; he hated seeing him in such pain.

Before he could ask the surgeon for more details, the sounds of carriage wheels on the pebbled lane out front caught his attention. That could not possibly be the dowager. There hadn't been time enough for her to have made the journey. Indeed, his letter explaining the situation would likely only just have arrived at Lampton Park.

He crossed to the window. The master's bedchamber where Charlie had been placed afforded a view of the drive below. He knew the fine traveling coach and Kielder heraldry on the instant. His family, it seemed, had chosen to return to Falstone Castle by way of Shropshire.

An unexpected surge of bone-deep relief swelled inside. Persephone would know what to do.

He offered a quick excuse to the surgeon, glanced at Charlie sleeping fretfully, then rushed from the room, along the corridor, and to the main staircase. His family's voices floated up to him, pulling him down toward them.

They had all stepped inside, filling the small entryway. Servants scrambled to gather trunks and divest the travelers of their coats and hats. Oliver sat in his mother's arms, clearly a bit unsure of this latest excursion.

Linus met his older sister's eye. The smile of excitement that lit her face turned immediately to concern. "What's happened? You look distressed."

Adam's gaze was on him now as well, and Artemis's.

"There's been an accident. Charlie was injured."

"Badly?" Persephone asked.

Linus nodded. "He's broken both his legs and an arm. Cracked several ribs."

"Good heavens."

"I've sent word to his mother, obviously. The physician has been here. A surgeon is here now."

Persephone nodded her approval. "Did you write to Daphne?"

"Of course." The tension that had grown since Charlie's fall increased tenfold as he stood there.

Persephone handed Oliver to Adam, then moved with purpose to where Linus stood. She took Linus's hand and pulled him back around the corner and to the stairs. "How perilous is his situation?"

"The physician and surgeon both believe his injuries will heal given enough time." That had been a relief yet not a true comfort. The panic Linus had felt at the sight of Charlie unresponsive on the ground had not subsided despite the passage of more than twenty-four hours.

"You mentioned leg, arm, and rib injuries. Does his mind seem intact?" Persephone had always been one for maintaining her calm in a crisis. Linus usually was as well, but his composure had fled.

"Charlie's in a great deal of pain, which makes him less conversant than he would likely be otherwise, but he has been able to speak, and what he has said is sensible."

They'd reached the top of the stairs. "Where has he been placed?"

"Father's roo—My room."

She slipped her arm free of his and faced him directly. "I will see to his care for the next while. You need a respite."

Linus shook his head. "I have a responsibility."

"Yes, you do. You are charged with running this estate, looking after all your guests—including those who only just arrived—and making certain you do not render yourself so exhausted that you cannot see to any of those tasks." She patted his cheek the way she'd done when he was a small boy. "Let me be your big sister again, Linus, and look after you for a change."

Relief warred with guilt at the escape, however temporary, she offered. "I spent far too much of my life when we were young letting you carry my burdens. I'm a grown man now; I cannot continue doing that."

She arched a single eyebrow. "I am a duchess now; I can do whatever I want."

He could actually smile at that, something he didn't think he'd done even once the last day and a half. "You sound like Adam."

"Good." She nodded crisply and turned toward the corridor. "Go see to it the others are settled. I will look after Charlie."

He remained in the corridor for a long moment after she'd disappeared inside the sickroom. Seeing Charlie so badly injured, so bent and broken, had shaken Linus deeply.

He rubbed at his weary face, trying to regain his lieutenant's demeanor. There was a great deal to be done: settling the rest of the family, sending the surgeon's instructions to the apothecary, bracing himself to face the dowager when she inevitably arrived.

Adam appeared in the corridor, Oliver in his arms, Artemis in his wake. Linus assumed a neutral expression, one he'd been taught to manufacture as he'd sailed toward battle.

His brother-in-law's mouth pulled in a stern slash across his face. "What happened to Mr. Jonquil?" Adam was nothing if not direct.

"He fell off a roof."

"He fell off a roof?" Artemis responded before Adam could. To her credit, she sounded sincerely concerned despite her unfriendly association with Charlie. "Will he recover?"

"The medical men I have consulted expect him to."

"Thank the heavens."

The opportunity to tease his sister proved too much to pass up. He needed a moment of levity. "*Thank* the heavens? I assumed you had been praying to them for something like this."

She angled her chin at him. "I would never wish harm on a person, no matter how aggravating and contrary he might be."

Linus looked at Adam. "That must be a relief to you, in particular."

"I'm not afraid of her."

Artemis shook her head in obvious annoyance. "The men in this family are impossible."

Adam set Oliver on his feet. "Go with your aunt. She'll take you to the nursery."

"I'm not afraid of her either, Papa," the little boy said.

"Thank you very much, Adam." Artemis held her hand out to Oliver even as she turned her back on the two of them.

"You're in her black books now," Linus said.

"Right next to you."

"And Charlie," Linus added.

"And half the population." Adam pushed out a breath that sounded a great deal like a growl. "She is going to be the death of me; I'm certain of it."

"Better you than me," Linus said.

"You look after the boy who fell off the roof," Adam said. "I'll look after the girl who likely would have pushed him if she'd been here."

Linus's amusement dissipated quickly. "I don't know that I've ever told you how grateful I am for everything you've done for my family. You've taken on responsibilities that ought not to have fallen to you. I'm their brother. I should have done more."

"For one thing," Adam said, "you were a child. For another, I didn't do any of it for you."

Linus knew his brother-in-law too well to be offended by the frank and gruff explanation. "I think you rather like Persephone."

"There is not anything in this world I wouldn't do for her. I endured Athena's miserable Season, Daphne's departure, and Artemis's drama because they are her family, and their happiness is crucial to hers."

"Is mine?" He'd intended the question to be a jest, but somehow the two words emerged with a ring of desperation to them.

"Why do you think I dragged you to that house party?" Adam didn't manage to keep the annoyance out of his voice. "I can endure Lampton, and Harry was distraction enough when necessary. But Persephone was worried about you being alone and unhappy." Adam shrugged. "I made certain you came along so she could see for herself that you were well."

"And you diverted your return to the Castle all this way so she could see her family home."

Adam didn't smile often, but he did in that moment, a soft, tender smile, one that somehow managed to soften the deforming impact of the web of scars on his face. "There is no undertaking so miserable that it isn't made endurable by having her with me. She makes my life worth living."

No undertaking so miserable. Linus was undertaking a few miserable things himself, things he wasn't certain he could endure. "I suspect I ought to find a Persephone of my own—one I'm not related to, of course."

Adam's gaze darted around the corridor. "I don't intend to stand about here while you make that search. Simply tell me where my wife is."

Linus motioned to the nearest bedchamber. He received a quick nod before Adam slipped inside.

Persephone eased Adam's burdens. He did the same for her. To have that kind of support and strength . . . Linus couldn't imagine Mrs. Blackbourne or Lady Belinda crossing the kingdom for him or enduring the company of a difficult family member for his sake. Miss Napper hadn't seemed willing to countenance the inconvenience of a conversation. If he were being entirely honest, he would not have happily upended his life for any of them either.

Unbidden into his thoughts came Arabella, as had happened often over the past fortnight. She had rescued Oliver, visited the children when they were ill, talked with him at length about his worries and difficulties. He'd gladly spent hours each day visiting her when she'd felt unwell, had listened to her struggles, and had wished he could do more to help. In the midst of it all, they had laughed and smiled. There'd been such joy between them.

Even with counties separating them, he thought about her, wondered how she was, wished she were nearby. She tugged at his heart in ways no one else had.

And by now, she knew that Charlie, whom she cared about, who belonged to a family that considered her one of their own, had nearly died while in Linus's care. Would she hold that against him? Blame him?

Would she forgive him when he was struggling to forgive himself?

Chapter Twenty-Seven

THE LAMPTON CARRIAGE PULLED UP to the house thirty-six hours after the Kielder carriage. Linus was watching over Charlie. Adam peeked inside the bedchamber.

"I'll sit with the boy," he said. "You had best go greet his mother. She deserves to hear what happened, and she deserves to hear it from you."

Adam wasn't wrong. Linus didn't shirk responsibilities, no matter how unpleasant, and he certainly didn't mean to start now. He rose, offered a nod of thanks, and made his way downstairs.

The dowager stepped inside just as Linus arrived in the entryway. Her heavy, worried gaze settled on him, not wavering in the least. "How is Charlie? I will have the truth, with no softening."

Linus took her hands in his. "He is in a great deal of pain. His wits are fully intact, even if the same cannot be said for all of his bones."

The dowager, though clearly concerned, showed no signs of faintness. "Your letter mentioned his legs in particular."

He nodded. "Both broken, as well as his left arm."

"Oh, my poor boy."

"His head, neck, and back were all spared," Linus quickly added. "Considering the height from which he fell, that is nothing short of a miracle."

"He will recover?" she pressed.

"Yes. My sister was impressed with how well he is doing already."

"Your sister?"

"The duchess," he explained. "They came here on their way home from your house party."

Some of the dowager's tension eased. "You haven't been left to look after him on your own, then."

"Another miracle."

"Let us go have a look at my boy," the dowager said.

Linus offered her his arm and walked with her to the stairs.

He did not have many memories of his mother, but in that moment, one flooded his mind. He could see so clearly his father and mother walking up those same steps, Persephone and Athena flanking them, Evander lingering a bit behind.

He missed his brother.

Persephone appeared on the landing above. "Lady Lampton," she greeted gently. "Your son will be so pleased you are here."

"He is sensible enough to realize who is present?" Worry laced the question.

"Quite." Persephone held out her hand. "I'll walk with you. Linus can see to your trunks and such."

The dowager accepted the change of plans without comment. Indeed, Persephone's presence seemed to bring her some measure of comfort. Persephone had that gift. Linus was ever more grateful for it and for her.

He returned to the entryway, determined to be helpful. The butler was directing a footman carrying a small traveling trunk. The housekeeper, ever dutiful, directed its placement.

She saw Linus and addressed him. "Where ought we to place the dowager? All the furnished bedchambers are occupied."

"She can use the room I moved to." It was not an entirely accurate statement. With Charlie in the master's bedchamber, Linus had been reassigned to the room he'd once shared with Evander. He hadn't made the switch though. He couldn't bear it. Instead, he'd slept in the armchair in the study, not telling anyone.

"We still don't have enough beds," Mrs. Tuttle said.

"I'll make do," he reassured her. "I did so enough at sea."

"Begging your pardon, sir. It wasn't *your* accommodations I was concerned over."

Linus quickly counted. Even with the addition of the dowager and one bedchamber lacking sufficient furniture, with Linus taking up residency in the study, they had enough room. "I believe we have—"

But someone stepped inside, someone who stopped his words. His thoughts. Very nearly his heart.

Arabella.

She stood in the spill of sunlight from the open door. The air around her danced with bits of dust rendered golden by the light. She slipped her bonnet from her head.

Her gaze fell on him in the very next instant, and she smiled, not in the practiced way Mrs. Blackbourne had, the indulgent way his sisters did, or the obligatory way the Misses Napper had. Hers was genuine, pleased, and, at least it seemed to him, personal. Seeing him *in particular* had brought her pleasure. He hoped so. Seeing her *in particular* had brought him a rush of unexpected emotion. Relief. Anticipation. Hopefulness.

"Welcome." Only after the word had slipped from his lips did he realize how inane he sounded. She had not come on a visit. This was a worry-filled time and warranted greater focus. "I can show you to Charlie's room. The dowager is there already."

She paused a moment in thought. Her hair glowed under the sun's amber influence. She stood alone, unsupported and unattended, yet she did not look defeated. Was she, too, beginning to find her place in this world? Had life been treating her better?

Mrs. Tuttle interjected apologetically. "Where should I put the dowager's companion? She's the one I hadn't found a place for."

Embarrassment flushed Arabella's cheeks. Her gaze dropped.

"Pose the question to Her Grace," Linus told Mrs. Tuttle. "Make certain she knows that Miss Hampton's accommodations are a priority."

Mrs. Tuttle curtsied. "Of course, Mr. Lancaster." She hurried away.

"Would you like to look in on Charlie?" he offered again. "Or would you prefer to rest from your journey?"

She didn't answer but met his gaze once more. Those blue eyes focused on him in that way that set his heart to hammering.

"How is Charlie?" she asked. "And do not think to spare my sensibilities. I am made of sterner stuff than that."

"The dowager said almost exactly the same thing."

"She has clearly had a good influence on me," Arabella said. "Before long, I will be dressing in all black and expressly forbidding unpleasant visitors from calling on me."

That was intriguing. "Who has she forbidden from calling?"

"My aunt," she said, "which has been quite a relief. She was making my life rather miserable."

He stepped closer, simultaneously fighting and mentally indulging the urge to take her hand. She, however, stepped a bit away, maintaining the distance between them.

"Your missive mentioned only a fall and broken legs, with no more detail than that." Nothing in her voice indicated she was as upended by their reunion as he was.

He kept his own voice even, hiding the effect she had on him. "I scribbled that note out in haste. I felt speed in that moment was more crucial than details."

She nodded. "Your methodology sounds to me like a naval one."

Her light tone kept his own thoughts from delving too deep. "How odd that I would behave like a navy man."

He motioned her toward the stairs. She, no doubt, would wish to look in on Charlie.

"How was he injured?" she asked.

"We were helping mend the roof of the vicarage, and he slipped."

Linus could still see that horrifying moment in his mind. Charlie had been on the other side of the roof's point. He'd turned. His face had registered a moment's panic, then he'd slipped downward and out of sight.

She glanced at him as they took the first of the stairs. "You were both on the roof of the vicarage?"

Linus rolled his shoulders against the tension there. "We've done a lot of manual work these past weeks. It is good for the body and mind. He's been lost, a little purposeless. The effort had been helping. Helping quite a lot, in fact."

Helping. The young man was lying in a bed, in pain and misery. How was that helping him?

"But he is expected to recover?" Arabella asked.

Linus nodded. "I've consulted a physician and surgeon, who both feel he will, in time, be quite whole. And this morning, I received very detailed instructions on tonics and tisanes from my sister Daphne, which will help tremendously, I'm sure."

"You further thought to send for his mother. It sounds to me as though you've done all you can for him."

"That might be comforting if I weren't responsible for his current condition." Guilt had hung heavy around his neck the past two days. He'd not felt able to speak about it with anyone else.

"You pushed him off the roof, did you?"

The unexpected comment caught him up short. He paused with one foot on the landing and one on the uppermost stair. A gentle amusement sat lightly upon her features. She was offering a way of relinquishing some of the heaviness he felt. For the moment, at least, he meant to accept the escape. "I am kin to the Duke of Kielder," he said. "Throwing people off roofs is a favorite pastime of ours. In fact, the family crest is nothing but an empty housetop."

"How regal."

He laughed for the first time since Charlie's accident. He'd almost forgotten how good Arabella Hampton was for his soul. He'd been drowning in the months leading up to the house party. During the gathering, he'd enjoyed a reprieve from that loneliness and lack of direction. Though he'd found purpose in his home and joy in Charlie's company, losing Arabella's companionship had taken more of a toll than he'd yet admitted.

"I should go make certain the dowager's bedchamber is prepared for when she is ready to rest." Arabella offered an apologetic smile. "I have very specific instructions from Lord Lampton to see that she does not overtax herself."

"Her sons are very careful of her, aren't they?" If his mother were yet alive, he would be every bit as protective.

"They have a great deal of their father in them," she said. "He treated people with such kindness."

"The Jonquil approach?"

Her expression softened further. "*His* approach. But one his sons inherited."

"I wish I could have known him," Linus said.

"So do I." After a moment, she shook off her abstraction. "If you could point me in the direction of the bedchamber assigned to the dowager, I would be most grateful."

He indicated his and Evander's childhood quarters.

He remained behind as she left, thinking on what she'd said. Kindness was important to her, no doubt owing in large part to her own family's unkindness. A caring heart. Loyalty. Compassion.

He valued those things as well. And he saw them in her.

Did she see them in him?

Chapter Twenty-Eight

"You have strict orders from Mater to drink all of this." Arabella carefully placed the cup of pungent liquid on the table beside Charlie's bed. "I have permission to plug your nose and pour it down your throat, if necessary."

He smiled weakly. "That won't be necessary. I will take my medicine like a big boy."

Arabella sat in the nearby chair. Mater was getting a bit of much-needed rest.

Charlie grimaced as he obediently drank the concoction. "What is this meant to do?" He eyed what remained in the cup.

"According to Mr. Lancaster's sister, it will help alleviate some of your pain."

"His sister?" Charlie very nearly rolled his eyes, she was certain of it. "Are you sure it isn't poison? She doesn't like me very much."

"I got the impression that the feeling is mutual."

One sip at a time, Charlie finished the last of his cup, then made a noise of displeasure. "That definitely tastes like something Miss Artemis would concoct."

"I beg your pardon." Artemis stood in the doorway, fists on her hips.

"I drank the foul liquid," Charlie said. "You don't have to yell at me as well."

"I had nothing to do with the tisane." Artemis stepped inside. "And I am not yelling at you."

"Bothering me, then."

She glared at him. Arabella likely should have intervened, but seeing so much life in Charlie was reassuring.

Artemis shook her head. "I told Adam we shouldn't have come here. You are always so sour."

"I'm allowed to be sour," Charlie said. "I'm dying."

Artemis folded her arms across her chest. "I interrogated that surgeon for thirty minutes yesterday, and I know perfectly well that you are not dying."

"I am sorry to disappoint you."

Artemis threw her hands in the air. "Why is it everyone thinks I would be happy to hear you had one foot in the grave? I am not a terrible person, Charles Jonquil."

"I am too tired to argue with you." Charlie lowered himself from his seated position to lie back on the pillows. For a person with as many broken bones as he had, he'd grown quite adept at moving about within the confines of his bed. He sighed, the sound full of weariness and pain. "Arabella?"

"Yes, Charlie?"

"If Miss Artemis's concoction proves fatal, ask my brothers to avenge me."

"And what am I to tell Mr. Lancaster?"

Charlie's eyelids had grown heavy and his speech slower. "Tell him it couldn't be helped; his sister brought it on herself." He fell asleep before he could say more.

Artemis watched him, brow pulled, lips downturned. "I don't understand why he dislikes me so much." She turned to Arabella. The young lady looked genuinely hurt. "Do you know why?"

She shook her head no. "I don't."

Artemis brushed a loose curl away from her face. "Perhaps it has something to do with this room. It was my father's. He didn't like me either." Emotion broke her words, and the air of indifference she attempted to strike as she left did not ring true.

How well Arabella knew the pain of longing for a father's affection. Her father had died when she was tiny. Her uncle had offered no paternal kindness. The man she'd come to think of as a father, whom she'd loved deeply, hadn't truly belonged to her, nor she to him.

"Please don't make me go back to my uncle's house," she'd begged him when she was all of seven or eight years old. "Please let me stay with you."

"It is not as simple as that," he'd said. "Family lives with family."

Though she'd known the truth of his words, hearing from his own mouth that she wasn't family had shattered her, and the cracks hurt still.

She rubbed at her face, forcing away her heavy thoughts.

Only a moment passed before Linus stepped inside the room. Her heart had positively fluttered when she'd seen him in the entryway the day before, something she hadn't been at all expecting. Seeing him now, her heart raced again. Her affection for him had been quite real during the house party. The intervening two weeks had convinced her that she would do best to let go of those fledgling feelings.

Her heart apparently had not listened to her head.

"How is our patient?" Linus asked.

"Not enamored of your sister," she said. "I thought they were going to come to blows right here in the sickroom."

He smiled. Heavens, that smile. His twinkling green eyes. The one golden curl that was forever falling down across his forehead. The gentleman was handsome; there was no denying that. "Artemis does find him exasperating."

She glanced at the sleeping young man. "And he suspects she might be a murderer."

"He *what?*" Linus's laugh startled Charlie enough to wake him a little but not so much that he became at all sensible. Linus tiptoed to the chair in the corner and pulled it up beside hers. "I had intended to ask how the remainder of the house party went. Did my fearsome brother-in-law behave himself?"

"He did, more's the pity."

Linus grinned unrepentantly. "He is a great deal of fun when he is at his most irritable."

"I was a little afraid of him when he first arrived at Lampton Park," she admitted.

"And *I* was a little afraid of him when I first met him at his formidable fortress of a castle." But he smiled at the memory.

"How old were you?" she asked.

"I was thirteen."

"Thirteen? And you faced down the infamous Duke of Kielder?"

"I was a midshipman in the Royal Navy, and he had just married my sister." He spoke with utter firmness. "I intended to make absolutely certain he was good enough for her and that she was happy."

"If you had discovered he wasn't good enough and she wasn't happy, what would you have done then?"

"I would have made every attempt to beat the tar out of him," Linus said. "And I would likely have been thoroughly flattened, tossed in his gibbet, and left for dead."

Linus was wonderfully humorous. She loved that. "I, for one, am grateful that you did not meet your demise all those years ago."

He looked over at her, his expression more than a little flirtatious. "Is that so?"

His tone set her pulse to simmering. Afraid he would see her reaction, she moved quickly to a jest. "If you had died in that gibbet, you wouldn't have been here to push Charlie off a roof."

"I'm certain he is deeply grateful for that as well," Linus said drily.

She recognized the guilt still hovering in his words. It had been there the day before as well. "His injuries were not your fault."

He shook his head. "I'm not sure it matters."

"Would talking about it help?"

He leaned forward, his elbows on his knees. "In the moment before he fell, he looked terrified. That expression . . . I know it so well. It is eternally burned in my memory."

"Charlie is like a brother to me," she said. "I have been trying not to think on what happened to him. I can only imagine how awful it was for you, watching it happen."

"I don't mean the look on *Charlie's* face," he said. "My brother's. At Trafalgar, when he was—when he was shot. I was looking at him when it happened. The same horror crossed his face then that I saw in Charlie's on that roof: the realization that something terrible had just happened." Linus swallowed. "It was the look of someone who is realizing he's about to die."

Arabella had never heard him speak at length about his brother. It was a subject he never dwelled on, never discussed.

"I climbed off the roof and rushed to where Charlie lay. His face was twisted in agony. His limbs were bent in ways they should not have been." The recollection brought fresh pain to his voice and heaviness to his posture. "I was absolutely certain for a horrifying moment that he was dead."

Emotion clogged Arabella's throat. She reached for Linus's hand, as much for her own comfort as any she might offer him. He didn't flinch, didn't pull away. Without looking back at her, he threaded his fingers through hers.

Linus took an audible breath and pushed forward. "While the vicarage housekeeper ran for help, I held on to Charlie, just as I held Evander on the deck of the *Triumphant*." He clung more tightly to her hand. "Sitting there with Charlie, I could hear my thirteen-year-old self begging my brother not to die. I could see his face again, the life draining from it."

He didn't speak for a long, drawn-out moment. This was a difficult subject for him. She didn't know if he would change the topic as he so often did or press onward. Was she offering him any degree of comfort?

"He died," Linus said after a time.

"I am so sorry," she whispered.

"He died in my arms." The pain in his voice pierced her heart. "I lost him. Like everyone in my family, everyone I care about. I lose them all."

"You didn't lose Charlie," she reminded him.

"That is true." A little hope had reentered his tone.

"And your sisters are here," she added. "The duchess and the murderer."

He allowed the briefest of laughs. "Does Charlie truly believe she's a murderer?"

"I suspect he doesn't know what to think of her, or she of him."

He rubbed the back of her hand with his thumb. "The ladies who make a man wonder are often the ones most worth knowing."

She could scarcely think for the pounding in her head and the fluttering in her chest. "What kind of things does a lady worth knowing make a man wonder about?"

"Quite a lot." He didn't look at her, didn't turn at all in his chair, but neither did he release her hand. "He wishes to know what catches her eye when she's out in the world. Where she would choose to go if she could go anywhere." His thumb continued tracing its slow, gentle circles. Good heavens, she could hardly breathe. "He wonders what makes her happy." He looked at her once more. His emerald gaze held hers. "He wonders what she dreams about."

Her pounding pulse nearly drowned out his words. "Why?"

The question clearly surprised him, but she didn't wish it unasked. She understood so little of these things. Her past didn't give her confidence. She'd been wrong too many times.

"Why? Because he hopes, however silently, that he might have a place in those dreams."

Arabella's breath caught in her tense lungs. Each beat of her heart echoed in her head. Did he have any idea how often she'd let herself imagine that perhaps she was part of *his* dreams?

A voice interrupted the moment. The housekeeper stood in the doorway. "Miss Hampton," she said. "You have a visitor."

A visitor? "You must be mistaken."

Mrs. Tuttle shook her head. "Dr. Scorseby was quite specific."

"Dr. Scorseby has come?"

A nod.

Linus released her hand.

"The doctor wishes to see me?" Arabella asked.

"In particular," Mrs. Tuttle said.

Arabella looked at Linus.

He motioned toward the door. "Go ahead. I'll keep an eye on Charlie."

I'll keep an eye on Charlie? Was that all the more he meant to say in parting, especially after having spoken so tenderly and held her hand as he had? Surely she had not heard more in his words than he'd meant. Surely.

Did he have any idea how bewildering he was?

Chapter Twenty-Nine

Linus paced the length of the room. Scorseby had come to further his cause with Arabella; Linus was certain of it. He seemed a decent enough person, yet Linus didn't like the idea of his courting her. He didn't like it at all.

Persephone's voice floated in from the doorway. "From the look of things, I'd say you have been informed about your newest visitor."

Linus was in no mood to match her laughing tone. "Scorseby knows we have a local physician. I said as much in my letter to the dowager."

"I doubt he's come for professional reasons."

Linus doubted that as well, though he wasn't ready to admit it. "I should go greet him."

Persephone didn't bother hiding her grin.

"You're laughing at me," he assessed out loud.

She nodded slowly and with emphasis.

Linus shook his head. "I'm only going to greet the new arrival."

"And study your competition," Persephone added under her breath.

"Greet a guest." Linus's firm insistence inspired a laugh from his sister.

"Well, then, make certain you 'greet' the dowager as well. She too has offered Miss Hampton a future and is in as much of a position to be accepted as Dr. Scorseby is."

"Has his suit progressed as far as that?" Linus hadn't heard as much.

Much of Persephone's laughter dissipated. "Not as far as I have heard. I do, however, believe both Miss Hampton and the dowager countess are happy with *their* arrangement. The good doctor would have to offer enough happiness to pull his would-be bride away from a situation she is already perfectly content accepting. That is a significant obstacle when a lady has lived a life of uncertainty."

Linus had not thought of things from that angle. "A doctor would have income enough to provide a wife with stability."

Persephone shook her head. "Miss Hampton has stability, my dear. And before you lodge any further guesses, she also has kindness, respect, friendship, and purpose in a household. Any gentleman who harbors ambitions of pulling her from her current position must offer all of that and more."

Linus knew perfectly well what his sister meant, but he was not ready to discuss the state of his heart nor offer conjecture on the state of Miss Hampton's. "He must offer diamonds, no doubt."

Persephone smiled a little and swatted at him. "You are impossible sometimes."

"I do my best."

"I will stay in here." She took a seat. "You go 'greet your guest.'"

Linus exited the bedchamber and reached the threshold of the drawing room, intending to do his duty as host. He didn't get a single step inside though. Scorseby stood near Arabella. The two were deep in conversation. This was a far more personal arrangement than he'd expected to find.

Of course, Scorseby was not holding her hand, something she seemed to enjoy when Linus had done it only a few minutes earlier. Linus knew with certainty that Scorseby had an interest in Arabella, but his suit did not seem to have progressed over the past weeks.

He stepped back into the corridor unnoticed. His mind spun, and his heart thudded out a rhythm of uncertainty.

You are Lieutenant Lancaster, he silently reminded himself. *Cowering before a battle is not in your nature.*

He did not know the extent of her feelings for Scorseby, but he knew well enough his own hopes and wishes. He further knew Arabella's character well enough to believe she would not have held his hand nor had so personal a conversation as they'd shared, veiled though it had been in pronouns and hypotheticals, if her heart belonged to another.

Adam had spoken of the strength to be found in the companionship of a lady who lifted one's burdens, who brightened even the darkest corridors of one's life. Linus had found that in Arabella. With her hand in his, he'd even managed to speak of Evander, something he could seldom endure.

If there was any chance of fully laying claim to her affection, if he could offer her the strength and comfort she offered him, if there was any chance she might learn to love him, then he did not intend to let Scorseby make his case unopposed. Here, away from the interference of her aunt and uncle and the potential entrapment of the eager gossip to be found at house parties, Linus resolved to see if there was any chance he might be granted a place in her heart.

Arabella stood with a blanket at the ready as the duke, butler, footman, and coachman carried Charlie, careful of his heavily splinted legs, into the drawing room. While the poor young man was still in a fair bit of pain, Mater had sensed in him an impatience to be included in the evening's conversations and diversions.

"Being the youngest, and by so many years, has left him a little sensitive about being overlooked or excluded," Mater had explained. "I wish I could say those worries were unfounded, but I fear I did not realize how lonely he often was."

Dr. Scorseby had agreed that so long as Charlie was carried to and from his bedchamber and agreed to keep quite still, he could join the family.

They had Charlie settled and as comfortable as he could be in a matter of moments. He was in remarkably good spirits, all things considered. Mater took up her place beside her youngest and saw to his every need. The duke and duchess sat on the other sofa in the room, her hand in his. Miss Artemis chose a seat a bit removed. Whether she was feeling petulant or simply wished for a bit of privacy, Arabella did not know, neither was she afforded an opportunity to interact with the young lady enough to sort the matter out.

Dr. Scorseby's full attention was on Arabella, anticipating all of her possible needs—tea, a place to sit, a lap blanket. While the efforts were meant as a kindness, she, nonetheless, found them a touch aggravating.

Why was that? She was unused to people looking after her, which was certainly part of her annoyance. But Mater had looked after her toward the end of the house party when she had been ill, and that had not irritated her. Linus had sat with her during her convalescence, and that had been a welcome salve to her discomfort. Was it the oddity of being aided when she was fully healthy that bothered her, or was it the fact that Dr. Scorseby, in particular, offered the help?

Linus, who had not joined them for dinner, arrived in the drawing room some thirty minutes after everyone else had. He strode in with confidence and authority. How easily she could picture him issuing orders to a crew, overseeing a journey across treacherous waters. A man of his capability could do anything he put his mind to. Why, then, did he insist he would make such an incompetent landowner?

His eyes met hers as he crossed toward her, pleasure sparkling in their depths. She felt an answering blush steal across her features. In the moment before he arrived at her side, Dr. Scorseby took his place there.

"It is a pleasure to have everyone assembled, is it not?" Dr. Scorseby said. "And it is a relief that young Charlie is well enough to join us."

Arabella nodded. Nothing in his tone was truly off-putting, neither was his presence odious or unpleasant. Yet she wished he hadn't sat beside her. The memory of being at Linus's side in the sickroom had filled her all day with the oddest mixture of hope and regret. He was not the sort of person to show her such personal affection if he felt nothing but friendship for her. Leaving the comfort of his company and his tender touch had left an ache in her heart, one she felt certain could never fully be healed by anything other than being at his side once more.

But Dr. Scorseby was there instead.

"Good evening, Miss Hampton." Linus gave an acceptable bow and offered another to Mater, the duchess, and Artemis, then dipped his head to each gentleman. "My apologies for being late. I was detained on estate business."

"You have truly taken up the mantle it seems." Arabella was pleased at the idea. Perhaps the pain he felt here at being reminded again and again of his brother was beginning to ease.

"The mantle has taken up me." Linus chuckled. He never seemed more himself than when his expression and tone turned lighter. "I brought Charlie here with every intention of forcing him to oversee this wretched mess, but he went and threw himself off a roof to avoid the work."

"That sounds about right," Artemis muttered.

"Hush," Her Grace said.

Linus moved past Arabella and placed himself within easy conversational distance of Charlie. "It's a shame you took such drastic actions." He pointedly eyed Charlie's splinted legs. "I was going to invite the Nappers and their daughters over for an impromptu bit of dancing."

Charlie laughed. "Well worth it, I assure you."

Mater closed her eyes for the briefest of moments, a look of absolute relief crossing her features. Arabella knew the expression for what it was: the easing of a worried mind. Charlie had sustained a number of injuries, but his ability to jest about them spoke volumes of his quick healing.

"You seemed to enjoy the attention of the Napper sisters," Linus said, sitting in the chair opposite Mater's. "Has your opinion changed so drastically?"

Charlie shrugged. "They were interesting enough, I suppose."

"*Interesting?*" Linus shook his head. "That is how one might describe a treatise on the changing of crops or a lecture on mathematics. One ought to feel something far deeper and more personal about a potential love interest."

Charlie's brow pulled low as his eyes narrowed on Linus. "Love interest? How did we jump to that?"

Linus didn't seem the least put out by the objection. He leaned against the arm of his chair, his posture growing a little casual. "Simply an observation." His gaze flicked to Arabella.

Their eyes met for only a fraction of a moment, yet the impact was undeniable. Her heart hammered. *One ought to feel something far deeper.* Did he feel something deeper . . . for her? He'd been affectionate during the house party, before the rumors had driven a distance between them. She'd felt that connection again as she'd sat with her hand in his. Had he?

Mater caught Arabella's eye. "Would you be willing to play for us? I would so enjoy a bit of music."

"Of course." Though she was not treated as a servant, Arabella was still keenly aware of the fact that her role in Mater's life was that of a helper, an easer of burdens. That she truly adored the dear lady made her efforts as a companion a joy rather than an obligation.

In that moment, Mater's request was also a relief. Linus's words and expression had set her a little aflutter. Taking her place at the pianoforte would be a welcome escape. And she felt certain that playing would show her a little to advantage. She was a fine pianist; she had often been told so. Linus, she hoped, would be impressed.

She had a number of pieces memorized and chose one to begin her impromptu recital. Not a dozen notes into a rondo by Pleyel, she stopped, horrified at the sound she'd produced.

Had she remembered the piece wrong?

She shook off the confusion and started again only to produce the same result. A third try proved no better. She looked back at the others, humiliated. They all watched her, wide-eyed and wincing.

"I don't know what is the matter," she said. One more attempt ended just as badly. *What was happening?* She kept her gaze on the keys, unable to look at the gathered guests again. How very certain she'd been of impressing them—impressing *him*.

Footsteps approached. Even without looking, she knew Linus had come to the instrument; she recognized the spicy cinnamon scent that always clung to him. She closed her eyes in horrified embarrassment. He must have thought her absolutely pathetic.

"I usually play much better," she said quietly. "I don't know what happened."

"I do."

How easily she heard her aunt's voice in her mind. *They will send you back in disgrace.*

Linus leaned against the edge of the instrument. "I have not had the pianoforte tuned since returning home. And as my sister Daphne, who was mistress of the house before my return, does not play the pianoforte, I suspect she did not have the instrument tuned either."

Whether or not his guess was accurate, she latched on to it. "My poor performance is your sister's fault, then?"

"Entirely."

She met his eye. The laughter she saw there washed away the last remnants of her humiliation. His companionship did that for her. He relieved her worries, her insecurities, her uncertainties with hardly any effort. There was never any disapproval in his eyes when he looked at her. He never seemed to find her burdensome or beneath his notice. She'd known very few people who consistently treated her that way; her dear earl had been the first. Mater was proving to be another. The Jonquil brothers were equally kind and considerate. And now Linus's name was etching itself onto that list.

"I don't know what I did to earn the look you're giving me," he said, "but I'm enjoying it."

She never had been good at hiding her thoughts and feelings. Her aunt and uncle had always known when their words had hurt her or embarrassed her or when she was angry with them. That transparency had made punishing her painfully easy.

As quickly as he had lightened her mood, her memories had dampened it.

She rose from the stool at the pianoforte and faced the rest of the room. "I am sorry there will be no music."

Mater waved that off. "It isn't your fault Mr. Lancaster has an irresponsible sister."

The duchess laughed. "Poor Daphne, to have her reputation so sullied."

Mater grinned unrepentantly. "If she would have tuned the pianoforte, we would not be having this discussion. We would be having music instead."

"Ask Linus to play his lyre," Artemis said. "I know it's here; he doesn't go anywhere without it. He's quite talented." Artemis turned a glare on Charlie that the duke would have been hard-pressed to match in ferocity. "And if you are even thinking about making a comment expressing shock that I would say something kind about someone else—"

Charlie held up his unbroken arm in a show of innocence. "I wasn't going to say anything."

"You were thinking it."

"No, I wasn't."

"Enough," the duke grumbled.

Arabella met Linus's eyes. "Those two are going to kill each other," she said quietly.

He nodded. "I know."

"Do play for us, Linus," the duchess said. "You haven't in ages."

"I am to be the court minstrel?" he asked with more than a hint of laughter.

"Yes." Mater spoke quite somberly. "And I intend to mistreat you terribly if I am disappointed in your performance."

Linus shook his head, his mouth downturned. "We Linuses simply cannot win. I am to be punished if I do not live up to expectations, while Linus of old was strangled with his lyre for playing too well."

"It seems you have a very fine line to walk," Arabella said.

He smiled at her, broadly, fully. She'd never known a man with green eyes and, thus, had not realized before meeting him what a preference she had for them, especially when lit by genuine amusement.

"Never let it be said a man of the navy shied away from a challenge." He winked at her, setting off a wave of warmth inside. "I will return shortly with the instrument of either my triumph or my untimely demise." He left, a bounce in his step.

"I don't know why Linus chose the lyre," Her Grace said with a half smile. "This family lives far too many of our namesakes' myths. If that instrument is his downfall, I will be sorely tempted to have 'I told you so' inscribed on his grave marker."

The Lancasters lived their myths. It was an intriguing idea, though not one to be taken too literally. As far as Arabella knew, Linus's oldest sister was not held prisoner in the underworld, his second sister had not been born from her father's forehead, his younger sister was never turned into a tree, and, though his youngest sister was young yet, Artemis clearly had not and did not seem likely to violently decry the notice of men.

It was a shame the myth of Linus didn't include his falling in love with a servant. She might have allowed herself to believe that the family's lives were influenced by mythology. She would have prayed for it to be true.

"I have never heard anyone play the lyre," Dr. Scorseby said. "This should be very interesting."

"Historical texts are *interesting*," Artemis said. "Mathematics is *interesting*. My brother's music is *mesmerizing*."

Arabella was ever more intrigued. "He is truly that talented?"

Artemis met her eye. With pride so obvious it was palpable, she said, "Linus of old would have been impressed. Perhaps even envious."

Arabella took the vacant seat beside Mater. She clasped her hands, hoping to hide her growing excitement. A man of the military who was kind to children, devoted to his family, responsible, friendly, tender, made her laugh, and gently and affectionately held her hand, who *also* apparently played beautiful music. How could she help but love him?

He returned in the very next moment, a wooden lyre tucked carefully under his arm. "Have you sufficiently prepared yourself for the musical genius you are about to experience?"

Charlie answered first. "Your sister extolled your abilities for hours on end. Our expectations are very high."

"Not 'hours,'" Artemis insisted.

"It felt like hours."

Arabella eyed the two combatants. "If the two of you continue to prevent him from playing his music, I swear to you I will make your next few minutes feel like hours."

Mater grinned. His Grace offered a silent round of applause.

Linus took her hand in his free one and bowed over it. "My most sincere gratitude, Miss Hampton." He did not immediately release her hand but lingered over the touch. "Do you have any tunes you'd like to hear?"

"Any you'd like to play." Her words emerged nearly breathless.

He nodded, smiled, and slipped back. He pulled the stool away from the pianoforte and sat on it. He rested the lyre on one leg, situated perpendicular to his body. A quick succession of strums sounded before he settled in more comfortably.

The others in the room might have been watching him as closely as she was, but she refused to look away long enough to find out. Every thought was focused on him.

Linus met her eye. "I learned this one in Naples."

He played a piece unlike anything she'd ever heard. The melody was unusual but undeniably pleasant. Lilting and light, precisely the sort of tune one would wish to dance to but wouldn't for fear of missing its beauty. Artemis's description had been entirely accurate. Her brother's music was, indeed, mesmerizing.

Furthermore, watching him was utterly enthralling. Some musicians grew tense and focused as they played. Some seemed to be aware of nothing beyond their effort. But Linus grew more relaxed. His expression turned to one of complete contentment as he swayed to the music. He looked happy.

She raised her clasped hands to her lips, pressing them there as she watched him. She already loved what she knew of him. To see his appreciation of music, an affection she shared, only endeared him to her further.

The tune ended.

"Marvelous, Mr. Lancaster," Mater said.

Dr. Scorseby said something vaguely complimentary.

The rest of the Lancaster family had more enthusiastic praise.

Linus didn't look at any of them. His eyes lighted on no one but her. How easily she could recall the feel of his hand in hers and his delicate kiss on her fingers.

"Play another, Mr. Lancaster," Mater requested.

Linus still held Arabella's gaze. "I think Miss Hampton will enjoy this one in particular."

Why was that?

The corner of his mouth tipped upward. He plucked a string. "This is called"—he met her eye again—"'Walking in a Country Town.'"

Walking. She bit her lips closed against the laugh that bubbled up. He chose a song for her about walking.

The song was lovely, buoyant in a way the previous hadn't been, but not loud or overbearing. It was a pleasant melody. She enjoyed it for more than that though. The song, one about walking, had made him think of her. He knew that she walked. He had noticed. Yet he hadn't mocked the need or the undertaking as so many others did.

She would think of him every time she walked, and she would think of this song he played just for her.

Her song.

Chapter Thirty

A LOCAL FAMILY, THE NAPPERS, called the next day. Arabella watched them all, once more uncertain of her place.

Mater chatted amiably with Mrs. Napper. Dr. Scorseby found in Mr. Napper a fellow science-minded gentleman. Charlie, who had once again been carried down from his bedchamber, seemed particularly pleased to see the younger daughters, something Artemis apparently found particularly ridiculous. Linus took great pains to interact with the oldest Miss Napper, a lady likely only a bit younger than Arabella, who did not seem to be putting any true effort into capturing Linus's interest.

She was quiet and appeared a little uncomfortable. Indeed, the more Arabella watched her, the more familiar the lady became, not because they were acquainted but because she saw so much of herself in Miss Napper. Quiet. Reserved. A bit out of place amongst the people with whom she associated. In need of a friend and a kind word.

And Linus was showing her attention and cordiality. Just as he did for Arabella when she most needed it. She knew compassion was part of his nature; it was one of the things she loved best about him. But certainly that was not all he felt for her?

How was she, who struggled to understand the minutia of interactions and relationships, supposed to be certain of Linus's feelings for her if he offered such contradictory versions of those feelings?

I am so confused.

"Mr. Lancaster, you should play your lyre for us," Mater said. "I so enjoyed the music last evening. The Nappers would as well; I am certain."

"My amateur efforts hardly deserve such praise."

"Do play for us," the eldest Miss Napper said. "I would enjoy hearing the lyre. It is not an instrument with which I am very familiar."

He offered an amused smile, the one that always set Arabella's heart flipping around in her chest. But it was not directed at her. Miss Napper was the recipient.

Arabella looked away. She did not like these feelings of doubt, but she didn't know how to rid herself of them. The Nappers were shifting about, switching seats and rearranging their positions. When Mrs. Napper vacated the chair nearest Mater, Arabella took advantage of the opening. She would feel better situated near the lady who came so close to being a mother to her. And Charlie sat on the sofa on the other side of the chair Arabella took. She would be flanked by Jonquils. A person couldn't help but feel safe in such a position.

The younger Misses Napper had moved to surround their sister. They were whispering and fluttering whilst their oldest sister simply smiled quietly. Mrs. Napper, now sitting nearer the fire, met her husband's eye. They exchanged pointed, knowing looks.

"Mr. Lancaster is very indulgent," Mater said to Arabella.

"He does like to play the lyre. I don't imagine he needs a great deal of convincing to do so."

"Especially since Miss Napper seemed keen on hearing him play," Charlie added.

Despite her wariness to receive a further explanation, Arabella looked to him for one, praying it proved innocuous.

"We had dinner with the Nappers the night before—" Charlie motioned to his broken legs.

"Before Mr. Lancaster pushed you off a roof," Arabella finished for him.

Charlie laughed. "You're funnier than I remember you."

"Mr. Lancaster is shocked that the lot of you don't think I am endlessly hilarious. He, apparently, has thought so from the very beginning."

"Maybe he's just more observant than the rest of us," Charlie said.

Mater's brow pulled in an expression of pondering. "I don't believe that's it."

Charlie shrugged. "I don't know if he thinks Miss Napper is hilarious. At the dinner we had at their home, Linus talked to almost no one other than her. He was so persistent, so determined to hold her attention."

"She seems a little timid," Mater said.

Charlie nodded. "And he seems a little interested."

Linus returned with his lyre and set himself down in the midst of them. He had the eldest Miss Napper's full attention. He strummed the strings a moment, just as he'd done the night before. The tune he played first was the one he'd begun with the previous evening. The second and third were familiar as well. Then he played her song, the one about walking, the one that had set her heart to fluttering. He had looked at her as he'd played, his expression warm and personal, at least it had seemed so to her.

He wasn't doing so now, but neither was he looking at anyone else.

As the tune ended, Miss Napper declared herself quite thoroughly impressed. Linus declared himself pleased that she approved.

Arabella's heart sank. His music the night before had touched her. His declaration that the song he'd chosen for her had, indeed, been *for her* had swelled in her. She'd felt special, important, noticed. She still believed it, and yet . . .

It was all very confusing and a touch overwhelming.

She rose. With a quick quarter smile of apology, she made her excuses to Mater, insisting her long walk had left her weary.

She'd gone no farther than the corridor directly beyond the sitting room door when Dr. Scorseby caught up with her. She'd all but forgotten he had joined the gathering.

"Miss Hampton, are you feeling unwell?" His assessing gaze swept over her, taking stock of her condition.

"I am only in need of a brief moment to lie down," she told the doctor.

His brow pulled low. "Are you certain? I cannot like the idea of you feeling unwell, not if I might be able to alleviate some of that suffering."

His solicitous treatment of her served as something of a balm in that moment. "I thank you for your concern and kindness. I really do need nothing more than a bit of quiet."

He nodded, not pressing her, though he clearly disbelieved her minimizing of her suffering. "I hope we will see you at dinner."

"I am certain I will be feeling quite well by then." She fully intended to have herself sorted out enough by then to return.

He offered a bow and she a curtsey, and they parted.

She slipped into the quiet sanctuary of the room she had been assigned, a peaceful, tranquil bedchamber draped in sheer white. She had loved it from the moment she'd stepped inside, yet it seemed to have lost some of its soothing ability. Her mind and heart, she feared, were too burdened.

Life had afforded her so few opportunities to truly come to understand people and relationships. Every hope she had harbored for a connection as a child had ended with four simple words: Family stays with family.

The only thing she knew with absolute certainty was that sometimes, no matter the closeness she might feel to someone, there was simply not a place for her. It was not an easy lesson to unlearn.

Chapter Thirty-One

WITH CHARLIE OUT OF DANGER and the dowager insistent that she was fully capable of seeing to his recovery, Persephone felt it best if those bound for Falstone Castle continued their journey. Linus stood in the front entryway as his family prepared to leave. The house would be very quiet after they left, especially once Mater, Charlie, and Arabella were gone as well. Linus hadn't found the loneliness of his house as overwhelming the past weeks as he'd expected it to be. But, then, the house hadn't been empty.

Persephone arrived in the entryway, Oliver on her hip. Adam was directing the footmen as they put trunks and bags on the carriage.

"You will, no doubt, be grateful to have us out of your hair," Persephone said.

"Nonsense. I've loved having you here."

She eyed him doubtfully. "Even though you've been sleeping in the study ever since young Mr. Jonquil's family arrived?"

"A few days sleeping in a chair won't kill me."

She shifted Oliver to her other hip. "And what about all the days before that?"

Did she know he hadn't been sleeping in his childhood bedchamber? He'd tried to keep that hidden, not wishing to explain.

Persephone gently touched his cheek. "Is there any corner of this estate where Evander does not haunt you?"

"He is everywhere," Linus confessed. "But I'm wading through those waters and making my way to shore."

"He would not have wanted you to be unhappy, Linus. None of us have ever wanted you to be anything other than joyous."

"Joy is in relatively short supply in the navy during a war," he said.

Regret and sadness filled her expression. "I know. If there had been any other option—"

He'd not meant to cause her remorse. "In the end, I loved my time in the navy. It made me who I am."

"And I love who you are." Persephone pulled him into a one-armed embrace.

Oliver set his arm around Linus as well. "I love you too, Uncle Linus."

"Will you come back and visit me again, Oliver?" he asked.

His little nephew nodded.

Linus looked to Persephone. "Will you?"

"Of course. And we hope to see you at the Castle for Christmas and Twelfth Night."

"I wouldn't miss it."

Adam stepped inside, eyeing them all with his customary impatience. "Where is Artemis? I'll leave without her if I must."

"You aren't leaving her here." Linus pretended to be horrified at the possibility.

"If she's not in the carriage in five minutes, I am."

Linus turned a grin on Persephone but found she did not share his amusement. "He is in earnest?"

She nodded. "If you don't want to keep her, you'd best find her and send her down."

He sketched a brief bow, ruffled Oliver's hair, and hurried around the corner and up the stairs. The house was small. Finding his sister would not be difficult. Indeed, he needed only to follow the sound of her voice directly to the master's bedchamber.

Why was she visiting Charlie? Had she decided to kill him before leaving for Northumberland?

Linus peeked inside the room. Charlie was sitting up, pillows tucked behind him. The dowager sat nearby. Artemis stood at the foot of the bed.

"Mrs. Tuttle's sister-in-law's father was a thatcher," she said. "He tied himself to the chimney when working on roofs. If you mean to go up on another roof, you might consider a good, sturdy rope."

"If I didn't know better, I'd say you didn't actually want me to fall to my death."

Artemis shook her head, a few loose ringlets bouncing about as she did. "Don't be ridiculous. I'm only worried about Linus. If you are tied to the chimney, he's more likely to be as well."

Charlie laughed. "I don't think Linus or I will be on another roof anytime soon."

"Good." She tipped her chin upward. "It's dangerous."

"We'll climb the Cliffs of Dover instead."

Linus looked at the dowager in the exact moment she looked at him. She appeared on the verge of laughter.

"That was a joke, was it?" Artemis did not sound impressed.

"Not a very good one, apparently." Bless him, Charlie was being very patient.

Linus stepped inside. "Adam is threatening to leave you here, Artemis."

She turned to face him. "He is always irritable before a journey."

"He also does not make idle threats," Linus reminded her.

She nodded her understanding. "It has been a pleasure to spend time with you these past days, Lady Lampton."

"A *mutual* pleasure," the dowager replied.

Artemis faced Charlie once more. "It has been a . . . trial to spend time with *you* these past days, Mr. Jonquil."

"A *mutual* trial," Charlie said.

Artemis turned a dry look on Linus, even rolled her eyes. "We had best not keep Adam waiting."

Linus offered his sister his arm. They stepped out into the corridor and toward the stairs.

"Are you certain you won't come with us?" Artemis asked.

"This is my home," he said. "I need to stay and take care of it."

"Won't you be lonely?"

His sister did not need to know the extent of the loneliness he anticipated. "Charlie will not be able to travel for weeks yet. The dowager won't leave without him. I'll have plenty of company."

"And Miss Hampton won't leave without the two of them, but Dr. Scorseby isn't likely to leave until she does." Artemis eyed him sidelong. "That might be one too many people for your taste."

"Especially since we have a doctor in the neighborhood already."

Artemis laughed and bumped him with her shoulder. "I do not think you object to that redundancy."

"Oh, you don't, do you?"

She embraced his arm as they descended the stairs. "I like Miss Hampton. I like the way she looks at you."

"How does—how does she look at me?"

"Like you being in a room makes it her favorite room in all the world." Artemis sighed. "And you look at her like you'd do anything at all to see her happy."

"Are you matchmaking? I think I had quite enough of that in Nottinghamshire."

Artemis set her head on his shoulder. She'd done precisely that during the carriage ride from London and a few times while they'd both been in Town. In those moments, she almost felt like little Artemis again, the loving and tiny sister he'd left behind so many years earlier.

"Do you really need me to matchmake, Linus? It seems to me you've made your mind up already."

There was a great deal of truth to that. "My heart made that decision weeks ago."

"Do not let her slip away," Artemis said. "You are happier when she is with you, and you deserve to be happy."

They'd reached the entryway, now empty, the rest of the family outside climbing into the carriage.

Linus pulled Artemis into a true embrace. "You deserve to be happy as well. Do not settle for anything less than that."

She pulled back and grinned mischievously. "I don't intend to."

Artemis waved as she walked through the door and out to the carriage. Only a moment later, Linus's family drove away, leaving him behind.

You deserve to be happy. Arabella deserved happiness far more than he did. How could he show her that they could find that happiness together?

The question remained heavy on his mind as he wandered inside once more. He stepped into the sitting room and found the dowager there. He offered a quick smile of apology and made as though to leave.

"Sit with me, Mr. Lancaster," she said. "I intend to ask you a few prying questions." No sooner had he taken the seat near hers, than she launched into her inquiries. "When did you last see Arabella?"

That was innocuous enough. "Yesterday when the Nappers were here."

"I have seen her since then," the dowager said. "And I am worried."

The military man in him jumped into action. "What's happened?"

"She spent four hours yesterday walking around the grounds of your estate. She is doing so again now."

He knew perfectly well what extensive walking meant for Arabella Hampton. What misery was she fleeing now?

"My husband used to find her, as a tiny girl, walking miles from her uncle's home, tears running down her face, broken by her unhappiness. It tore at his heart. She was running, surviving, but at such a cost. She was so often alone and so often hopeless."

"Your husband cared about her."

"Immensely," the dowager said. "He adored her, in fact. 'Such a sweet little dear.' He referred to her that way more times than I can remember. If he had been alive to witness the new Mrs. Hampton's treatment of her and Mr. Hampton's indifference to her suffering, he would not have minced words, I assure you. And if he had seen her return to her desperate walking these past twenty-four hours, he would be heartbroken."

"What precisely do you think has sent her fleeing this time?"

"Honestly," the dowager said. "You."

That was not at all what he'd wanted to hear, yet he didn't find it surprising.

"I believe you have laid claim to a bit of her heart."

Hope swelled, though with it came a growing confusion. "Why has that sent her out on her walks again? Is she afraid of me?" Heaven, he hoped not.

The dowager shook her head. "I would wager she is uncertain, nervous. Such attachments do not always end well, especially when a significant difference in station is involved."

"You make us sound like a master of the estate and a chambermaid, rather than a gentleman and a gentleman's daughter."

She smiled kindly. "I am well aware that yours is not a difference as wholly insurmountable as a lord and a servant. She, however, was brought up in a household where she was treated as an unwanted, unworthy hanger-on. While I do not think she truly believes that of herself, it is not difficult to understand why she might worry that others do. You, after all, have two titled sisters and are kin to the Duke of Kielder."

"She is fleeing because she thinks other people will consider her a ladder-climber?"

"I believe she is worried that you will not return her regard and that she is foolish to hope you might."

That was decidedly lowering. "Then she believes *I* consider her beneath me."

"I can see I am not doing a very good job of explaining this." She thought a moment. Linus kept his peace and allowed her to ponder. If she had an explanation that didn't reflect so poorly on him, he would happily wait for it. "I know with utmost certainty that you have never, nor could you ever view her as being unworthy of regard. I further am certain that you have never treated her in a way that would give her reason to believe otherwise. But a few weeks of kindness and acceptance does not undo years of rejection. Her uncle, who ought to have cared for her and treated her well, never did. His late wife did not either. His current wife certainly doesn't. She has known very little kindness in her life. That would make even the most optimistic of people wary in the face of hope. And in light of the Nappers' visit . . ."

"The Nappers?"

"You played your lyre for Miss Napper," she said.

Linus shook his head. "I didn't play *for her.*"

The dowager eyed him doubtfully. "Didn't you?"

Did she truly think he had? "Were you under that impression?" Nothing could be further from the truth.

"A little. Arabella certainly was."

Shock tied his tongue a moment. "Miss Napper was welcome to listen, but I chose songs Arabella would enjoy. I thought only of her."

"That is not quite the impression you gave."

The lyre had been Linus of old's downfall. It seemed destined to be his as well.

"Arabella has known great heartache in her life," the dowager said. "She worries that those she loves will hurt her."

That made a good deal of sense. "If not for your husband, she likely would have no reason to hope for anything else. She has spoken often of his kindness toward her."

The dowager nodded. "I doubt even she realized the depth of his attachment to her."

"Likely not, considering she thinks of herself as something resembling a servant in your household."

Sadness touched her expression. "I have wanted to talk to her about him, to tell her how he felt. I can't seem to manage it. Even after more than a decade, I often struggle to speak of him."

He patted her hand. "My brother died eleven years ago. I don't speak of him often either."

She sighed. "Grief can remain surprisingly raw."

"Yes, it can."

They sat a moment in silence. A light, cool breeze rustled the trees outside the sitting room window. The weather was pleasant and the sky clear. It was not unlike the afternoon he'd spent looking out over the grounds of Lampton Park, imagining life in such a peaceful place. He would not have imagined then that his own home would have begun to feel so tranquil.

Without warning, the dowager spoke again. "Have you told Arabella that you are in love with her?"

"In love?" The words sputtered out.

She gave his hand a maternal pat. "I have seven sons. I know all too well the symptoms of a young gentleman in love."

Would his own mother have seen the state of things so clearly? He imagined she would have. And she might have offered him a bit of much-needed advice. Perhaps the dowager would be willing to fill that role, at least for the moment.

"When I left the house party, I knew I had grown very fond of Arabella. Not until her arrival here did I truly realize the depth of my feelings."

She nodded slowly. "And you haven't told her as much?"

"That is a task easier said than accomplished. There is a risk there."

"I know," she said. "My dear husband and I wasted a great deal of time when we were young not telling each other how we felt. It seemed to us too great a risk."

"You are telling me to be brave?"

"I am telling you that it is worth it."

Chapter Thirty-Two

ARABELLA SAT ON A ROUGH-HEWN stone bench a few yards from the road, resting after hours spent walking. She'd doubled back on her path a few times, chosen narrow footpaths, sometimes walking alongside the larger roads. This had always been her escape, her way to breathe. Her troubles never magically disappeared or resolved themselves simply because she'd been away, but being out of reach of those people and circumstances with the power and ability to hurt her was a welcome gift. So she walked. Sometimes all day, and she pretended there was no pain to return to.

The strategy was not proving as effective this time. Her worries were not coming at her from without but from within. Her heart and her mind were at war, and she hadn't the first idea how to reconcile the very strong arguments they both made.

She loved Linus Lancaster and had reason to believe he might feel the same. Again and again her heart insisted upon that.

Then her mind interrupted with an equally inarguable fact: she had loved a gentleman before, though not at all in the same way as Linus, and what she had needed most from him he hadn't, in the end, been able to give her. *Family stays with family.*

The earl had had a family of his own to look after, an estate to run, obligations in London and at his many holdings. That he had made time for her was both a kindness and a sacrifice.

But I needed so much more than his time. She had prayed for an escape more permanent than her daily walks. She'd needed to be able to leave and not return to a home where she was neglected on the best of days, made miserable on the rest. She had been too young and too powerless to save herself. She'd looked to him. But he hadn't been able to help.

She wondered in all the years since then how much she dared trust the people she cared about, how much to lean on them in her difficulties. If even her beloved earl, who had loved her as no else had, hadn't helped her when she'd needed him most, however unavoidable that disappointment had been, then whom could she possibly rely upon?

She wiped away the moisture on her cheeks, forcing herself to take a deep breath. These were insecurities she had struggled with all her life. How did one go about shaking free of them? She needed to be able to trust her own judgment but didn't know how.

She took a long breath, deep enough to lift her shoulders. She straightened her spine. A bit of courage and determination ought not be impossible to come by. The past weeks had seen her face any number of unexpected situations, none of which she'd proven truly disastrous at facing. She could confront her current uncertainties as well.

Yet when she considered the possibility of ending her walk for the day and returning to Linus's home, her stomach clenched.

It seems I am not as brave as I'd like to believe.

Nearby, a twig snapped. Footsteps crunched the first of the autumn leaves scattered about. Frustration bubbled. It was, no doubt, Dr. Scorseby. He had run her to ground the day before, waxing long and insistent about the inadvisability of her long excursions. He had insisted she cut her walk short. No amount of persistence on her part had been sufficient. In the end, she had done as he'd bade simply to stop the debate. She was not, however, ready to return yet today.

Dr. Scorseby was not the one who stepped into view.

"Linus." Only his name emerged in her surprise.

"You are a difficult lady to track down." Without preamble, he sat beside her on the bench. "I have had report of you passing by nearly every home, cottage, shop, and barn throughout the area. You've covered miles and miles."

Her fingers clutched at one another. Her heart hammered against her ribs. "I like to walk."

He set his hand atop hers, wrapping his fingers around hers, halting their nervous movement. "I know why you walk," he said quietly. "That is why I have been trying to find you this past three-quarters of an hour."

"You have been looking for me?"

His gaze held hers for a long moment. "Why does that surprise you?"

"Because . . . because few people ever have."

He moved his hand enough to intertwine his fingers with hers, and every bit of her melted. "Did the earl?"

She shook her head. "He was always welcoming. If I happened upon him along the river or sought him out after services, he was unfailingly kind and attentive. But I don't remember him searching me out." Oh, it hurt to admit it out loud. "It was not a matter of unkindness on his part," she was quick to specify. "I am simply not the sort of person one thinks of when I am not present."

"I can assure you that is not the case."

She wanted to believe him. How did one stop wondering about one's value when life itself had infused that doubt into nearly every moment?

"Why have you begun walking again?" Linus asked. "The dowager said you had not undertaken such long outings lately."

"I am attempting to sort through some things."

He looked straight ahead, though she did not think he was truly focused on anything. "Do those things involve me? Because I have a terrible suspicion that they do."

"They mostly involve me," she said.

"Will you come back home, Arabella? The dowager is worried. I am worried."

Her heart dropped to her feet. "I am causing trouble, aren't I?"

"Not at all." He turned and faced her. "We care about you, Arabella. Sometimes caring means worrying. Sometimes caring means chasing after someone when they run away."

"I'd like to keep walking."

"You've been walking for hours," he said.

She stood, pacing away from the bench, her hand pulling free of his. "Dr. Scorseby already scolded me for this. Please don't you do so as well."

"I wasn't scolding." He rose but did not close the distance between them. "I simply don't wish for you to walk so long and so far that you are too exhausted to return home."

Home. What home did she truly have? The Park had not proven the place of refuge she had expected. The dower house did not entirely feel like home either. Linus spoke of his home, but it was not hers.

"Arabella?"

As always, her emotions betrayed her. Why was it she could never seem to keep her thoughts and feelings hidden? "I am going to walk a little more." She didn't wait for a response but took up her trek again. To her great surprise, Linus walked alongside her. She eyed him sidelong, unsure what to make of his continued presence. "Are you walking with me?"

"If that is acceptable to you."

Though solitude had always been an integral part of her daily walks, she found herself perfectly content with this unusual arrangement. "I don't mind."

"I am glad." He smiled at her. "So long as I am out here, I can ignore the ledger that is awaiting me at the house. Balancing the books is not at all my idea of an enjoyable pastime."

"You will likely think me the strangest creature in all the world, but I do enjoy balancing ledgers." She glanced at him long enough to catch his look of shock, which brought a laugh bubbling to the surface. "Mine was not an extensive education, but I was taught to keep household accounts. I quite unexpectedly discovered that I liked the undertaking."

"It seems you and Charlie are cut from the same cloth. That boy is enamored of mathematics."

"And you are enamored of the sea." She sighed as if it were a great tragedy. "We all have our oddities."

"Oddities?" He chuckled low. "A love of the sea is not a quirk; it is an inevitability."

"I would not know," she said. "I have never seen the sea."

Again, his gaze turned surprised, only this time without the theatricality. "Oh, Arabella, you simply must see the ocean. To stand on the shore and look out over the vast expanse of water. There is something both humbling and exhilarating about it. While I was always anxious to board and launch, Evander loved to stand on the shore and simply breathe it all in."

She knew how difficult speaking of his brother was for him, not unlike her struggle to reflect on the earl and all he'd meant to her. Not wishing for him to be disheartened, she slipped her arm through his as they continued to walk. The physical connection proved comforting to her as well.

"What was it Evander liked most about watching the sea?" she asked.

"The sound of the waves crashing against the shore." His smile was a fond one, though a little sad. "'It is as if the ocean is announcing its long-awaited arrival home,' he would say. I imagine that is why he liked the sound so much. It was a promise that those things that sail out to sea can and will return again."

She leaned her head against his shoulder, not knowing what she could say to counter the heartache she heard in his voice. His brother, after all, had not come home. "Does the ocean make that same crashing sound when one is out in the midst of it?"

"During storms, it is quite loud," he said. "But, no, the sound is not the same as it is on shore."

"The sound of home."

"No." The single syllable emerged with almost no volume. "The sound of home was always my family's voices. It filled my mind and my heart during long voyages. It was what I dreamed of hearing again. But those voices are gone now."

"Home, for me, was always the sight and sound of the Jonquil brothers larking about on the back lawn of the Park while the earl joined in their fun." She pushed down the lump in her throat. "Even more so when they invited me to be part of it."

"If you had lived in this neighborhood, I would have made certain you were part of every bit of mischief my siblings and I undertook."

Oh, how she adored him. He soothed her worries without being suffocating, knew what she needed to hear without being patronizing. Returning to Nottinghamshire meant likely never seeing him again. The idea pained her deeply.

"And would you have walked with me?" she asked.

"Perhaps you wouldn't have needed to walk so much. You wouldn't have been so lonely."

She wrapped her arm more tightly around his arm, nearly embracing it. "I will be lonely again when I return to the Park. I rather dread it."

"You will have the dowager for company and Lord and Lady Lampton."

"It will not be the same," she whispered.

"No." He spoke as quietly as she did. "No, it will not be."

"Will you miss me?" The question would likely have been viewed as overly bold by most of Society, but she knew too little of attachments and fondness to be at all able to guess at his feelings. A direct question seemed her best option.

"I missed you when I left Nottinghamshire," he said.

"I missed you *before* you left Nottinghamshire," she countered.

"Before?" He clearly didn't understand.

She threw caution to the wind. "You sat with me every day when I was ill. You talked with me and laughed with me. Then, suddenly, I was more like a stranger than a friend. You seldom spoke with me or sat near me. I was the poor relation in the corner again."

He stopped walking, so she did as well. He moved to face her. "People were gossiping. They were speculating about you and me."

Oh, the misery of that explanation. "I realize I am comparatively insignificant, but I didn't think I'd given you reason to be ashamed of me."

"Arabella." He took her hands in his, his gaze earnest and pleading. "I could never be ashamed of having you my life. I consider it an honor."

She struggled to believe that. "Why, then, did the whispers drive you away?"

"I know the power of rumors. If the gossip took hold, we'd have had no choice but to . . . I did not wish for either of us to be forced into a situation not of our choosing."

That was a better explanation than the one she had imagined. "You didn't object to me personally?"

He raised her hand to his lips and kissed her fingers. "I didn't object in the least."

She tried to breathe but wasn't entirely successful. She had dreamed of his affection. The realization of those hopes was proving almost overwhelming.

"I have something for you," he said.

"You do?"

He released her hands and fished about in the pocket of his outer coat. They'd stopped beneath the wide branches of an old oak tree. The air was cool. Tiny pockets of light broke through the leaves above. After a moment's searching, he presented her with a small drawstring bag made of simple muslin. It was tiny enough to fit in the palm of her hand.

"This is for me?" Her heart thudded against her ribs. "Thank you."

"You don't even know what it is yet."

She lifted a single shoulder. "I happen to be very fond of muslin bags."

Linus leaned one shoulder against the thick tree trunk and watched, waiting.

The bag was light and nearly flat. Whatever was inside was not large. What could it possibly be? She tugged the top of the bag open and glanced inside. She couldn't see anything.

She met his eye once more. "Is it really just the bag?"

He laughed. "No."

Arabella turned up her palm and tipped the contents of the bag onto her hand. Two beads, deep green and no larger than the tip of her smallest finger, poured out.

"They're jade," he said. "I saw them in a shop years ago in a port in the east. I can't say exactly what I, a then fifteen-year-old boy, saw in a pair of jade beads, but I returned to them again and again. Most of the baubles I picked up over the years were subsequently gifted to my sisters."

"But not these?" Had his sisters not wanted them? Arabella couldn't imagine they wouldn't; the deep-green stone beads were gorgeous.

"There was always something special about these beads, though I never could say with certainty what."

She closed her fingers around them, pressing the spheres into her palm. "I can't possibly accept them."

"Why not?"

She set her fist, the beads clasped inside, against her thudding heart. "They are special to you."

He pulled away from the tree and closed the gap between them. He leaned close and dropped his voice to a whisper. "*You* are special to me, Arabella Hampton. You have been from the moment I met you. I suspect you have been since before I met you, since I was fifteen and standing in a shop on the other side of the world knowing without realizing that somewhere, someday I would meet you."

She looked up into his eyes, very nearly the color of the beads. Sincerity filled his gaze. He ran his hand the length of her arm. "I am not good at expressing what is in my heart—I never have been—but these were always meant for something greater than a mere token. I held on to them for years, waiting . . . for you."

He slipped his hand around hers. "I missed you while we were apart. And when you return to Nottinghamshire, I will miss you again until I am able to be there with you and see you again."

"You would come to Nottinghamshire?"

He raised her hand to his lips. "If need be, I would sail the world to be with you."

"And would you walk with me?"

"Every day." He kissed her fingers. "And would you make paper boats with me?"

She laughed lightly. "Every day."

His arms wrapped around her, pulling her fully into his embrace. "Will you wear my beads?"

"People might whisper," she said.

"We've time yet before you must return, time enough to decide our own futures. Then they can whisper all they'd like; we will know what we want."

Arabella leaned into his embrace, fully wrapped in his arms. They had time, yes, but she already knew her heart.

Chapter Thirty-Three

ARABELLA EYED HER REFLECTION IN the mirror hanging in her bedchamber. On either side of the earl's bead were Linus's. She ran her fingers over all three. Life had left her so often questioning if she was loved or even cared for. Yet here was a reminder of Linus's affection.

She smiled to herself. The man she loved cared about her in return. Years of heartache eased at the simple but profound realization. She, who had always longed to be loved, could clearly see that possibility in her future at last.

"Shall we go down to dinner?" Mater stood in the doorway.

Arabella stepped away from the mirror and toward the door. "Will Charlie be joining us?"

"I believe he will be." Mater's gaze fell on Arabella's necklace. "You've added new beads to the one my husband left for you."

Arabella set her hand over the adornment. "You knew about his gift to me?"

Mater smiled gently. "My dear Arabella, his fondness for you was not a secret. Neither was he the only one who cared for you."

"The boys did enjoy having me join in their battle reenactments." Those had been happy times. "The earl was always very kind to me. I wondered what it would be like if—Had I been—" She had never spoken aloud her wish to be part of his family. She found she couldn't now. "He was always kind when he saw me, but he never sought me out. He never . . . I have always been very easily forgotten."

"My husband visited your uncle's home many times." Mater sat on the edge of Arabella's bed and folded her hands on her lap.

"He visited my uncle," Arabella clarified.

"Do you know why?"

She had never been made privy to his reasons. "Estate business?"

"Your uncle's estate held no sway over any of my husband's holdings, neither would my husband have responded to a summons from your uncle."

She hadn't thought of that. What influence could Uncle have possibly had that would have brought the late earl to Hampton House? She sat beside Mater. "He came quite often though."

"He was attempting to negotiate something of great importance but also of a tremendously sensitive nature." Mater set her hand on Arabella's. "He was trying to arrange for you to come live with us."

Every thought fled. Her heart seized painfully. She had begged the earl to let her live with his family at Lampton Park. But he had told her no.

"We made every attempt to convince your uncle to legally grant us guardianship. He was willing, provided we paid regular sums of money to him, the amount of which he increased every time we discussed the arrangements. Though we were not unwilling, we knew perfectly well that he would continue to demand more and more, knowing that he stood in a position to make you unhappy and that your happiness mattered to us."

"Blackmail," Arabella whispered.

"Essentially." Mater shook her head, her eyes unfocused. "He would never have stopped. Lucas very much feared that if we were to pay the ransom your uncle demanded, it would only be a matter of time before that information was bandied about the neighborhood. Those rumors would have shadowed you all your life. He could not bear the thought of causing you such misery."

Mater turned her gaze on Arabella once more. "He never stopped trying though. He did manage to arrange it by convincing your new aunt that should you be attached to Lampton Park, you would be granted a London Season and she would benefit from that social standing. Your aunt, in turn, would prevent your uncle from demeaning you and your presence at Lampton Park, as that would interfere with the benefit she would receive from your situation."

"I was to come live with you?"

Mater nodded. "Lucas bought that necklace as a 'welcome home' present to give to you on the day you were to come to our home."

Arabella wrapped her fingers around her beads. She tried to swallow, but her throat had grown too thick. "But I never came to live with you."

"No, you didn't." Mater's voice lost most of its volume.

"Why not?"

Mater blinked a few quick times in succession. Redness touched the rims of her eyes. "He died." She took a breath and pressed on. "The law does not truly permit a lady guardianship of anyone, not even her own children. My husband had arranged for trustees who would not interfere with my efforts to raise our sons should he be taken from us unexpectedly. That foresight proved almost prophetic. He had no ability, however, to make arrangements for me to be appointed your guardian, despite his agreement with your uncle. My husband's passing put a permanent end to our hopes for you. I could not bring you to the Park, though I wanted to."

"You did?"

Mater sighed. "It breaks my heart that you are unsure of that."

"I never knew." She had never been told any of this.

"We did not wish to raise hopes in you that would be dashed should our efforts fail. And after Lucas's passing, I couldn't bear to tell you what had almost been. I could hardly think of it myself."

She had come so close to her dreams. So very close.

"I should have attempted to bring you home long before now. I believe your aunt and uncle would have parted with you, but there was no explanation for it that would prevent the neighborhood from speculating. Then Philip married, and I prepared to remove to the dower house."

"And the neighborhood could be made to believe that you wished for a lady's companion."

Mater nodded. "I ought to have explained it to you. I tried more than once. But discussing those last months of Lucas's life is still difficult. The words simply would not come."

"Did—Did he love me?"

"Oh, Arabella." Mater squeezed her hand. "He loved you so very much. He thought of you as his own child. If he were still here—" Emotion cut off her words. "He likely would be disappointed in me that I left you to wonder about his feelings for so long."

"And in me for doubting him in the first place." Tears started in her eyes. "He showed me such love, yet I didn't allow myself to believe it."

Mater smiled, the expression a little sad but also a little wistful. "Were he here, he would take the two of us in his arms, tell us he loved us, and insist we trust the depth of his regard. And then he would do everything in his power to make certain we believed him."

Oh, how she had loved him.

"He would be heartbroken to think you spent so many years feeling forgotten," Mater said. "He would never want you to feel anything less than cherished."

"Do you think he would have liked Linus?"

Mater raised an eyebrow. "He is 'Linus' now, is he?"

Heat filled Arabella's face. "Mr. Lancaster."

Mater laughed. "You might as well call him Linus. I know full well how the two of you feel about each other. I've known for ages."

She couldn't hold back a pleased smile. "*We've* only known for a few hours."

"You've known," Mater said. "You simply hadn't admitted it yet."

Heavens, that was true. "He gave me the new beads."

Mater nodded. "I suspected as much."

Arabella slid one jade bead along the chain. "I think the earl would approve of him."

"If my Lucas could see your Linus's tenderness for you, he would more than approve of him; he would love him."

Arabella closed her eyes, memories of the earl filling her thoughts. "I wish he were here."

"So do I," Mater said. "I wish it every day. Every single day. But I see him in his sons. I see him in you."

That pulled Arabella's gaze to Mater once more. The fondness she saw there soothed so many of a lifetime's uncertainties.

"To know that the influence of my beloved Lucas is still being felt comforts me beyond words. He lives on, and he has not been forgotten."

"And he never will be," Arabella said. She put her arms around Mater and received a tight embrace in return. Years of loneliness were fading away.

She was loved.

Chapter Thirty-Four

LINUS NEEDED TO MAKE THE better acquaintance of a few more of his neighbors. The Nappers were pleasant enough company, but having them as guests yet again left much to be desired. Mr. and Mrs. Napper clearly had hopes of both him and Charlie taking an interest in their daughters. Charlie was too young for a serious attachment. And Linus's affections were fully focused elsewhere. Perhaps he needed to make that a little clearer.

"What shall we do for entertainment this evening?" the dowager asked when they'd all gathered in the drawing room. "Loo or whist, perhaps?"

Linus had been working on a surprise for Arabella. Now was the perfect opportunity. "I had hoped we might have some music."

"Excellent," Mrs. Napper said.

"I would very much enjoy hearing your lyre again." The eldest Miss Napper had spoken to him more about his music than any other topic. He hadn't intended to pique her interest; he had something else in mind entirely.

"I had hoped," he said, "that Miss Hampton would favor us."

Her eyes pulled wide. He likely should have warned her.

"Miss Hampton plays the lyre?" Mrs. Napper asked.

Linus shook his head. "She plays the pianoforte, and I understand she is quite talented."

He turned fully to Arabella. "Would you be willing?" He held his hand out to her.

She allowed him to help her to her feet. Under her breath, she said, "Your pianoforte is not playable. This will end in humiliation."

He tucked her arm through his and walked her to the instrument. "I would never ask you to embarrass yourself," he whispered.

She sat on the stool. Her fingers hesitated over the keys.

"Trust me," he said.

Arabella squared her shoulders and set her hands in position. She did, indeed, trust him. The realization touched him deeply; he knew full well how difficult that was for her.

She began to play. After only a few notes, though, she stopped. With amazement in her voice, she said, "You've had the pianoforte tuned."

"Today during your walk," he said.

Rather than the excitement he'd expected, he saw concern in her expression. "But you don't play."

"I don't."

"And no one who lives here does."

He smiled gently. "It will bring you pleasure. That makes the effort more than worth it."

She absentmindedly touched her fingers to the beads on her necklace—his beads. "Thank you."

He nodded. "Please play. I've wanted to hear you ever since the dowager told me of your talent the night she introduced us."

"I do like to play."

"Then I will not keep you." He offered a small bow, then took a seat at the front of the group, where he could watch and hear.

She took up a tune. Her playing was every bit as pleasurable as the dowager had said it was. More wonderful even than that, she clearly enjoyed playing the music. They shared that. Perhaps they could learn a few duets for his lyre and her pianoforte. How easily he could imagine it.

Mr. Napper sat near enough to quietly comment to him. "She plays well."

"More than merely 'well,'" Linus said. "Lovely. Beautiful."

"The music or the musician?" That was certainly pointed. Still, it was an opportunity for offering clarity.

"Both," he said, holding Mr. Napper's gaze.

His neighbor made a gesture of understanding. "I had begun to suspect the wind blew that way."

"And I've begun to suspect some in your family believed it might blow another direction entirely." He hoped the frank observation did not give offense. Rumors had caused him and Arabella trouble before. He would not risk it happening again. "I trust any misconceptions there can be easily cleared up."

Mr. Napper gave a single nod, one devoid of malice. It seemed he, at least, hadn't pinned too many hopes on Linus.

Arabella continued to play. Linus could fully listen once more. Her music was lovely. And watching her was a joy.

He hoped his offering—an instrument she could play—brought her some happiness while she was here. More than that, he hoped her time in his home, in his life, brought her peace and joy and the assurance she was loved. There was no other word for what he felt. Love.

Her song ended. She rose and, with a bit of a blush on her cheeks, curtsied as her audience applauded. Linus moved to escort her to a seat, but Dr. Scorseby arrived at her side first.

"Yours is an impressive talent." Dr. Scorseby placed himself directly between Linus and Arabella, something that likely wasn't accidental. There was no mistaking the message. Scorseby was well aware that Linus was courting Arabella, and he didn't mean to abandon his own efforts. "I feel quite privileged to have heard your performance," the doctor said to her. "I hope you mean to favor the neighborhood with a performance once we've returned to Nottinghamshire."

Scorseby might have held Arabella's attention at the moment, but she was wearing Linus's beads. She had stood in his embrace the previous afternoon. That was reason enough to believe his suit was not being rejected or brushed aside in favor of someone else's.

"Dr. Scorseby," the dowager spoke loud enough to prevent the physician from continuing his commentary. "Forgive me for depriving you of your partner, but I need Miss Hampton to fetch my shawl for me."

The doctor graciously stepped aside. Arabella left quickly. Linus had not been granted even a moment of her time. Perhaps she would sit by him when she returned.

The second of the Nappers' daughters took her place at the pianoforte. She played well, but Linus found his interested waning.

"Psst," someone whispered behind him.

He looked back. Charlie motioned him over. Curious, he moved to the sofa where Charlie sat, his splinted legs stretched out in front of him.

"What are you waiting for?" Charlie whispered. "This is your chance."

"I don't understand."

"Arabella."

What was Charlie pushing at? "She went to fetch your mother's shawl."

"Mater has her shawl."

Suddenly it all made sense. "The dowager created a ruse."

"She created an opportunity."

"Thank her for me."

Linus slipped slowly from the room, not drawing attention to his departure. He took the stairs two at a time. Arabella stood a few feet from the top of the staircase. She watched him approach, brows pulled low. She looked uneasy.

"Is something the matter?" he asked.

"You tuned the pianoforte," she said, "but you don't play."

"I don't play, but you do."

"You tuned it for me?" She stepped closer, narrowing the distance between them.

"Exclusively for you." He moved closer as well.

"Because you like music?" She closed the gap between them, standing so near he could hear every breath she took.

"Because I like you." He slipped an arm around her waist, his hand splayed against her back. "I like you very much, indeed."

She set her open palms on his chest. Her eyes met his. "I like you very much as well."

"Do you?" A smile tugged at his lips.

She raised herself up on her toes and pressed the briefest, lightest of kisses to his cheek. "I very much do."

He pulled her more fully into his embrace, but she stepped back, slipping away.

"Arabella," he called after her.

She paused halfway down the stairs and looked back up at him.

"May I join you on your walk tomorrow?"

She smiled. "Of course."

"And the day after that?" He descended to the step she stood on.

"Of course."

He moved one step lower, putting him nearly eye-to-eye with her. "And the day after that?"

"Of course." She gently touched his cheek.

"You'll find I'm a bit wind-bitten, my dear," he said. "Years at sea take a toll."

"Do you know what I thought the first time I saw you in the Lampton Park entryway?"

He pretended to ponder it. "You likely thought, 'Who is that old man?'"

She tipped her head, her blue eyes bright with amusement. "I thought you were the most beautiful man I'd ever seen."

"Beautiful?"

She laid her head on his shoulder. "I know it is not quite the right word, but it was the first one that came to mind. Certainly not wind-bitten."

He wrapped his arms around her. "Do you know what I first thought?"

"'Who is that mouse in the corner?'"

He breathed in the scent of her, cherishing the moment. "I thought of how much I wanted to meet you, how intrigued I was by you."

"A woman hiding in the shadows?"

"You tugged at me in ways I could not begin to explain." He pressed a kiss to her temple. "I was embarrassingly nervous every time I spoke to you."

"I am glad you spoke to me anyway."

"So am I," he said.

With a small sigh, she stepped back, out of his arms and down the stairs. She looked back at him once more before disappearing down the corridor below.

Linus slowly followed in her wake. He'd held her. She'd leaned into his embrace. He had every reason to hope that while she was in Shropshire, he would find a way to prove himself worthy of her affection.

He reached the corridor below. Arabella had already stepped inside the drawing room. Dr. Scorseby stood not far away, watching him.

Linus squared his shoulders. He'd faced down foes before. This one, however, didn't look as though he meant to scuffle.

Scorseby eyed him for a drawn-out moment, then taking a breath, he nodded. He walked down the corridor, not into the drawing room but toward the entryway. He looked back at Linus. "Be good to her."

"I have every intention of being far more than merely 'good.'"

Scorseby held his gaze firmly. "See to it that you are." He slipped from the house.

Linus made his way into the drawing room. His eyes found Arabella on the instant. She smiled at him from her place beside the dowager. His heart warmed at the sight of her.

Oh, yes. He meant to be far more than "good" to her; he intended to do everything in his power to be worthy of her love.

Chapter Thirty-Five

ARABELLA WAS LEAVING.

Charlie had healed well over the past six weeks, thanks to the care of his mother and the attentions of the local physician, Scorseby having long since returned to Nottinghamshire. Charlie had missed the start of the new term at Cambridge and would not be returning until after the Christmas holiday. His prolonged absence had increased his enthusiasm for taking up his studies once more. The time away from his brothers had increased his enthusiasm for their company. He was ready to return to Lampton Park, as was Mater. Linus would miss them. But Arabella's departure weighed far more heavily on him.

Six weeks he'd had her company. Six weeks of walking through the neighborhood and leisurely strolling the gardens and estate. Six weeks of holding her hand each evening after dinner. Six weeks of growing attached to the idea of her in this home, at his side. And she was leaving.

The past month and a half had changed them both. She had shed much of the uncertainty that had once hung heavy in her eyes. He had slipped free of the loneliness that had dogged his heels the past eleven years. They were happy together, comforted by each other, strengthened. He could not imagine his life without her in it.

He was running out of time to secure that future.

The first item of business was running Mater to ground, which proved quite easy. He found her in Charlie's room. Somehow, over the course of the last two months, Linus had begun to think of the bedchamber he had once shared with his brother as Charlie's. It was not the place of pain and regret it had once been, neither did he rush past the door or refuse to step inside. He would always feel Evander there. He would always miss and mourn his brother. But he no longer feared those emotions. There was happiness in this home now.

"Linus." Mater had begun calling him by his Christian name. Indeed, she had taken on a role in his life one could only describe as maternal. "Have you come to help us pack?"

"No."

Charlie laughed as he put yet another book inside his small traveling bag. He had received a steady stream of texts from Cambridge to study during his convalescence.

"What has brought you in, then?" Mater asked.

"I have come on a matter of business." That was not quite the right word, but his nerves rendered his thoughts a little muddled. "I know that Arabella's nearest male relative is her uncle, but as I have no intention of giving him the false impression that he has any say whatsoever in her life or decisions, I will not be presenting this bit of business to him. And though your oldest might be the substitute Society would consider most acceptable, you are the one I feel best suited to this particular matter of . . . business."

Lud, he was rambling. And Charlie, blast the boy, was grinning quite unrepentantly.

"I realize it is customary when undertaking this type of business"—he really needed to come up with a different word—"to seek the blessing of the lady's family. I would like to know that you approve, that you support this possibility. She would be unhappy if her decision did not meet with your approval, but I do consider her more than able to make this decision without—I am not asking you for permission; I—not that I don't value your thoughts, but—"

Charlie actually snorted.

Mater swatted at him before crossing to Linus. She set her hands on his upper arms. "Arabella is more than capable of choosing her own future. That you know that and acknowledge it only endears you to me further. And your concern that our position on the future you mean to propose to her might bring her unhappiness does as well."

"You do not think me entirely terrible, then?" he asked with a laugh.

Charlie chimed in. "Not entirely."

Mater shook her head. "Do not listen to him. Now that he is feeling better, he is choosing to be troublesome."

"As any younger brother worth his salt would," Linus said.

Charlie wandered over, moving slowly and using his cane. He would require time yet to fully heal. "How do you intend to ask her?"

How? He looked from Charlie to Mater and back again. "I was simply going to ask."

Charlie rolled his eyes.

Mater eyed her son. "I suppose you, when the time comes, intend to undertake something grand and spectacular."

"One ought to make a gesture," Charlie said as if any other opinion was simply absurd. "Proposing a future together should be memorable."

Linus couldn't help a laugh. "You sound like Artemis."

Charlie's expression turned stern. He pointed a finger at Linus. "Keep spouting nonsense like that and I'll brain you with this cane. My sister-in-law showed me how, and she is an expert."

"As much as I would enjoy an impromptu duel, I have far more important . . . business to attend to."

Mater patted his cheek. "Arabella does not require gestures or grand productions. She simply needs to know you love her. Remind her of that."

"*Remind* her?"

Mater smiled kindly. "You have shown her again and again these past weeks the truth of your love for her."

Quite to his surprise, Mater pulled him into an embrace. Memories of his mother doing the same when he was a little boy flooded over him. Linus put his arms around her and cherished the moment.

"Thank you, my dear Linus," she said, "for loving Arabella. For seeing my Charlie when his own family didn't always." She pulled back enough to look him in the eye. "For being a welcome and wonderful addition to my beloved boys."

"And thank you for letting me be part of your family at a time when I desperately needed one and for giving me a mother again. That is something I have not had since I was very little."

"It seems I was wise to hold that house party."

He nodded. "I will be forever grateful that you did."

She set him a little away. "Go find Arabella. I will write to my son Jason. He can procure a special license, then we need not wait to plan a wedding."

"Do you not think you are getting a little ahead of yourself?"

"Not in the least." She moved to the writing desk. "I have no doubt of the outcome of your endeavors."

"I will rely upon your confidence, then, as I am not nearly as sure she will be pleased at the idea."

Mater smiled at him fondly. "I certainly wasn't when first confronted with the possibility of a match between myself and the gentleman I would eventually marry. I threatened to run away from home."

Linus laughed. "You are not helping my confidence."

"Yes, but you see, our situation was not at all the same as yours. You love her, and she knows you do. That makes all the difference in the world."

"Well"—he returned to the doorway—"wish me luck."

"Without a gesture, you'll need it," Charlie called after him.

"Stop it," Mater laughingly scolded.

Linus shook his head in amusement as he stepped into the corridor. Being part of the Jonquil family these past weeks had been a joy and a blessing. He'd begun not only thinking of himself as one of them but also growing more anxious to make the needed effort to rejoin his own family, finding for himself a place amongst them rather than simply bemoaning the gap created by years of separation.

He meant to spend Christmas at Falstone Castle. If all went well, he *and* Arabella could spend Christmas there. Though he wanted to brush aside Charlie's insistence, Linus suspected he needed to find a better way to pose the possibility other than simply searching her out and saying, "If you don't have plans for Christmas, we should get married and then visit my family."

He ought to do something, but what? He was not a very romantic person, having so little experience with such things. There must have been something he could do or arrange that would help his cause, something that would further show her he cared.

On the instant, he knew.

He ducked into the study and pulled open the top desk drawer. A former shipmate of his lived in neighboring Cheshire. Linus had written to him three weeks earlier, knowing that the retired sailor had amassed a collection of oddities from around the world. Just as Linus had hoped, his one-time associate had amongst his international trinkets a particularly unique bead, one he had been willing to sell. The bead had arrived only two days earlier, but Linus hadn't found the right moment to give it to her.

This was that moment.

He pulled the package out and tipped the bead into his hand. It wasn't colorful like the bead Arabella had received from the earl, neither was it impressive like the two jade beads he'd given her weeks ago. It was not fancy or fine, but it was unique and interesting. He felt certain she would love it.

A quick glance at the clock told him where he would find her. She no longer spent hours of each day walking for miles on end, but she did walk around the gardens or the open meadows of the estate each afternoon. Linus had joined her on many of those excursions. Doing so had relieved his concerns. She no longer looked weary and afraid and worn down. She seemed content. More than content, she seemed happy.

He made for the garden first in case she'd chosen a path closer to the house. Fate was on his side. He found her sitting beneath the branches of an oak tree on the west side of the garden. Autumn had edged the leaves in red. The nearby bushes had undergone the same transformation. The scene was tranquil, captivating, more so for her being in it. How easily he could picture her in that very spot in the white of winter, the budding greens of spring, the vibrant sunshine of summer.

She looked up as he approached. Her eyes lit with pleasure.

"Good afternoon, Linus." She slid to the end of the bench on which she sat, making room for him without hesitation. With Arabella, there was always room for him, something he'd not always been granted by his loved ones.

He sat beside her. She laid her head on his shoulder and threaded her arm through his. They had established that pattern between them. He would normally have laid his hand atop hers and adjusted his position until they were tucked cozily together. This afternoon, however, he had pressing matters to attend to.

"I have something for you," he said. Charlie would likely have dismissed the beginning as too ordinary. Artemis certainly would have.

"Have you?" Though she sounded interested, she didn't pull away. His company appealed to her more than a gift. Was it any wonder he loved her so dearly?

He reached into his pocket with his free arm, grateful that their current arrangement allowed for easy access. His fist clenched tightly around the small bauble, afraid of both losing it and discovering she was unimpressed by it.

"It must not be very large," she said.

"It isn't." He set his fist on his leg, suddenly nervous.

She reached across and gently, tenderly turned his hand over and peeled back his fingers one at a time until his hand lay open, the bead in the middle of his palm. Carefully, she placed her thumb and forefinger on either side of the bead and picked it up.

"It comes from Greece," he said. "It is made of boxwood, the same variety as my lyre."

"I love when you play your lyre." She closed her fingers over the bead and pressed it to her heart. "This is the same wood?"

He nodded.

"It will be like having a piece of you with me."

He took her hand in his and raised it, the bead inside, to his lips. "I don't imagine I will ever be able to pass up another bead as long as I live. Soon enough, you'll have the oddest necklace in all the world."

She smiled. "I would love that."

"Of course, giving them to you will be difficult if you are in Nottinghamshire."

Her countenance fell. "And we are leaving soon."

"Do you have to?" He turned, necessitating that the arm threaded through hers pull free. He took hold of her hand instead, now holding both of hers in both of his.

"My family—" For a fraction of a moment, she paused, amazement pulling at her features. "My family is leaving."

He knew full well what it meant to her to be part of the Jonquil family. She'd told him in detail the dreams she had harbored all her life. Belonging to a family, being loved and cherished and cared about, mattered to her deeply.

"Don't you see, Arabella? My family is leaving as well."

Her brow pulled low in confusion. "Your family left weeks ago."

He slipped a hand free and brushed his fingers along her cheek. "*You* are my family. You are home to me."

"And you are home to me."

Relief and hope pulled a sigh from him. He knew enough of her history to have wondered if she could ever learn to trust his declarations of devotion. It seemed she had.

"Have you been happy here?" he asked.

"Have you?" It was not at all the answer he'd been expecting. His confusion must have shown. She smiled a little. "I know returning was difficult for you, and the memories you've been confronting are often heavy."

"I've made it my own, as you suggested all those weeks ago. And you've allowed me to speak of my brother without pressing me or insisting that I suddenly stop grieving." He pressed a kiss to her forehead. "Have I thanked you for that?"

"You have now."

For one who had arrived with a very specific purpose in mind, he had wandered far afield. She was happy with the bead he'd given her, had expressed tenderness for him, had sat in his embrace. Everything indicated she would accept his proposal, yet he was still nervous. Were all gentlemen uneasy when undertaking this momentous task?

"I didn't seek you out only to give you the bead," he said. "I wanted to ask you something."

A tiny, silent laugh shook her frame. "You have actually asked a lot of questions since you joined me here: Do I have to leave? Have I been happy? Have you thanked me for being a wonderful person?"

"I'd like to ask one more."

She watched him, waiting.

"Will you—Would you consider—?" He shook his head at his own ridiculousness. He was a man of the navy. He had fought in wars. Losing his nerve, especially when reaching for something he wanted this desperately, was not acceptable. "Will you stay with me?"

Hope warred with uncertainty in her eyes. "In the garden?"

"In this home. In my life."

Her hand, still clutching the bead he'd gifted her, pressed once more to her heart. She took a shaky breath. "I have been wrong about important things before, Linus. Please, don't make me guess."

That was fair. He slipped one arm around her middle, then the other. He pulled her close to him, so close the flowery scent of her tiptoed over him. "Arabella Hampton, I love you. I cannot imagine my life without you in it. The two of us have spent so many years searching for a place in our families. In meeting you, I found my place. I found my family. I found where I belong. If there is any chance you might have found the same—"

"Linus." His name emerged as a scold and a plea.

He was still wandering around his point. The time had come to be bold. "Will you marry me?"

An exhaled breath lowered her shoulders as if a world of tension had suddenly dissipated. "Linus." This time, she spoke his name with contentment. She leaned into his embrace, her head resting against his chest. "Linus."

"Now it is my turn to plead for you to not make me guess."

"I love you," she said. "And I cannot imagine my life without you."

"Are you saying yes?" His heart pounded even as his lungs contracted.

She pressed a feather of a kiss on his cheek. "Yes."

"Yes?"

"Yes," she whispered.

He brushed his lips over hers. "I love you."

She wrapped her arms around his neck. He kissed her more fully, more deeply. She held fast to him and he to her. For so long, he had silently cursed fate for tearing him away from home and family, yet fate had brought him to her. His life, with its holes and gaps and loneliness, had filled with love and joy and hope.

"I love you," he said again. "And I will love you forever."

About the Author

SARAH M. EDEN IS A *USA Today* best-selling author of witty and charming historical romances, including 2019's *Foreword Reviews* INDIE Awards Gold winner for romance, *The Lady and the Highwayman*, and 2020 Holt Medallion finalist, *Healing Hearts*. She is a two-time Best of State Gold Medal winner for fiction and a three-time Whitney Award winner. Combining her obsession with history and her affinity for tender love stories, Sarah loves crafting deep characters and heartfelt romances set against rich historical backdrops. She holds a bachelor's degree in research and happily spends hours perusing the reference shelves of her local library.

www.SarahMEden.com